ABOUT THE AUTHOR

Shirley Wells was born and raised in the Cotswolds, where her headmaster wrote on her school report—*Shirley is content to dream her life away.* Years later—as an adult living in Cyprus—it dawned on her that this wasn't necessarily a bad thing and that fellow dreamers, in the guise of fiction writers, had been getting away with it for centuries.

A move to the Orkney island of Hoy followed and, during the twelve years she spent there, she wrote short stories, as well as full-length romance fiction for U.K. women's magazines. She's now settled in Lancashire, where the Pennines provide the inspiration and setting for her popular mystery novels. She and her husband share their home with an ever-changing selection of deranged pets, who often insist on cameo roles in Shirley's novels.

When she isn't writing, Shirley loves reading (anything and everything), listening to live music, watching TV, eating chocolate and drinking whisky—though not necessarily at the same time. She's also a season ticket holder at Burnley Football Club and can often be seen in the biting wind and pouring rain, cheering on her favorite team.

And she's still content to dream her life away.

SHIRLEY WELLS

Silent
Witness

CARINA
PRESS™

For Kate, Joe and Elle
Love you.

CARINA
PRESS™

Recycling programs
for this product may
not exist in your area.

ISBN-13: 978-0-373-06265-2

SILENT WITNESS

First North American Publication 2012

Copyright © 2012 by Shirley Wells

www.CarinaPress.com

Printed in U.S.A.

Silent Witness

Acknowledgments

Many people have helped bring this story to you and although I take the credit (and the blame for any errors), I'd like to thank the amazing team at Carina Press for their hard work, commitment and professionalism. Special thanks go to my fantastic editor, Deborah Nemeth, who puts the commas in the right place, has faith in my writing and is great fun to work with.

As always, I'm grateful to Nick. His love, support and willingness to cook makes anything possible.

ONE

DYLAN LIKED DOGS. Most dogs, at least. The sort he didn't like were Rottweilers weighing in excess of a hundred and fifty pounds. Like the one showing him yellow, sharklike teeth right now.

"Okay, Sunshine, we're keeping this gate between us." Dylan tried to speak with authority, to show it who was master here.

The dog already knew who was controlling the stand-off and it wasn't Dylan. Mud puddled around the creature's enormous feet as it emitted a menacing growl that shook its well-muscled body.

"Right. I can stand here all day," Dylan said.

The evil-eyed creature came a step closer. Still growling. Still putting Dylan at the top of the day's breakfast menu.

Dylan couldn't really stand here all day. Rain was soaking through his jeans, and a force eight was threatening to knock him off his feet.

The house he was trying to reach looked like something from a child's painting. Square and built of red brick, it had four symmetrical windows, two on the ground floor and two above. The front door was in the middle of the windows, and a chimney was dead centre in a red-tiled roof. A curl of smoke twisting skyward completed the picture.

That front door was about twenty yards from the gate. Dylan wondered if he could find a stone to throw at the door and alert the occupant's attention. Another thought came—

"Right, Sunshine." Dylan wandered into a lane where a

vehicle had churned up deep ruts in the mud. He picked up a stone and hurled it the length of the garden at the side of the house. "Fetch!"

The dog simply curled its lip and gave a warning growl.

"Fallen for that one before, have you?" Dylan asked.

A large blue-and-white painted sign told him he was outside the Pennine View Rescue Centre so he couldn't even hope he had the wrong property. Another sign begged for donations. Anything from blankets to pet food and cash was welcomed.

"Hello!" Dylan called as a figure, it was impossible to guess the gender, came into view at the corner of the house.

"Trudy, are you up to your old tricks? Come here, sweetheart." It was female, and she walked up the path, laughing at Dylan's plight. "Don't worry about Trudy. She only wants to play."

Who in hell's name would christen the evil creature *Trudy?* Probably the same person who thought Dylan was daft enough to open the gate.

"It looks like she'd rather have breakfast than play," he said.

"Nonsense. She'd play all day." The woman fondled Trudy's ears. "Wouldn't you, sweetheart?"

"I'm looking for Mrs. Kaminski," Dylan said as the woman reached for the gate.

"Oh, my—" A shocked hand went to her mouth. "You must be Mr. Scott. You're early. Thank you. I mean, thank you for being early. Thank you for coming at all. Sorry, I'm Mrs. Kaminski. Sue."

She thrust out a hand. The closed gate was still between them, the way Dylan would like to keep it.

"Good to meet you, Sue. I'm Dylan." He shook her hand.

She nodded at his car, a 1956 Morgan in Daytona Yellow. "Is that what the best private investigators are driving?"

"It's what *I'm* driving."

"Aw, isn't it pretty?"

He was about to explain that under no stretch of the imagination could his pride and joy be described as *pretty* when she yanked open the gate. The dog lunged. Dylan sucked in his breath, waiting for the crunch of teeth on bone, but the dog merely sniffed at his sleeve and wagged its vast backside in greeting.

"You see?" Sue said. "You're friends already. Come into the house, Mr. Scott. Dylan. This rain's getting heavier. We'll be soaked through."

Dylan, the dog trotting at his side, followed her along a path littered with rope toys, balls and bones that had been well chewed.

"I wanted to keep myself busy until you arrived," Sue said, "so I've been painting one of the kennels. You know what they say about a watched clock. Still, you're here now. And I'm so pleased to see you. I was too excited to sleep last night."

"Oh, I really don't think—"

She was striding on ahead and Dylan's words were lost to the wind.

He followed her around the side of the house to the back. Here, the garden looked like a mini show-jumping arena. There were small red-and-white painted jumps, a long plastic tunnel and a see-saw. Beyond that was an untidy range of mostly wooden outbuildings. Kennels, Dylan assumed. From what he knew of Sue Kaminski, which wasn't much, she devoted all her time, energy and money to caring for the area's stray dogs and cats.

She pushed open a door and led him into a small porch crammed with several pairs of Wellington boots, more dog toys and several waterproof jackets for humans. She yanked off her boots and added them to the pile.

"Come in," she said. Another door led to a large square kitchen. "It's nice and warm in here."

"So it is." Dylan made for the large cream-coloured Aga that was throwing out the heat. Several towels hung from its rail to dry.

"Here." Sue handed him a towel. "It's clean. You can at least dry your hair."

"Thanks." He rubbed at his hair but his jeans were uncomfortably damp.

"Sit down and I'll make us a drink."

Dylan sat at a pine table, making sure he was close to the Aga. The dog, bored with Dylan, thank God, stretched out on the floor in front of the heat source.

Sue pulled off a blue knitted hat, black gloves, red-and-white scarf, dirty blue anorak and thick black sweater, dumping each item on a chair. Dylan had thought the outdoor clothing was responsible for adding inches to her size, but he was wrong. She wasn't fat, but she was quite tall and certainly stocky. Her short fair hair was cut with a view to easy management rather than any thought of fashion.

Her chunky sweater looked hand-knitted and, given the rainbow of colours, Dylan wouldn't have been surprised to learn that she'd used up scrap wool. Black jeans were plastered in mud and her feet were clad in scarlet woollen socks. The only visible jewellery was a scratched band of gold on the third finger of her left hand.

"I'm so excited to see you," she said.

"I don't know what you've been told, but I haven't agreed to take on the case yet." And probably wouldn't. "Unless something convinces me that your husband is innocent—"

"But he is."

"Maybe he is," Dylan said, "but the police and jury thought otherwise. Nothing convinced them he was innocent. Maybe nothing will convince me."

"You're visiting him tomorrow, aren't you?"

"Yes."

"Then you'll see for yourself. Once you've talked with him, you'll know he's innocent."

Such belief was touching, but it meant nothing. Having been a respected member of the police force, Dylan knew that men weren't convicted of murder without good reason. On the other hand, a spell in prison had taught him about the flaws in the judicial system.

"Right, let me make you that drink. Tea or coffee?"

"Whatever you're making. Either would be welcome. Thanks."

"Coffee okay then?" she asked, and he nodded.

"Thanks."

While she filled the kettle and took mugs from a cupboard, Dylan looked around the kitchen. Cluttered didn't begin to describe it. A total of three calendars, two showing pictures of dogs and one adorned with cute kittens, hung from the wall. The sink held around a dozen mugs and a plate waiting to be washed. A pile of mail sat on the table. One envelope contained a red final warning notice from her electricity supplier. Two jackets hung from the backs of chairs. Three plastic dog beds of different sizes were vacant. A vase of wilting daffodils sat on the window sill and blocked the light.

The room was untidy—or perhaps lived in was a better description—but it had a certain homely appeal. Although the surfaces were clean, the floor was speckled with muddy paw and boot prints. Dirty marks on the door frame showed the height of resident dogs.

"There you go," she said. "Here's the sugar."

"Thanks." Coffee came in a thick blue pottery mug. Dylan stirred in a couple of spoonfuls of sugar and cradled the mug in his hands for extra warmth.

The door opened and closed, letting in a blast of cold wind and a tall, rangy man.

"Hi, Jamie," Sue greeted the stranger. "Sorry, but you'll have to make do with Anne today. I'm tied up for the moment."

Jamie was early thirties, and he had to be at least six feet tall. He wore his sand-coloured hair short. Rimless glasses gave him a geek look. Beneath a green wax coat he wore a canary-yellow jumper. His trousers looked as if they'd quarrelled with his shoes and weren't going within four inches of them.

Trudy roused herself to inspect the visitor. He was presumably known to her, judging by the way her rump wriggled as he stroked her ears. Losing interest in him and spying Dylan's briefcase, the dog picked that up and began to circle the room. Dylan wasn't about to argue with a Rottweiler, especially this one, but he didn't want his briefcase decorated with bite marks.

Sue smiled indulgently, removed it from the dog's jaw and put it on the table out of harm's way.

Jamie was too busy looking miffed with his rejection to notice. "Anne's nowhere to be seen."

"She's definitely here. I expect she's walking one of the dogs." Sue reached for a mobile phone, searched for a number, hit a button and held it to her ear. "Hi, Anne. How far away are you? Jamie's here. Can you deal with him? Yeah? Great. Okay, I'll send him down."

"I'll go and find her then, shall I?" Jamie asked.

"Yes, she's only out in the field," Sue said. "Give me a shout if there are any problems."

He nodded and, with the colour high in his cheeks, left them alone.

"That's Jamie, our vet," Sue explained. "He comes regularly to check out the animals, but I'm sure there's nothing

Anne can't cope with." She pulled a chair closer to Dylan, was about to sit and said, "Sorry, I haven't offered you anything to eat. I forgot you'd had such a long journey."

"I'm fine, thanks. I stopped at a service station on the way."

Satisfied, she sat down. "How long are you staying up here?"

"That depends." He was booked into a hotel in Dawson's Clough, and was due to visit her husband, Aleksander Kaminski, at two o'clock tomorrow afternoon. Unless anything interesting was said, he'd drive straight back to London after that meeting. "As yet, I don't know much about the case. I'm only here as a favour to my mother really. And to Aleksander's parents. My mother used to live in Birmingham and knew Aleksander's parents quite well."

She'd know all that, just as she'd know that Aleksander's mother had tried to get other people interested in her son's case. They'd all turned her down. Dylan probably would too.

"At least you're here," she said. "At least you're willing to see Alek."

"Yes, but it's only as a favour."

That wasn't strictly accurate. He had two reasons for coming to Lancashire and neither had any bearing whatsoever on Aleksander's innocence or guilt.

First, Dylan was broke and this was the first offer of real work he'd had for months. That alone wouldn't have convinced him to make the long journey north though. From the little he knew about Aleksander Kaminski's case, it had been cut and dried. There had been no doubt from either police or jury that he was a cold-blooded killer.

"Have you left family behind in London?" she asked.

"Yes. A wife and two children."

A wife and two children. It was the first time he'd said that. Ever.

It was also the second reason he'd been persuaded to come

to Lancashire. His house had become a never-ending discussion of baby's feeding times and bowel movements.

"I've got a thirteen-year-old son, Luke," he said, "and a daughter, Freya. Freya is six days old."

Sue had taken a sip of coffee and she almost choked on it. "Six days?"

"Yeah."

"Oh, my God. Well, congratulations!"

What she probably meant was what the hell was he doing in Lancashire when his wife needed him. That was more or less what Bev had wanted to know.

"Thanks," he said.

"And your wife doesn't mind you coming here?"

Dylan wouldn't go that far. "It's fine."

No point telling her that Bev had thrown a vase of flowers at him, complete with water, and called him the most selfish, self-centred bastard she'd ever met.

"Right then," he said. "Perhaps you can begin by telling me why you believe your husband is innocent."

She smiled at that. "Alek couldn't hurt a fly."

How many mass murderers had been bestowed with that particular compliment? Not that Kaminski was a mass murderer. As far as Dylan knew.

"You'd be surprised how few people really know the person they live with." Dylan sometimes had his doubts about Bev. "Okay, tell me all you know about the case. What happened? How did Alek come to be suspect number one?"

She nodded at his briefcase. Surprisingly, there were no teeth marks on it. "Don't you want to record this or make notes?"

"No. Just tell me your story."

"Right." She tugged on the sleeves of her sweater. A scarlet-sock-clad foot strayed to the Rottweiler's back and she ran it back and forth. "Carly Walsingham, Alek's first wife, was murdered in her own home one afternoon. It's eight months ago now. The third of August to be precise. We saw it on the news that evening. We were in here, in this very room." She nodded at a small TV on the counter in the far corner of the kitchen.

"We? You and Alek?"

"Yes." She stood and crossed the room to a notice board where she jabbed a finger at a photo pinned there. "This was taken the same day."

She took the photo from the board and handed it to Dylan. It showed Sue with an elderly lady. They were celebrating a birthday, judging by the candle in the centre of a decorated cake.

"It was a happy day," Sue said. "I always visit my great-aunt, that's my dad's aunt, on Wednesdays, have done since she went into the care home a couple of years ago, and it was her ninetieth birthday that day. I'd baked the cake and made up little bags of chocolates for the staff. They're really kind to her so, on her birthday and at Christmas, I like to bake a cake and give out small gifts. It was a good day, and I was telling Alek all about it when the news of Carly Walsingham's murder came on TV."

"How did you both feel?" Dylan asked.

Her foot resumed its work, stroking the dog's ear. "Horrified, naturally. Not that we had much time to feel anything. Poor Alek was still reeling from the shock when the police arrived and took him off for questioning."

"What made them think he had anything to do with it?"

A wave of colour flooded Sue's face until it matched her socks. She ran her fingers through her short hair. "He'd been there. With her."

"He'd been in Mrs. Walsingham's home? That afternoon?"

Sue nodded, her gaze resting on her socks and her dog.

"Why?" Dylan asked.

She was taking so long to answer that Dylan lost patience. "Okay," he said, "perhaps we should start at the beginning. How long was Alek married to Mrs. Walsingham? How long have you known him? Give me a history lesson, will you?"

Sue took a breath. "Alek, as you probably know, was born in Poland. His dad was offered work on a big building site in Birmingham and the family moved there when he was three. Alek met Carly there. Of course, she was plain Carly Smith then. They were married in 1992 and divorced in 2005."

Perhaps, after all, Dylan should be making notes. Remembering dates was never his strong point. So far this year, and they were only into April, he'd forgotten Bev's birthday, Valentine's Day and their wedding anniversary. Not that it seemed to matter as she'd bought herself jolly nice—and highly expensive—presents before the events.

Dates weren't too important, though. Carly Walsingham, formerly Carly Kaminski, formerly Carly Smith, had married Aleksander Kaminski twenty years ago and been divorced from him for seven years.

"What brought them both to Lancashire?" he asked.

"Her job. She trained as a radiologist and got a job at the hospital in the Clough. Alek's a builder, like his dad, so he can work anywhere. He's self-employed and works mainly on extensions, conservatories, that sort of thing."

"I see." Dylan was making plenty of mental notes. "So they divorced seven years ago. Any reason? Did she meet someone else? Did he? Was it his relationship with you that—?"

"Oh, no. He'd been divorced for a couple of years before I met him."

"So what were the grounds for the divorce?"

"It's difficult to say." The words came grudgingly. "I do know that she wanted children. Nothing was happening though, so she insisted they both go for tests. They found out Alek can't have children. That didn't suit her and soon after they found out, she told him she wanted a divorce. Alek's loyal, he would have stayed with her, but she wanted out. Within a very short time, though, she was married to Dr. Walsingham so, if you ask me, she'd already been seeing him behind Alek's back."

Dylan really should be making notes. He forgot that people led such complicated lives.

"What about you, Sue? How did you meet Alek?"

"He came here to adopt a dog." Her face took on a dreamy expression. "We got talking as we filled in the paperwork, and he came back a couple of times to let us know how Charlie was doing. Sometimes I'd meet up with him when I was out with the dogs."

"I see."

"He was divorced and I—I was a widow."

"Oh?"

She nodded. "My husband Keith died twelve years ago. A pileup on the motorway. He was only twenty-six."

"I'm sorry, I didn't realise."

"We'd only been married for four years. Still, there's nothing we can do about it, is there? I wasn't the only person to lose someone that day. Five others lost their lives and there were a lot of injuries."

Dylan shivered, despite the warmth of the kitchen.

"Life goes on," she said, brightening, "and a few years later, I met Alek."

"Love at first sight?" Dylan smiled.

"More or less, yes. I was wary at first because Alek's twelve years older than me, but love doesn't care about age, does it?"

"No."

Alek was forty-eight, which meant Sue was thirty-six. Dylan had thought she was younger.

Her phone rang and as she spoke to her caller, she was

frowning in Dylan's direction. "That's okay," she said finally. "I'm on my way."

She finished the call and looked at Dylan. "I need to walk a dog. Sorry, but it has a skin complaint and we need to keep it moving to stop it licking off ointment. It's a Yorkshire terrier who can't wear a head collar."

Dylan was happy enough to wait. He'd make himself another coffee and enjoy the warmth. So long as she took the Rottweiler with her.

"We can talk while we walk," she said. "I've got spare wellies and coat. Socks too."

Dylan's gaze flew to the window. He looked beyond the daffodils and saw that it had stopped raining. "Okay," he said, reluctantly getting to his feet.

True to her word, she found a pair of huge grey socks, a pair of Wellington boots and a cavernous black anorak.

"We always keep plenty of spares around," she said.

They walked across the back garden, past the ramshackle kennels to a brick building. A corridor ran through the centre of it. One side housed half a dozen dogs, all leaping up at their doors to see what was going on and all barking at the disturbance. On the other side was a small office and, further on, an examination room where Jamie and a girl Dylan assumed was Anne were inspecting a small Yorkshire terrier.

Jamie smiled at Sue. "I'm really pleased with her. She's looking great. Another week or so and I think she'll be ready to leave."

"Great. So all I have to do is find a home for her." She stroked the dog. "You're a little sweetie though, aren't you, Sophie? I'm sure we'll soon find somewhere nice for you. You'd like a warm bed of your own, wouldn't you? Lots of cuddles too? Maybe a fire to curl up in front of?"

It drove Dylan mad to hear dogs being treated like babies. Come to that, it drove him mad to hear babies being treated like babies. What was it that turned grown women into coo-ing, dribbling idiots?

"Half an hour should do it," Jamie said.

"Great. Thanks, Jamie."

Sue put a pink collar around the dog's small neck, attached a pink leash and turned to Dylan. "Let's go then."

Once they were outside in the damp air and howling gale, Sue nodded back at the building. "Alek built that."

"It's nice."

"It's perfect. He's so clever." She strode to the front of the house and into the lane where Dylan's car sat—*pretty,* indeed—and on down a muddy lane overhung with dark, dripping trees. The dog pranced along, oblivious to the mud.

"To get back to Mrs. Walsingham," Dylan said, "you said you and Alek heard about her murder on the TV news?"

"That's right. We were sitting in the kitchen and the news was on. I was telling him about Aunt Joyce's birthday party so we weren't paying attention until we heard her name men-tioned."

"What happened after that?"

"The police came to question Alek the next day. They'd been asking questions in her street, and a neighbour claimed to have seen someone who looked like him leaving the house. And, um, they found his fingerprints there."

"He was definitely there that afternoon?" Dylan asked.

"He was, yes." She kicked out at a stone, startling the tiny dog. "I don't know much about it because Alek doesn't like to talk about it. Obviously he doesn't. I mean, he wouldn't want to upset me, would he? Alek's trouble is that he's too kind for his own good. If she said she wanted to see him, he'd go. Not because she had any hold over him, but because he's good like that. He likes to help people, you see. But—" She cleared her throat and tried again. "But he went to see her.

He would have felt obliged. And she—she managed to get him into bed with her. There. It's said."

It certainly was and Dylan knew exactly what it had cost to say it. "He—" It was difficult to put his question into words. "Did they make love the afternoon she was murdered?"

The answer was a long time coming. "They had sex, yes."

Sue was walking so quickly now that Dylan was struggling to keep up. The Yorkshire terrier had broken into a gallop.

"When did you find out that he'd—seen her?" Dylan asked.

"I was eventually allowed to see him. They were holding him in custody, but I was allowed a short visit. He told me then." She stopped walking so abruptly that the dog was yanked off its feet. "He's ashamed, of course, but I know it meant nothing. It was just sex. Men will be men, won't they? All Alek wanted was to be rid of her."

Not the best choice of words. "He got his wish then, didn't he?"

"No!" Her eyes showed signs of moisture. "Not like that. I told you, he couldn't harm a fly. No, he would have just wanted her to stay out of his life."

So he'd silenced her for good?

Not for the first time, Dylan wondered what the hell he was doing in Lancashire. Police had gathered enough evidence to put Aleksander Kaminski behind bars for life. The jury had been happy to put him there. What did people expect him to do about it?

"Was that the only time he visited her?"

Sue shook her head. "He saw her a couple of times, I gather."

"And they—had intercourse?"

She nodded, and bit on her bottom lip.

"Is there anything else you can tell me?" he asked.

"No."

"I used to be in the police force, Sue, and—"

"A policeman? You?"

"Is it so surprising?" He smiled. "I was trying to arrest a known criminal—well, to cut a long story short, the criminal accused me of using excessive force and I found myself on an assault charge. I spent time in prison and lost my job."

"Really?" She carried on walking at a more sensible pace.

"Yes. Anyway, as I was saying, I'm seeing an old colleague of mine this evening. He's retired from the force now, but still has plenty of contacts. He's going to introduce me to the senior investigating officer on Alek's case."

She nodded, but didn't comment.

"So if there's anything else you can tell me before I see him, I'd be grateful."

"There's nothing else. Alek was there the day Carly was murdered and the police found evidence of that. Not that he would have denied it. He had nothing to hide. Anyway, from that, they decided he must have killed her."

"I see."

"You must believe me, Dylan. Alek is innocent." Her voice dropped to a whisper. "You have to get him out of there. You have to."

TWO

JAMIE TINSLEY WAS still at the kennels when Sue returned with a muddy Sophie. He'd made sure of that.

"Everything okay?" he asked.

"Fine, thanks. She's a bit dirty, but at least the ointment's had a chance to work."

Jamie was giving a new dog, a shaggy collie cross, a thorough checkup. The animal was probably eight or nine years old, but he was in good shape.

"How did this one come to be here?" he asked.

Sue stroked the dog's ears. "He was tied to the gatepost. I saw him when I woke up yesterday morning. The poor thing must have been there all night because he was soaked right through to the skin. He was starving too, poor baby."

People's cruelty made Jamie wild. He would love to catch the humans responsible and tie them to a gatepost during a long, cold and wet night. He'd like to frighten them and make them go without food and water.

"He's all right though, isn't he?" she asked.

"Yes. Yes, he's fine. He's in good shape so someone must have been looking after him before they dumped him."

"Money's short, Jamie." Sue continued to stroke the dog. "People are losing jobs, they can't pay rent or mortgages, and I suppose even the price of dog food becomes a burden. At least they left him where they knew he'd be well cared for."

Sue saw nothing but good in people. No matter the cruelty she witnessed, and there was plenty, she could come up with excuses. Jamie wondered if that was why everyone loved her.

"His coat's matted in places, but other than that, I can give him a clean bill of health." He helped the dog jump down from the examination table before handing him a meaty treat.

The dog reminded him of Ben. He too had been a shaggy collie crossbreed. He'd had the same huge brown eyes, the long feathery tail that never stopped wagging, and the grey muzzle. Jamie and Ben had been constant companions from the moment they met when Jamie was nine. They'd only had five years together, but Jamie would never forget his special friend. Many dogs had come to him and been helped since then, but not one had touched his heart like Ben.

Jamie leaned against the table, arms folded. "So how are things going? Is everything set up for Monday?"

Sue had been working toward Monday's event for months. She'd breathed a sigh of relief when the Christmas fundraiser went well and then started making plans for this Easter one.

She gave him a rueful smile. "As set up as it ever will be. I just hope the weather improves a bit. No one will turn up if it's like this."

"Oh, I don't know. The weather wasn't great at Christmas but you had a good turnout. Besides, people like to get out on Easter Monday."

"I hope you're right. Well, I won't keep you, Jamie."

"That's okay. I'm not rushing off anywhere." He was due to take the evening's surgery but that didn't start till five o'clock. "Who was your visitor? Someone wanting to adopt an animal?"

"No."

He thought that was all she intended to say on the matter, and that her silence was a polite way of telling him to mind his own business.

"He's a private investigator," she said at last. "Honestly, Jamie, I've been too excited to sleep or even think straight.

He hasn't actually agreed to take on Alek's case yet, but I'm sure he will. He's going to the prison to visit him tomorrow."

Her words shocked him to the core. He'd assumed Kaminski would fester behind bars until he was an old man. Why the hell did she have to rake it all over again?

"Really? I didn't know you were thinking of employing someone. I didn't think you could afford to—with this place to worry about, I mean. Still, why not, eh?"

"It isn't costing me a penny," she said. "I would pay. God, I'd give every penny I had, borrow as much as I could. I'd do anything if I thought it would bring Alek home. But no, this is all thanks to Alek's parents. They used to live near Dylan's mother. That's the investigator's name, Dylan Scott. He says that's why he's come up to see Alek, as a favour to his mother and to Alek's parents."

"That's handy then. As they say, it's not what you know, it's who you know."

"Quite." She chewed on her bottom lip. "I daren't even think about it. If I start to imagine Alek coming home—God, I'll die if it all comes to nothing."

"Don't be ridiculous. Of course you won't." He smiled to take the sting from his words. "You're tough, Sue. Strong and brave."

She laughed that off. "I wish. Anyway, I'd better get on."

"Me, too." He checked that he'd put everything in his bag and reached for his coat. "I'll see you on Monday, if not before."

She grinned at him. "Don't forget to bring your wallet."

"I won't."

Sue led the dog to its kennel and, with no excuse to linger, Jamie walked back to his car. The sky was grey, the land wet and dreary. It suited his mood.

Sue had said this private investigator hadn't agreed to take on the case. Hopefully, he wouldn't. Jamie felt sure it would come to nothing but, all the same, he didn't want Dylan Scott or whatever his name was poking his nose where it wasn't wanted.

He'd put a stop to it if he had to.

THREE

DESPITE THE COAT and socks Sue Kaminski had loaned him, Dylan had been chilled all day. Now, finally, he was thawing out. After leaving Pennine View Rescue Centre, he'd checked into his hotel and spent the afternoon on the internet, finding out as much as he could about Aleksander Kaminski and the ex-wife he may or may not have butchered. He searched for information on Sue Kaminski and her animal rescue centre, as well as Dr. Walsingham, the victim's husband. Nothing of interest had come to light, nothing he hadn't already known.

He was meeting ex-DCI Frank Willoughby and ex-DI Lewis Cameron at seven-thirty. Dylan was half an hour early but that was okay. On previous visits to Dawson's Clough, the Dog and Fox had become one of his favourite pubs. Passing time in the company of a pint of good beer was no hardship.

This corner of east Lancashire, with its stunning views and hardworking, close-knit community, had grown on him. He found the tall chimneys, relics of a long-dead cotton industry, strangely romantic. Some of the old mills had been left to take their chances with the elements, but others had been turned into luxury apartments. The area was a mix of old and new, and he liked it.

He'd chosen a table at the far end of the pub's lounge, one close to a crackling log fire. A gale still raged outside, hauling rain clouds across a threatening sky, and the fire provided cheer as well as warmth.

A few customers crowded round the bar but, other than

that, the place was quiet. From experience, he guessed more people would call in later.

He'd settled down with his second pint when Frank and a man Dylan assumed was Lewis Cameron came in. With a wave of his hand, Dylan indicated that he didn't need another drink.

He wondered if anyone else was watching the two men at the bar and thinking they both looked like coppers. Dylan didn't know what it was, perhaps the erect carriage or the well-polished black shoes, but they oozed policeman from every pore.

Unlike Dylan, who'd been kicked off the force in disgrace—not that he was bitter, or not *too* bitter—these men had retired with commendations. A heart attack had forced Frank to retire, whereas Lewis Cameron had decided to spend more time with his family after years of excellent service.

Ex-DCI Frank Willoughby was sixty and, thanks to a stringent diet and exercise regime, looked good. His hair was short, thick and dark, his back and shoulders straight. Ex-DI Lewis Cameron was a couple of years younger, not as tall as Frank, and about twenty pounds heavier. Dylan wondered if he kept his hair slightly longer to conceal the fact that he was going bald.

"Well, Dylan." Frank gave him a hearty pat on the back. "Long time no see. This is Lewis Cameron. Lewis, Dylan Scott."

Once the handshaking was out of the way, they took their seats around the table.

"So how's life treating you, Dylan?" Frank asked. "Congratulations, by the way. How's the new baby?"

"Life's good, thanks, mate." Dylan couldn't resist. He reached for his wallet and took out the small photo of his daughter. "The new baby is gorgeous. Here. We've called her Freya."

"Freya?"

"Yeah. Apparently, it comes from Norse mythology. I think Freya was the goddess of fertility as well as being the most beautiful of the goddesses."

Lewis Cameron smiled as he looked at the photo. "She's lovely."

"She is." Dylan returned the photo to his wallet. "It just goes to show that not all babies look like Winston Churchill."

"How's Bev?" Frank asked. "Is she okay with you coming up here when you should be helping with the new addition?"

"Okay isn't quite how I'd describe it." Dylan took a swig of beer. "She hasn't forgiven me for missing the birth yet so everything I do is wrong at the moment."

"How come you missed it?" Frank asked.

Dylan had asked himself that same question a dozen times and he still found it hard to answer. "In my defence, Freya was a couple of days early. She was born Wednesday night, when Arsenal were playing Chelsea at home. I had my phone with me, of course, but there's a lot of noise when Arsenal play Chelsea and I didn't hear it ring. I came out of the ground, checked my messages and raced to the hospital. It was all done and dusted by that time. The birth was short and quick, and my mother was there to take charge of everything. Bev was in hospital less than forty-eight hours so it's all okay."

"You like to live dangerously." Frank shook his head and added for Lewis's benefit, "Dylan's wife chucked him out. She went the whole way—even found him a flat of his own. It took months for him to worm his way back into her good books. If he's not careful, he'll be back in that flat again."

"Don't." Dylan shuddered at the thought.

He hadn't been in "that flat" above five minutes when his mother moved in, and if there was anything worse than living with his mother, Dylan hadn't yet stumbled across it. He loved his mother, God knows why, but he couldn't live with her.

He often thought that if Bev hadn't got drunk that night nine months ago, and if that night hadn't resulted in her falling pregnant, he'd still be living in that shoebox the bastard of a landlord chose to call a studio flat. The whys and wherefores didn't matter though. He was back in the marital home and, God willing, he'd stay there.

He made a mental note to keep on the right side of Bev. He'd take flowers when he went home.

"What about you, Lewis?" he asked. "You're obviously married. Any children?"

"Two boys. One's in Scotland and the other's in Canada. Why obviously? You said I was obviously married." He glanced down at his left hand as if he expected to see a shining band of gold on his finger. It was bare. "How can you tell?"

"You winced. When I was explaining how I missed Freya's birth because of the Arsenal game, you winced."

"Christ, you must be a direct descendent of Sherlock Holmes." He laughed loudly at his own joke.

Dylan smiled, but they clearly didn't share the same sense of humour. "How are you liking retirement? Do you manage to fill your days?"

He knew a lot of coppers who were totally lost without the job.

"Easily." Lewis tapped the side of his nose. "I do some consultancy work. Security, you know? It has its perks."

"Lewis's just back from a fortnight in New York," Frank explained. "All expenses paid and a decent bonus."

Dylan tried to look suitably impressed. And failed.

"I had a chat with Sue Kaminski this morning," he said, keen to get to more important matters. "She's adamant that as soon as I see her husband, I'll know he's innocent. Is that likely?"

"No." Lewis was firm on that. "Kaminski will tell you

he's innocent, but even he doesn't sound terribly convincing. It was one of the most straightforward cases I've ever worked on."

"Tell me about it." Dylan sat back, glass in hand.

"Carly Walsingham was supposed to collect her children from school. They're five years old. Twins." Lewis pulled a face. "William and Harry."

"After the royal princes?" Frank asked.

"Yes. Apparently, Carly was a huge fan of Princess Di. She even had the same hairstyle. She was obviously an impressionable teenager when Diana married her Prince."

"Wait a minute," Dylan said. "How come the kids were at school? It was August."

"There was a series of activity days for anyone interested. It was supposed to benefit the working mothers but anyone could pay a fiver to dump their kids there. A poet visited, a drama society put on a show, that sort of stuff. Anyway, when Carly didn't turn up to collect them, a teacher tried phoning the house. There was no response so she tried Carly's and then Neil Walsingham's mobile phones. She got hold of Neil and, as he couldn't raise a response from his wife either, he left work, collected the children and took them home. He found her in a bath of blood. Her throat had been slit."

Dylan hated this. Instead of hearing stories second or third-hand, he liked to be at the scene. Failing that, he liked to see photographs. Cameras didn't miss things.

"Okay. No sign of a break-in?"

"Nothing. The front door was locked but the back door wasn't. She'd go to the garden via the back door and her husband said they rarely locked it when they were at home."

She'd been killed in early August when the warm weather tempted people into their gardens. "Did you find the murder weapon?"

"No. And believe me, we searched every inch of the surrounding area. Fingertip search. Dogs. The lot." Lewis ran a finger around the rim of his glass as if bringing the murder scene to mind. "She was in the bath. Her attacker had come at her from behind and put a pillow over her face. There was a large bruise on one wrist and, from that, we were able to get a print." He looked incredibly pleased with himself. "Her other wrist had been cut, but not fatally. The same weapon—small, sharp and precise, like a surgical blade—cut into her carotid artery. She would have died in seconds."

At times like this, Dylan wished he was still a member of the police force. No officer, regardless of the number of years he'd served, liked seeing a body. Especially a body in a bath of blood. If Dylan was still on the force, though, he would have been able to see the bathroom with all its clues.

"Where was the pillow?" he asked.

"On the floor by the side of the bath," Lewis said.

"Why cut her then? Why not just put the pillow over her face and drown her? It would have been a lot less messy."

"It takes a long time," Lewis said. "Carly was young and fit, and would have put up a fight. It would have taken too long, possibly ten minutes."

Dylan supposed he was right. Also, if the killer was angry, drowning her wouldn't satisfy him. He'd have to slash, to hurt, to make her bleed.

He drew a mental picture of the bathroom that was probably totally inaccurate. There was no probably about it. The room could be fourteen feet square or a cramped six by six.

"Anything else odd in the room?" he asked.

"Nothing." Perhaps Lewis knew that Dylan wanted to visualise the room. "The Walsinghams' house is large, spacious and worth a fortune. The bathroom is attached to the main bedroom by the only door. When you open that door, you see a huge bath in the centre of the room. Anyone lying in that bath would have their back to the door, as Carly did. To the right is a large walk-in shower. There are plenty of cupboards filled with white towels. More cupboards crammed with expensive toiletries. Electric toothbrushes for Mr. and Mrs. Walsingham only, as the children used the family bathroom."

The room had made a strong impression on Lewis Cameron. It would, though. Even the longest-serving detectives rarely saw a body in a bath of blood.

"There were fingerprints everywhere," Lewis said, "so that was easy enough. We were soon able to eliminate the victim's prints, her husband's and the cleaner's."

"I assume her husband had a watertight alibi?" Frank voiced the question Dylan wanted answering.

"He'd been at the hospital since eight o'clock that morning." Lewis emptied his glass and Dylan supposed he ought to show willing.

"Are we ready for another?"

They were, so Dylan walked up the bar and waited to be served. He'd been right in that trade would soon pick up. The pub was becoming more crowded as the evening wore on. He wasn't surprised. The Dog and Fox offered clean, warm, convivial surroundings, service that was quick and friendly, and, most important, good beer. There were no televisions, no loud music blaring out and no slot machines. Several pubs were closer to his hotel, but the Dog and Fox made forking out for a taxi worthwhile.

Dylan carried their drinks back to the table and retook his seat.

"So," he said, "you had your murder scene with its array of prints. What next?"

For some reason he couldn't fathom, he was becoming intrigued by this case. It was madness, surely? Lewis Cameron was an experienced detective and, as senior investigating officer, would have handpicked an equally experienced team.

There was no way Kaminski could be innocent, despite what his wife claimed.

Dylan would do well to remember that he'd only come to Lancashire to escape the madhouse that was currently his home. That, and as a favour to his mother and her old friends. Getting involved in this case on anything more than a superficial level was absurd. There was no mileage in it.

"We started on the usual house-to-house questioning," Lewis explained. "A neighbour had seen a man leaving the house around a quarter to four that afternoon. He left through the back garden. Because she was up a ladder, hosing leaves off her conservatory roof, she had the perfect view of him. If she'd been standing in her garden, she wouldn't have seen a thing. No one would."

"Her description matched that of Kaminski, I take it?" Dylan said.

"It was a good description, yes."

"He must have been walking away from her though. She couldn't have seen his face, could she?"

Lewis smiled at that. "She saw a man wearing black jeans and a grey hoody striding down the garden. We checked with some CCTV of Kaminski that day and he was wearing black jeans."

"And a grey hoody?"

"We didn't find that on CCTV, no, but it was a warm day. He would only have pulled that on to try and hide his head and hair as he left the house."

"So the neighbour saw a man in black jeans?" He glanced down at his own black jeans. "That description would fit about forty percent of the population. And isn't it a bit odd? Not volunteering the information until your officers went knocking on doors, I mean. Didn't it occur to her that something might be wrong?"

"No. She said she assumed it was a tradesman. The houses

have large gardens, and gates in the fences at the back of those gardens lead onto Peebles Road. There are shops there and, sometimes, tradesmen nip out the back way to buy sandwiches or newspapers."

"Right," Dylan said. "So the shops on Peebles Road must have cameras?"

"Unfortunately, there's very little CCTV in the area, but we checked with all nearby shops, offices and garages to see what they had. Kaminski had gone into a newsagent's and bought a packet of cigarettes. That's how we caught him on film. Better still, the newsagent knew him. Kaminski's a builder and he'd done some work for him."

As Dylan took a swallow of his beer, he was shocked to realise how badly he wanted to find a hole in Lewis's reasoning. Perhaps he was more bitter and twisted about his dismissal from the force than he'd believed. No, surely not. While he couldn't find a good thing to say about those at the top—those who, for purely political reasons, had him banged up on an assault charge on the say of a habitual criminal—he'd always admired and respected the hardworking detectives.

Frank wasn't saying a lot, he noticed. Perhaps, like Dylan, he was trying to find arguments in the case.

"There's more," Lewis said. "Neil Walsingham told us how his wife had been on the phone the night before. He came home from work and heard her talking to someone. She was agitated and upset, apparently, and was telling the person on the other end to stop threatening her. When she realised Walsingham was in the house, she cut the connection and, when he questioned her, she said it was a salesman trying to force her to buy health insurance. Walsingham didn't believe her."

"And?" Dylan asked.

"It was easy enough to check the phone records and there was only one outgoing call made from the Walsinghams' house that day. Mrs. Walsingham had phoned Aleksander

Kaminski's mobile. It was Kaminski who was threatening her." Lewis took a long appreciative swig of beer. "In less than twenty-four hours, we were able to pick up Kaminski and get his prints checked. A perfect match. Not only were his prints all over that bathroom, including the edge of the bath, his thumb was also responsible for the bruise on Mrs. Walsingham's wrist."

Lewis didn't so much look pleased as smug.

"Prints on skin," Dylan said. "They don't last long, do they?"

"An hour and a half maximum on living flesh," Frank said. "Is that right, Lewis?"

"Yes. A little longer on a corpse. We were lucky with that print. No doubt about it."

If Dylan hadn't been drinking, he would have saved Kaminski's parents the cost of a hotel room and driven straight back to London. The case was cut and dried. Dylan was wasting everyone's time.

"What was Kaminski's story?" he asked.

"He claimed he'd been seeing his ex-wife a couple of times a week for months."

Which wasn't what Sue Kaminski believed. According to her, he'd only visited Carly Walsingham a couple of times because he was a good man who liked to help people.

"Did Walsingham know his wife was seeing her ex-husband?" Dylan asked.

"There was nothing to know," Lewis said. "He was aware that Kaminski had phoned his wife a few times, but that was all. Apparently, Kaminski wouldn't let her go. He couldn't accept their marriage was over."

"How does Walsingham know she wasn't seeing Kaminski?" Dylan asked. "After all, the spouse is always the last to know about these things."

"She wasn't interested." Lewis was adamant about that.

"So why did she phone him? Surely, if he was the one making a nuisance of himself and threatening her, *he* would have phoned *her*."

"We'll never know," Lewis said. "We know from Walsingham that Kaminski used to phone her. He used to follow her too. We can only assume she phoned to try and get through to him, once and for all, that it was over."

"Yet Kaminski claims they had sex regularly?"

"All lies. When asked about the bruise, Kaminski claimed she liked rough sex. Walsingham maintained he had a good sex life with his wife, and that there was nothing rough about it."

"Hmm. Did Kaminski admit to being in the bathroom?" Dylan asked.

"Yes, but he had little choice given that his prints were over everything. He claims that, when he left, she was still enjoying a nice hot soak."

"Your house-to-house inquiries," Frank said. "They didn't bring up anything else at all?"

"Nothing."

One of the bar staff came to put logs on the fire. Talk turned to the weather, how spring was supposed to have arrived and how the forecasters were predicting gales and heavy rain for the next couple of days. Dylan wasn't paying attention. He was more interested in the murder of Carly Walsingham.

Having dealt with the fire and satisfied himself that the logs were sufficient, the young man left them alone.

"Tell me," Dylan said, "why would Aleksander Kaminski use a surgical blade to murder someone?"

Lewis shrugged. "Why not?"

"If I were a builder," Dylan said, "I'd use a hammer or a saw—"

"Or something equally easy to slip in a pocket." Lewis grinned and Dylan supposed he had a valid point.

"I know what you mean, Dylan," Frank said, "and I'd expect a builder to use one of the tools of his trade. Surgical blades, scalpels, small sharp knives—they're common enough in the building business though."

"I suppose so." Dylan's mind flitted to something else. "Am I to assume then that Kaminski is a bit dim, a sandwich short of a picnic?"

Lewis frowned. "Not especially. What makes you ask?"

"The fact that he had a surgical blade with him hints that the murder was premeditated," Dylan said. "Given that, you'd think anyone but a moron would wear gloves. Even the least clued-up on forensics know about fingerprints. Perhaps some people don't know about getting prints from flesh, but everyone knows you can lift them off doors and furniture. If I was murdering someone, I'd either wear gloves or, if that was impossible because I fancied sex with the victim first, I'd wipe the place clean afterwards."

Smiling, Lewis shook his head. "Anyone can plan a murder. Carrying it out takes a lot of balls. Hanging around with a corpse and cleaning up the evidence takes even more balls. He will have panicked and got the hell away."

Dylan tried to put himself inside the killer's mind. And failed. If he, Dylan, was planning on murdering a woman, he knew damn well he wouldn't be able to have sex with her first.

"A doctor would use a surgical blade," he said.

"I used a scalpel at the weekend to trim some wallpaper," Frank said.

"And Dr. Walsingham was at the hospital at the time of the murder," Lewis said.

"Says who?" Dylan asked.

"I can't remember but, trust me, his alibi was watertight."

Dylan knew all about watertight alibis. During his time on

the force, he'd poked and prodded at them until they leaked like sieves.

"You'll see Kaminski for yourself tomorrow." Lewis's smile was wry. "I'm surprised he managed to convince his own mother that he's innocent."

FOUR

DYLAN WAS STILL pondering Lewis Cameron's words when he joined the queue of visitors at Strangeways. Or, to give the building its correct name, HM Prison Manchester. They could call it what they liked but, to most people, and certainly to the people who saw its tall tower on the skyline every day, it would always be Strangeways.

Built in the late 1800s, it was an impressive building. A tour, preferably when empty of inmates, would be great. An overnight stay would be bearable. Just. A life sentence behind walls that were rumoured to be sixteen feet thick in places would be one of the worst things imaginable.

Dylan had arrived early because he knew how long it took to process all visitors, especially first-timers, but he was still surprised by the length of the queue. Eventually, it was his turn to hand over his visiting order and be subjected to a surprisingly thorough search.

It was the first time Dylan had been inside a prison since his own stint behind bars and the experience sent shudders down his spine. He'd never suffered from claustrophobia, but he was getting close. He'd thought he'd be okay. He wasn't. His plan had been to drive straight home to London after this visit but, sod it, he'd return to his hotel, treat himself to several stiff drinks and drive home in the morning.

With the preliminaries over, Dylan soon found himself sitting at a table opposite Aleksander Kaminski. Despite the width of the table, designed to keep prisoner and visitor apart, the man was too close. Dylan needed space.

He hadn't known what to expect but Kaminski came as a surprise. He was tall, thin and gaunt, and was wearing jeans a couple of sizes too big and a sweatshirt of indeterminable colour. He had dark hair and his eyes were like chips of ebony. Dylan would bet he was one of those men Bev would class as sexy. Bev liked her men "weathered," as she put it, with faces that looked "lived in." "Every woman fancies a bit of rough," she'd say. Which rather begged a question Dylan didn't feel like answering.

It wasn't Kaminski's appearance that took him by surprise though, more the expression of boredom he wore. Or perhaps it wasn't boredom. Perhaps it was despair.

"How's life in here?" Dylan asked.

Kaminski shrugged. "Room service is a bit slack but the rates are reasonable."

It wasn't boredom but Kaminski was showing a distinct lack of interest in Dylan's presence.

Dylan decided to get to the point. "Did you murder Carly Walsingham?"

There wasn't so much as a flicker. "No."

Dylan was finding it difficult to sit still. He wanted to push back his red plastic chair but it was attached to the table. Kaminski, on the other hand, was calm and still. CCTV cameras captured their every gesture. Prison warders watched on. They'd be extremely interested in Dylan because, try as he might, he couldn't stop putting his hands in his pockets and taking them out again. Despite the search he'd been subjected to, warders must think he was trying to pass drugs to Kaminski.

"Look, Mr. Scott, I appreciate you coming to see me but really, there's no need. I keep trying to tell my mother that we just have to put up with it, but—" He left the sentence unfinished.

"Mothers aren't very good at putting up with things."

Dylan leaned back in his seat but still couldn't settle comfortably. "My mother visited me when I was in prison." He saw a touch of surprise on Kaminski's face and ignored it. It amazed Dylan, too. First that he'd ended up behind bars and second that his mother had been allowed to visit. She usually carried enough marijuana to keep every inmate happy for a month. "She liked to tell everyone who'd listen that I was innocent. It didn't help. In fact, it was downright embarrassing. Once a judge has spoken, there's little that can be done."

Kaminski didn't comment and Dylan thought again of Lewis Cameron's words. Lewis was right in that Kaminski would have a hard job convincing his own mother of his innocence. He'd managed that, though.

Dylan wanted to escape this place, get back to his hotel, enjoy a few drinks and a good night's sleep before driving away from Lancashire. There was no point getting involved. There was especially no point when the man sitting opposite looked as if he couldn't care less.

The cameras watched on and Dylan supposed he should go through the motions.

"Tell me about Mrs. Walsingham then," he said. "You married her when you both lived in Birmingham. Is that right?"

"You're wasting your time, mate."

"Not at all. Your parents are paying me well so I should give them their money's worth."

Kaminski looked at him for long moments and Dylan thought he could easily be a murderer. He'd bet those dark eyes were no strangers to anger.

"Okay," Kaminski said. "Yes, I married Carly when we lived in Birmingham. I thought we'd live happily ever after, but we didn't. We moved up to Dawson's Clough, realised I couldn't have kids, started fighting and got divorced. Then she married her doctor and had the kids she wanted."

Kaminski spoke in an offhand way yet he couldn't quite conceal a depth of feeling that surprised Dylan.

"She was happy presumably?" Dylan asked.

"Not really, no. She loved the kids but felt nothing for her husband. He bored her. Just as I knew he would."

"Was she easily bored then?"

Kaminski thought about that and chose his words with care. "No, but she wasn't the type to be content with a role as a doctor's wife either. She had her own life and liked to live it to the full."

"I see."

"She loved the kids, though," Kaminski added. "Idolised them."

"How long had you been having an affair with her?"

Kaminski smiled at that, a wry painful smile. "It seems like all my life."

"That sounds a bit dramatic." To put it mildly.

"Our whole relationship was a bit dramatic. Okay, we met at secondary school. I was fourteen, Carly was eleven. We hung out together and started seeing each other seriously when she was sixteen and I was nineteen."

"Childhood sweethearts."

"Yes."

"Yet she divorced you," Dylan said. "Why?"

"She wanted kids and I couldn't have them."

"Hadn't she heard of adoption?"

"She'd heard of it."

"But she wanted a child of her own?"

"Yes, and she refused to go through all the adoption rigmarole and spend years waiting, possibly in vain because age was creeping up on her."

"Okay." Dylan supposed it was feasible. "So you divorced. Carly married her doctor and you married Sue."

"You've got it."

Dylan wondered why he didn't just leave him to it. If Kaminski wasn't bothered about any of it, why the hell should anyone else care? If Kaminski was happy to rot behind these sixteen feet thick walls, why not let him?

"So how did you suddenly end up in her bed again?"

"After we got divorced, she refused to see me, but she'd phone me all the time to tell me she was dating Neil, marrying Neil, having Neil's baby. I met Sue and thought we could move on. We couldn't though. A month or so after I married Sue, Carly suggested we meet up. We went for a coffee, then back to her place."

"Wait a minute. You'd been seeing her that long?"

"Yes."

"But Sue said you'd only seen her a couple of times."

"Christ, what else was I going to tell her? It was bad enough as it was. They let her visit me when I was in custody and, despite the fact that it had been splashed across the front page of the local rag, she wouldn't believe I'd seen Carly." He expelled a long breath. "It was bloody difficult convincing her it was true. I could hardly pile on more grief by telling her I'd been seeing her for years, could I?"

"She really had no idea? You see another woman for years and Sue doesn't once ask where you've been and what you've been up to?"

"No. I used to visit Carly's house and that's it. Her husband assumed she was flicking a duster round or cleaning windows, and my wife thought I was working. My job made it easy. I'd spend two days working on a porch for someone, a day fitting a door for someone else, then a week erecting a conservatory for yet another customer. Sue would have no need to know where I was working. I used to finish work early, go to Carly, and then return to Sue. I was never late home, I never spent the night or a weekend with Carly. There were no meals out or any of the usual romantic crap."

If Kaminski was telling the truth, and Dylan had heard so many conflicting stories it was difficult to tell truth from fiction, it was possible that Carly Walsingham was using him. Presumably, she enjoyed her children and life as the doctor's wife but liked to play games with her old childhood sweetheart. She wouldn't let him move on. She didn't want him, but she didn't want anyone else to have him either. No man would appreciate being used as a plaything.

Would they dislike it enough to commit murder? They might. Dead women don't play mind games.

"How often did you visit her?" Dylan asked.

"A couple of times a week. Every Monday and Thursday."

"I thought she was murdered on a Wednesday."

"She was. She'd phoned me the night before, the Tuesday, and said she'd arranged to meet up with an old friend on Thursday. She suggested I go round the following afternoon instead."

"Tell me about that phone call." Dylan tried to give the air of being calm and relaxed. He was neither. This place was freaking him out.

"There's not a lot to tell." Kaminski's tone was dry. "She phoned, explained she'd arranged to meet up with her friend Kirsten, and told me to go round the following afternoon instead. We were having a laugh, joking about not being able to wait, and then she dropped her voice and told me she had company. I assumed she meant her husband was home. We finished the call abruptly."

"You didn't threaten her?"

"No."

"Her husband claims you did. He also said she was upset. Agitated. That's why the police checked the phone records to see who she'd been speaking to."

"He's lying."

Was he? Dylan found it impossible to tell. That lie, if it

was a lie, had helped put Kaminski in this hell-hole. Yet Kaminski didn't seem bothered one way or the other.

"Why would he lie?" Dylan asked.

"I've no idea."

"Where did you meet up?" Dylan asked. "Was it always at her place?"

"Yes."

"Wasn't that a bit risky? Wouldn't the neighbours get suspicious if they saw you turning up all the time?"

"You haven't seen her house, have you?"

"No. Why?"

"There are trees in front of it," Kaminski said. "Tall, thick evergreens. On the other side of the road, there are more trees. If you stand in Carly's driveway, you can't see the houses opposite because of those trees. Alternatively, if you stand on the other side of the road, you can't see Carly's house."

"Yet a neighbour saw you leaving on the afternoon she was murdered. Or saw someone who looked like you."

"No. The neighbour saw someone walking down the back garden. I'm talking about the front of the house."

"Wait a minute. You used the front door?"

Another of those grim smiles. "Yes. Like I said, the front is far more private."

"You didn't use the back door?"

"No."

"Then your fingerprints—"

"Weren't anywhere near the back door. That's right. We went over and over that, and the police decided I'd left by the front door, walked along the side of the house and cut across the back garden."

For all Dylan knew, Kaminski could have done exactly that. Dylan liked to think he was a good judge of character. He was also a firm believer in gut instinct. With Kaminski, he felt nothing. Kaminski could be innocent. He could just as easily be as guilty as hell.

"You claim Mrs. Walsingham was in the bath when you left her," Dylan said.

"She usually was. It doesn't do to meet your children or your husband when you smell of another man, does it?"

He sounded bitter. He'd hated to think of her with her husband.

"How's your relationship with your wife?" Dylan asked.

"Sue? It's okay."

"Only okay?"

"It's no better and no worse than most marriages." Kaminski leaned toward Dylan. "Look, mate, you're wasting your time. Whoever killed her is long gone. You can't bring her back."

"It's not a question of bringing *her* back though, is it?" Dylan said. "The idea is to get *your* life back?"

Kaminski didn't bother to comment. He looked as if escaping these thick walls was of no interest to him whatsoever. Dylan didn't know whether to admire him or shake him until his teeth rattled.

"Tell me what you did the day she was murdered," he said.

Kaminski sighed, like a man who was tired of telling the same story over and over. "I did a morning's work. I was putting up a conservatory for a couple in Dawson's Clough. I finished at lunchtime and drove out to see Carly. I parked in my usual spot on a side street, Hilltop Avenue, and walked the half mile to her house. I stopped at the newsagent's for a pack of cigarettes but, other than that, I didn't see anyone to speak to. I got to her house, rang the bell and she let me in. I had a shower—she used to get off on the idea of me showering in his bathroom—and then we went to bed. She had a collection of sex toys and we messed around with those. She liked rough sex. It was always the missionary position with her husband, and that bored her. Anyway, at about three o'clock, it was time for me to leave so I ran her a bath and left her in it. I walked back to my car and drove home. I began preparing dinner and then Sue came home. It was her aunt's birthday and she was busy telling me about that. She visits her aunt—her great-aunt in a care home—every Wednesday and it was the old dear's ninetieth birthday that day. Sue was full of that. The next thing I knew, Carly's face was plastered all over the TV and they said she was dead. Murdered."

He might pretend to be in control of his emotions but the colour had slowly ebbed from his face with every word. His sickly pallor made those dark eyes even more startling.

If—and it was a big *if*—he was telling the truth, it was a shocking story. Reliving it would make anyone queasy.

"Her collection of sex toys. Describe them to me."

Dark eyebrows rose at the request. "She had handcuffs, a whip, a huge red vibrator—"

"Okay. And who knew you were seeing her?" Dylan asked.

"Apart from the lying doctor? No one."

"What do you mean? Are you saying Walsingham knew about it?"

"Me and Carly thought so. I don't know how he could have found out, but we were pretty sure he knew. Or at least suspected."

Walsingham knew that Kaminski had been phoning his wife. Stalking her. Could he have known they were having an affair? If, of course, they *were* having an affair.

"As far as I'm aware," Kaminski said, "no one else knew. I don't see how they could have. Carly liked to live dangerously, that's why she wanted me in his bed, why she insisted on my taking a shower in his bathroom, but she wouldn't have told anyone. She wasn't *that* crazy."

"Was she seeing anyone else?"

"No."

"Are you sure?" Dylan asked again.

"Yes."

"Were *you* seeing anyone else?"

Kaminski smiled that half-smile again. "No."

It was almost time to go and Dylan was more than ready.

"Okay," he said, "I'll think about everything you've told me."

"Please yourself," Kaminski said.

"What I can't understand is your attitude." Again, Dylan felt an almost overwhelming urge to shake the bloke. "You don't seem to care whether you get out of here or not. Are you really prepared to rot in this hellhole?"

Kaminski leaned in until he was inches from Dylan's face. "Tell you what, Mr. Scott, why don't you go home and put the television on? Catch the local news and imagine they're saying *your* wife's been butchered. Forget they're talking about yet another murder or a senseless stabbing in another anonymous city. Imagine it's *your* wife. Picture *your* wife lying in a bath of blood. See what you care about after that."

It was time to go and Dylan got to his feet.

"It's not the same though, is it? Mrs. Walsingham wasn't *your* wife."

Kaminski nodded slowly, looked as if he was about to argue and then couldn't be bothered. "No. She wasn't my wife."

Dylan really didn't know what to make of Kaminski.

"So," he said, "who do you think killed her?"

"I've no idea."

"What? None at all? You've been here all this time, with nothing to do but think, and yet you haven't come up with a single suspect?"

"I didn't say that." Kaminski was totally unruffled. "I said I had no idea who killed her. It could have been anyone. I'd start with her husband."

"What makes you say that?"

Kaminski shrugged. "It could as easily have been him as anyone else. Carly wasn't the only one looking elsewhere."

"How do you know?" Dylan asked.

Kaminski was standing. Time was up. "That he was seeing other women? Carly told me."

"He has an alibi."

"Yeah, I know. A nurse he was shagging vowed he was at the hospital when Carly was killed." Kaminski's smile was bitter. "Life's full of surprises, isn't it?"

FIVE

Bev pulled her fingers through her hair. She was quite probably going insane. So far today, she'd burst into tears three times for no apparent reason. And now—

God, now the TV was loud enough to split eardrums, Freya was screaming at the top of her exceptionally healthy lungs, Luke was yelling "Freya's screaming" above the noise, and the bloody phone was ringing.

Bev Scott, this is your life.

She snatched at the phone. "Yes?"

Although she hadn't bothered to look at the display, the surprised silence on the other end told her who was calling.

"Everything all right?" Dylan asked.

"Bloody hell, Dylan. Does it sound all right?"

"I've called at a bad time, haven't I? You get on with whatever you were doing and I'll call back later, okay?"

"Good idea, Dylan. You go and put your feet up. Have a drink, watch a film, enjoy yourself. Meanwhile, I'll deal with *your* family, shall I?"

"Bev, I'm only trying to—"

"Shut up." She bit back on her temper. "Have a chat with Luke while I try to stop Freya screaming. Then again, I might just join her." She held the phone at arm's length and called to Luke. "Your dad's on the phone."

Luke was smiling for the first time that day as he grabbed the phone, and Bev's mood softened slightly. It couldn't be easy for Luke either. As soon as she'd settled Freya and spoken to Dylan, she'd spend some quality time with him. Perhaps they could watch a DVD together.

That was assuming she could stay awake because, right now, exhausted didn't even hint at how she felt. Dylan's mum had been a gem and would have been here now if Bev hadn't sent her away until the morning, but Bev didn't want to take advantage.

This was no joke though. Even climbing the stairs took effort.

When she reached Freya's room, she was tempted to sit in the middle of the floor and howl. It wasn't only that Freya enjoyed exercising her lungs constantly, it was the lack of— something. Wasn't she supposed to experience a huge gut-wrenching rush of love when she saw her daughter? She felt nothing.

She couldn't remember how she'd felt when Luke was born, but she knew she hadn't been this empty.

"Okay, madam, what can we do for you?" She reached into the cot and lifted Freya out. Her baby's face was red from screaming, but there were no pointers as to what she might want. She'd been fed and changed less than twenty minutes ago.

Bev carried her round the room, rocking her in an instinctive manner and, gradually, the screams subsided to sobs. With the noise level bearable, Bev carried her downstairs and kept rocking her as she waited for Luke to finish talking to his dad.

Her baby was stunningly beautiful. She had huge eyes and a thick tuft of dark hair. Perhaps if she wasn't so noisy, so demanding, Bev would feel that overwhelming rush of love she kept waiting for.

Luke handed over the phone, grabbed an apple and went to the relative safety of the sitting room. Bev sat at the kitchen table, baby in one hand, phone in the other. She felt more like bursting into tears than talking.

"So what's it like to have peace, quiet and room service?" she asked.

"I'd rather be at home."

"Tell you what then, let's swap. You come home and I'll bugger off to Lancashire for weeks at a time." Even as she spoke, she knew there was no point taking everything out on Dylan. Who else was there, though?

"Bev, if you want me to come home, just say the word."

Really, when she stopped to think about it, all she had to do was cope with one small child. It wasn't as if Luke made huge demands on her. He was a sensible kid, old enough to be fairly independent, and even quite helpful when he put his mind to it. All she had to do was cope with a baby. She'd done it before. All over the world, women were coping. Some were doing all sorts of amazing things at the same time. Bev was on maternity leave so all she had to think about was one small child. It wasn't rocket science.

"Your mum's been," she said, "and she's coming round tomorrow. It's fine."

"Good."

"So," she said, "did you see Aleksander today? Can you prove his innocence?"

She didn't really care one way or the other, but even she was tired of her constant whining.

"You've been talking to Mum. Her friends—friends she hasn't seen for ages, I might add—believe their son is innocent. Therefore, Mum believes he's innocent. For all I know, he could have butchered dozens of people in his time."

"You think he might be guilty?"

"Of course he might be." She heard amusement in his voice. "The police thought him guilty, the jury decided he was guilty—"

"Well, yes, but what do *you* think?"

He was a long time answering. "I don't know. I truly don't know."

"So what are you going to do?"

Bev was torn. Half of her wanted him at home to share the responsibility. On the other hand, she liked him better when he was working. Added to that, babies were unbelievably expensive. They needed the money.

"I'm going to do a bit of digging around," he said. "According to Kaminski, Carly Walsingham's husband was having affairs and one of his women provided his alibi. I want to look into that, see what I can find out."

"You'll be home at the weekend though, won't you? It's Easter."

"Of course I will. Meanwhile, make good use of my mother. She's desperate to help, you know she is. She'd be more than happy to spend the night and—"

"I can cope." It was only one baby, she reminded herself.

"I know, but you may as well make the most of her. God, there has to be some advantage to my having her for a mother."

Bev had to smile. She knew how much Dylan loved his mother. She also knew that the woman drove him to distraction and he longed for what he called a *normal* mother.

Bev adored her mother-in-law. Yes, she still wore beads and flowers in her hair, a relic from the sixties, and she smoked marijuana like some people drank coffee, but she was fun. True, the ideas she came up with, like the camel-trekking holiday they'd survived in the summer, were a tad off the wall, but life was never boring around Vicky Scott.

Life was an exciting adventure as far as Vicky was concerned. No way would she let one small child turn her life and her emotions upside down. Bev could learn a lot from her.

"It's fine," she said. "Truly. Do what you have to do and I'll see you at the weekend."

As soon as she replaced the receiver, she took her sleeping baby upstairs.

Then she sat on the floor and burst into tears.

SIX

ALEK LAY ON his mattress and stared at the ceiling. The quick and no doubt cheap paint job was already failing. A crack in the shape of a V was getting bigger. Perhaps, in ten years, the ceiling would crash down on top of him.

He didn't have to be in his cell for another hour, but it was where he preferred to be. In an hour, at lights out, he'd have a peace of sorts. The constant talking—or, more often, shouting—would cease for a few hours and all would be as quiet as it got in this place. Meanwhile, he concentrated on blocking out the noise.

An unread letter from Sue scowled at him from the desk. It had arrived this morning—at least one arrived every morning—but he hadn't been in the mood to read it. He wasn't now.

It would be filled with the same old crap that was of no interest to him. She always started and ended her letters by telling him how much she missed him. The middle would be taken up with the minute details of her day, like *10:50 Jamie called and I spent an hour with him before taking Fido for a walk, 2:15 I nipped into town for groceries.* Always, hidden among the six or so pages, would be something along the lines of *Don't worry about writing to me, I know your time's taken up with stuff.* That always made him smile. If there was one thing he did have, the only thing he had, it was time. Days stretched endlessly toward the night and sometimes, he was convinced time had stopped. It was inclination he lacked, not time.

He received almost as many letters from his mother, but

those weren't too bad. His mother wasn't as needy or as clingy as his wife. He could write his mother half a page about how well he was doing, and she'd be content. Not content enough to give up on him without a fight though.

Dylan Scott was the third private investigator she'd spoken to. The first one had been a stiff, formal man who, after speaking to Alek, wrote to his parents saying that, regrettably, he felt unable to take on the case. The second hadn't even bothered speaking to him.

It didn't matter. Alek couldn't complain of being lonely because he had plenty of guilt to keep him company.

Guilt was another reason, possibly the real reason he couldn't bring himself to read Sue's letter. He'd lived with shame because, no matter how hard he tried, he'd never been able to love Sue. That was why he'd been so careful. He and Carly had never enjoyed nights together or romantic meals for two so he'd never had the usual adulterer's slip-ups to worry about, but he'd always made doubly sure there were no stray hairs on his jacket or lipstick smears on his collar. Although he'd never loved Sue, he'd cared about her enough to make sure she never knew about him and Carly.

Having to tell her he'd been screwing his ex-wife while she'd been visiting her great-aunt was one of the hardest things he'd ever done. It would have been easier perhaps if she'd walked out on him. But no. Shock and hurt had been there for all the world to see, yet there had been no recriminations.

Before this nightmare started, they hadn't been worrying unduly about finances. They'd had to stretch their money and make cutbacks, though. Thanks to the recession, people were panicking about their jobs and putting any plans they'd had to add extensions or conservatories to their homes on the back burner until the economy picked up. Now, Sue would be finding it almost impossible to cope without his income.

She'd go without food herself rather than let the strays starve. She had a roof over her head at the moment, but for how long?

And still there were no recriminations. Still she loved him. Still the letters arrived.

His parents didn't deserve this either. They were proud people who'd worked hard all their lives. The shame of having a son forever branded a killer would be more than they should have to bear.

The noise around him built to a crescendo. Voices were raised, heavy metal doors were slammed shut, locks were checked and double-checked. At last, a restless, uneasy quiet descended on the cells.

Alek didn't move. He knew from experience that, eventually, he'd drift off to sleep for a couple of hours, maybe even four or five. It was the dreams he dreaded. Some people, Sue for one, could sleep for eight hours solid without having a single dream. Alek envied her. He would love to sleep and wake up slowly feeling relaxed and refreshed. When he slept, he invariably woke bathed in sweat with his heart doing its best to leap out of his ribcage.

He'd never been a great fan of reading or watching television, but he'd done a lot of both in Strangeways. Biographies were his reading choice and he was halfway through Kirk Douglas's life story.

Many people thought it wrong that prisoners had televisions in their cells. They said prison was more luxury holiday than punishment. The argument was that the punishment was being relieved of freedom and that, if men were treated like animals, they came out fighting. Alek didn't know who was right or wrong. Nor did he know if he'd go out fighting when he'd served his life sentence.

"And that's another thing," the moaning brigade would cry. "Life should mean life."

In Alek's case, life meant at least twelve years. It would be long enough.

He closed his eyes but knew sleep was a long way off. He didn't mind. If he slept, he would dream, and the dream was always the same. He would hear Carly calling to him above the sound of running water. He'd watch that water turn red.

Sometimes, in his dreams, the hot red water swallowed them both.

SEVEN

EARLY THE NEXT morning, Dylan called Dr. Neil Walsingham's home phone. Receiving no reply, he called the hospital and was soon thanking God it wasn't an emergency. The phone rang out for a full two minutes before Dylan gave up and re-dialled. Again, it rang out unanswered. He ordered himself a coffee in the hotel's lounge, carried it to a table near the window, and tried the number again. This time it rang out for just over a minute.

"Dawson's Clough General Hospital. How may I help you?"

Dylan decided that "by answering the damn phone more quickly" wasn't a suitable response.

"I'd like to speak to Dr. Walsingham, please," he said.

"Just a minute." Papers rustled. "He's on duty in Accident and Emergency at the moment. I can leave a message for him if you like."

"Will you ask him to call me? My name's Dylan Scott. I'm a private investigator." He gave her his number and, because she didn't inspire confidence, he made her read it back to him.

"I'll pass on the message," she said.

"I'd be grateful. It's important. What time will he be off duty?"

"Six o'clock this evening."

Dylan thanked her and, as he drank his coffee, he wondered how to spend time until Walsingham called.

He still wasn't sure what to make of Aleksander Kaminski. It was impossible to know if he was innocent or guilty, or why he was so damned unconcerned about spending years of his life locked up like an animal.

Assuming he was innocent—Dylan's mantra was *Never Assume*—but assuming he was, the finger of guilt might point toward Walsingham. If he was having affairs, as Kaminski claimed, he'd be more or less guaranteed an alibi, and if he wanted his wife out of the way, he'd be a man with plenty of surgical blades at his disposal. How many people knew that severing the carotid artery would have a victim bleeding out in seconds? How many people even knew what or where the carotid artery was?

Or maybe the killer simply slashed and got lucky. Or unlucky. Maybe a burglar hadn't realised she was in the house, panicked, intended to cut her as a warning and watched her bleed out in record time.

Or maybe, and this was far more likely, Kaminski had tired of her games and decided it was time to stop them once and for all.

His coffee cup empty, Dylan returned to his room and switched on his newly acquired laptop. He was getting to be quite a whiz on the machine, even if he did say so himself. Admittedly, he had a good teacher in Luke.

He conducted another online search for Dr. Neil Walsingham. There were several mentions of him working at Dawson's Clough hospital. He also considered himself something of an artist and a couple of his works—awful, childlike daubs of red and blue paint—were showcased on a website promoting local artists' work. Dr. Walsingham was also on the committee of the local camera club. A head-and-shoulders shot showed a smiling slim man with fair hair flopping across his forehead. Another picture showed him with a medal round his neck after completing a marathon and raising over two thousand pounds for a children's charity.

Still he didn't return Dylan's call.

Dylan hunted out ex-DI Cameron's phone number. There were a couple of questions he wanted to ask him.

Here, at least, was someone willing to answer their phone.

"Lewis? It's Dylan."

"Hi. Are you back in London? You saw Kaminski, I assume?"

"I'm still in Lancashire but yes, I did see him. That's why I'm calling. I wondered if you'd clarify a couple of points."

"You surely didn't fall for his story, did you?"

"I'm keeping an open mind."

Dylan neither believed Kaminski's story nor disbelieved it. If there was a possibility that the man was innocent, though, it was up to Dylan to get him out of Strangeways. He knew only too well what wrongful imprisonment felt like.

"You've been off the force too long, mate."

Dylan didn't suppose there was any malice in his words, but he still resented them.

"Maybe. Right, first off, Kaminski claims that he left Mrs. Walsingham's property at about three o'clock. Now, your witness says she saw him, or someone else, leaving at around three forty-five. Is that right?"

"That's right." Lewis chuckled down the phone. "He says he left about three o'clock. About. That could mean anything from half past two to half past three. The neighbour says she saw someone at about a quarter to four. That little word *about* again."

He spoke as if he were trying to explain the theory of relativity to a four-year-old.

"What else do you want to know?" Lewis asked.

"Dr. Walsingham's alibi. Who verified it?"

"I can't remember offhand, but several people confirmed it. I tell you, his alibi's watertight."

Call me a bluff old cynic, Dylan thought, but all alibis were watertight until someone punched a hole in them.

"Hmm. What about motive?" he asked. "What was Ka minski's motive for killing her, Lewis?"

"Who knows? Maybe Carly had threatened to tell his wif he kept pestering her."

Dylan wasn't convinced. "Was there any money in it? Di anyone gain financially from her death?"

"Nope. The money was all the doctor's." He laughed, bu it was a tight, humourless sound. "I don't know how muc evidence the elite southern police forces need but, up north we find phone calls, witnesses and fingerprints pretty con vincing."

Dylan didn't miss the sarcasm. Or the resentment. Lewi Cameron didn't appreciate people looking for holes in hi casework.

They chatted for a few more minutes, but Dylan was n wiser when he ended the call than he'd been at the start.

Either Kaminski was lying or confused about the time h left, the witness was mistaken about the time, or someon else left the house that day. Or, as Lewis Cameron would sa all timings were approximate. In Dylan's book, approximat equalled meaningless.

Dylan called the hospital again and was told, again, that message would be passed on to Dr. Walsingham.

"He knows you want to speak to him," the receptionis said, "so I'm sure he'll call you back when he has a free mo ment. He's a very busy man, you know."

To pass time more than anything else, Dylan drove t Lakeside Drive and found number two, home of Dr. Wals ingham and his sons.

Kaminski was probably right in that the front of the prop erty was more private than the back. Dylan would guess tha the twelve houses making up Lakeside Drive had been buil between ten and twenty years ago. They sat on the edge of road that circled a manmade lake. Each was large, detache

nd sat within its own good-sized garden. Each was differ-
nt too.

To see the front of the Walsinghams' home, Dylan had to
ark the Morgan at the bottom of their driveway. Tall ever-
reen trees shielded the building from prying eyes. As Ka-
ninski had said, it was impossible to see the properties on
he other side of the small lake. They were a fair distance
way too.

Property prices in this northern mill town were lower than
most in the UK but—thanks to a good motorway network that
ave the town easy access to Manchester, Liverpool, Leeds,
reston and Glasgow—were increasing. These properties
ad five bedrooms minimum, double garages, large gardens
nd, more sought-after than anything else, privacy. A Lake-
ide Drive address wouldn't come cheap.

Dylan left his car blocking the driveway and walked a cir-
le round the lake. Each home boasted a sophisticated alarm
ystem. He supposed that meant very little though. People
ended to activate alarms when they went to bed at night and
when they left the property. If they were at home during the
ay, alarms were often ignored.

Feeling aimless, he returned to his car and drove into the
entre of Dawson's Clough. At least the weather was better
oday. The wind had died down a little and, although the sky
was still a menacing battleship grey, it wasn't raining.

He walked past the indoor market, bought himself a news-
aper and headed to Starbucks. The coffee bar was busy, tales taken mostly by female shoppers, but he got a coffee and
arried it to the one free table in the corner.

Still Walsingham didn't return his call.

It was unlikely that the doctor would tell him anything he
idn't already know. With or without talking to him, Dylan
eeded to make up his mind. Did he take this case or not? The
money would be more than useful and he had nothing else to

do. On the other hand, Kaminski's parents weren't wealth
and he didn't like the idea of wasting their life savings.

He'd talk to Walsingham and then make up his mind.

First and foremost, he wanted to hear more about the
phone call. Walsingham had said his wife was being threat
ened, and Kaminski claimed that all they'd done was arrang
to meet the following day. Who was lying?

A harassed-looking woman at the next table balanced sev
eral carrier bags on a chair before ticking items off on
shopping list. She peered inside one of bags and counte
the number of chocolate eggs she'd bought. Dylan mentall
thanked her for the reminder.

It was Easter which meant that flowers for Bev wouldn
be considered an unexpected treat, they were a necessit
Experience had taught him that he needed to buy her a car
flowers and a huge beribboned egg if he wanted to keep o
the right side of her.

Luke was the child in the house, but he'd be content wit
any old egg. Madness.

As he drank his coffee, he wondered how much the var
ous celebrations cost over the course of the year. Christma:
birthdays, wedding anniversaries, Valentine's Day, Easter–
the expense was vast. He'd just spent a fortune to celebrat
Freya's birth too.

He made another mental note. He must stop being such
grumpy bastard. He had a wonderful family, the best.

With his coffee drunk, he went on a shopping spree. Th
flowers would wait until he was on the way home, but he soo
had a suitably romantic card, two sickly chocolate eggs fo
Luke, a fluffy Easter bunny for Freya and the biggest, mos
expensive egg in the shop for Bev. Sorted.

He stowed his purchases in the Morgan and set off in
more determined mood for Dawson's Clough General Hos
pital.

The building was new and several people stood puffing
on cigarettes outside glass automatic doors. Inside, there was
less activity. He walked up to the deserted reception desk.
The phone rang out. Unbelievable.

A dark-haired woman in her thirties eventually strolled
over, nodded at Dylan, and answered the phone.

Dylan gave the hospital the benefit of the doubt. No emergency calls would come through on this number, and staff
would be too busy dealing with patients to worry too much
about people phoning with general enquiries. Presumably rel-
atives enquiring about patients would call the specific wards.

The call ended and she looked at Dylan. "Can I help?"

"I hope so." Dylan gave her his best smile. "I'd like to
speak to Dr. Neil Walsingham."

"You phoned earlier. You're the private investigator, right?"

"That's right."

Unimpressed, she turned away and flicked through charts
on a clipboard. "Just a minute."

She lifted a phone, and tapped in two numbers. "Is Dr.
Walsingham there?"

After a lengthy conversation, she ended the call. "Sorry,
but he's not on duty. He finished at twelve."

"Really?" It was almost two o'clock. "I was told he'd be
here till six."

She shrugged in a that's-your-problem way.

"I've tried his landline," he said, "but he's not home, and
I seem to have lost his mobile number. I don't suppose you'd
give me that, would you?"

"Sorry, I'm not allowed to do that."

"Ah, yes. Very sensible. You couldn't do me a huge favour and phone his mobile and ask him to give me a call,
could you?"

"Well—"

"Thanks. My name's Dylan Scott and if you could give him

my number again, just in case he's lost it, that would be great. He took his phone from his pocket and pretended to searc for his own number. "I always forget it—ah, here we are."

He wrote it down for her.

Still reluctant, but probably eager to get rid of him, sh turned to her side and called Walsingham's number. Dyla made a careful note of the number she tapped in on his ow phone.

The receptionist's call was answered immediately and sh passed on the message. Looking pleased with herself, sh finished the call.

"He's going to call you straightaway, Mr. Scott."

"Thanks so much. Right, I'll leave you to it. Thanks again.

Dylan ambled across the car park to the Morgan and waite for his mobile to trill into life. It didn't. Dr. Walsingham wa annoyingly slow at returning calls. Either that or he didn' want to talk to a private investigator.

Dylan decided that another trip to Lakeside Drive wa in order.

Once again, he parked in the Walsinghams' driveway. Thi time, he strode up to the front door and rang a bell. A lou irritating tune played inside but no one responded. Dyla walked round to the back of the house. The garden was larg with a couple of apple trees, a greenhouse and a wooden sum merhouse. Off to the right, above a wooden fence dividin the two properties, he could see the roof of the neighbours conservatory. Presumably, the witness who claimed to hav seen Kaminski had been washing leaves off that roof. On of the Walsinghams' apple trees was probably the culprit.

Anyone who knew the Walsinghams' property, anyon who wanted to remain hidden from prying eyes, would us the front entrance. Only someone who assumed, as is usu ally the case, that the back was more private would make hi escape this way. And that someone would have to walk th onsiderable length of the garden to reach the gate in the fence hat led to a road at the back of the properties.

Dylan returned to the front of the house and prodded the loorbell again.

A car horn sounded. Dylan turned round and saw that a nan with fair hair flopping over his forehead was leaning on he horn of a blue Mercedes.

"Sorry." Dylan waved his arm and dashed back to his car. le moved the Morgan five yards, allowing the man access o the drive.

The Mercedes slid into the left side of a double garage and)ylan had the feeling that the door would have been closed f he hadn't called out.

"Dr. Walsingham?"

"Yes." He came toward Dylan.

"Dylan Scott." He offered his hand.

"Ah yes, the private investigator." He looked Dylan up nd down, his gaze lingering on Dylan's scuffed shoes be-iore returning to his face. "What would a private investiga-or want with me?"

"I'm working for Aleksander Kaminski," Dylan explained.

Valsingham didn't even blink. "I'm sorry for your loss, Dr. Valsingham, truly sorry, but I wondered if I might ask you few questions."

"No. I'm sorry, but I don't have the time." Walsingham vas broader across the shoulders than was evident from the hotos Dylan had seen. His dark suit looked handmade. A old watch, slim and expensive-looking, peeped out from a risp white shirt cuff.

"I could come back later. Six o'clock? Seven?"

"No. Sorry."

"Tomorrow?"

"No. Look, Mr.—"

"Scott. Dylan Scott."

"Mr. Scott, I'm sorry but I have nothing to say to you or to anyone else. As you can imagine, it's all been very difficult. For my sons, too. We had reporters camped out on our doorstep for months. We're slowly starting to move on and get our lives back together and we don't want it all dragged up again. No. I'm sorry, but it's too distressing."

"I can appreciate that, and I promise it'll only take a couple of minutes. Five minutes tops."

"No. Sorry." Walsingham strode back to his car, took a sports bag from the passenger seat and headed for the front door. "I'm sorry you've had a wasted journey, Mr. Scott. Goodbye."

The front door that had once been covered with Aleksander Kaminski's fingerprints opened and closed. Dylan was left standing in the middle of the driveway.

It irked him that he'd learned nothing from Dr. Walsingham, but something, and he had no idea what, had convinced him to take this case.

For all he knew, Kaminski could have planned Carly Walsingham's murder for months and carried it out in a calm, coldblooded, exacting manner. On the other hand, Dylan wasn't convinced and, so long as that albeit small element of doubt remained, he wouldn't rest.

One way or another, he had to learn the truth. He had to prove Kaminski's innocence or his guilt.

EIGHT

JAMIE TINSLEY BOWED his head.

"For what we are about to receive may the Lord make us truly grateful." His father recited the words that came before every meal in this house. "We also ask You, Lord, to take good care of our son Peter, and we thank You for seeing fit to take him to Your side. We thank You for Peter and we ask that You watch over him."

"Amen," they said dutifully.

Jamie sat opposite his mother at the dining table that had dominated this room for as long as he could remember. His father took his place at the head of the table.

"It's good to see you, James," his mother said as they picked up cutlery and prepared to slog their way through roast beef with all the trimmings.

"And you, Mum." He nodded at his father. "You too, Father."

His father was sixty-two yet looked much older. He'd always appeared old to Jamie. The thick hair was completely white now. Lines were deep around lifeless green eyes. Not laughter lines. Never laughter lines.

His mother looked the same as she always had. A little nervous perhaps, but that wasn't surprising. Her every waking thought was concerned with trying to do the right thing, trying to win her husband's approval. It was an impossible task.

She wore the plain long-sleeved blue dress that she seemed to be wearing every time Jamie saw her. Looking at her now, her face pale, her hair pulled back in a severe style, a stranger wouldn't know how she loved to laugh. Jamie couldn't remember the last time he'd heard that laugh, but that was because, these days, he only saw her with his father.

He loved his mother, despite her funny ways, and longed to make her laugh. Sadly, that was out of the question.

The sun was shining today, but it never reached this room at the back of the Victorian terraced house.

They'd always eaten their meals in this room. The table could accommodate eight easily, but no friends came. Years ago, it had been just the four of them. These days, his parents had it to themselves except on the rare occasions Jamie knew he could put off visiting no longer.

The only thing that had changed was the number of photographs. The dresser was now filled with pictures of Pete, the son the good Lord had seen fit to take to His side. Or as Jamie thought of it, the poor bugger who'd been blown to pieces in Afghanistan.

There were pictures showing him swamped by a school uniform that he'd eventually grown into and looking dashing in his army uniform. Jamie couldn't bear to look at them. Pete, the favourite son, was smiling in every one.

"You're still keeping busy at work then?"

Jamie swallowed a piece of beef. "I am, Father, yes. It's very rewarding."

"That's good," his mother said. "And you managed to get to church before coming here?"

"Of course." He hadn't been inside a church since he'd left home, but it was easier to lie. He'd learned that long ago. "This is delicious, Mum. You've excelled yourself."

She smiled with almost childlike delight. "It's such a pleasure to cook for my boy. I only wish Peter—"

She broke off. Jamie sucked in a breath. They knew what was coming.

"How can you wish such a thing, you ungrateful woman?"

Victor Tinsley demanded. "Our son was chosen, Margaret. We're the *lucky* ones."

"Oh, yes." Now she was flustered. "Yes, of course I know that. Sometimes, I just wish that Peter could be here, just for a few minutes."

Jamie watched his father nod. He wasn't happy, but he wasn't going to make a scene. Not today. Not on Easter Sunday.

"So long as you're not questioning God's will," he murmured, spearing a roast potato.

"Of course not."

Silence descended once more. All Jamie could hear was the occasional chink of cutlery on plates and the angry thump of his heart.

He wanted to shout and scream at his father until he saw sense. Which side was God actually on? Of all the senseless killings in Afghanistan, who was to say that God was on the side of the British or the Americans? God hadn't *chosen* Pete. Even the young Afghan who'd planted the roadside bomb that killed Pete and one of his colleagues hadn't *chosen* him.

Everything in this house, from the weather to blasted wars, was God's will.

Jamie had been six when he'd first seen his father hit his mother. That had been God's will too. It wasn't his father behaving like the bully he was. Oh, no. It was God who wanted this tall, strong man to raise his hand and knock his wife to the floor.

Pete had understood Jamie's anger, but he'd never shared it. He'd been the special son, though, so he'd had more freedom and, therefore, more opportunities to make friends. People had laughed at their parents, and Pete, always the joker outside these four walls, had laughed with them. Jamie had simply cringed with a mix of anger, embarrassment and humiliation.

He'd spent years wishing his father dead. He looked at

him now and imagined him clutching his chest, exactly as people did in films, before falling headfirst into his beef and gravy. Better still, he imagined him having a stroke, of being paralysed and being taught to eat again in an anonymous nursing home.

Sometimes, he even fantasised about killing him. He'd give him a lethal injection perhaps. Once, he dreamed that his father fell down the stairs in this house and broke his neck, dying instantly. Years later, he could still remember the feeling of disappointment when he'd woken to find it was nothing more exciting than a dream. The bastard would live forever out of spite.

"I'm getting a dog," Jamie said.

Cutlery was stilled. The only sound was the relentless ticking of the clock.

"It's a collie crossbreed," he said. "It's the image of Ben."

"Have—have more potatoes." His mother pushed the bowl toward him. "A growing lad like you—"

"And how do you plan to fit that in your life?" Victor laid down his knife and fork. "As things stand, you're even too busy to visit your own mother. How will you find time for your mother, and for worshipping our Lord, for studying His Word? Hmm?"

"Plenty of people live good, honest, decent lives and have pets," Jamie replied.

"Some people do, yes. Not you though, James. You proved that you're incapable of such things, didn't you?"

In his imagination, Jamie was upending the table, sending plates, cutlery and food flying in the air. "I was fourteen," he was yelling at his father. "I was a fucking kid, that's all." In reality, his father was waiting patiently for his response, and his mother was holding her breath and in all probability praying to God that they didn't have a fight on Easter Sunday of all days.

"I've grown up since then, Father." He couldn't look at the
an whose blood ran in his veins. "I made a mistake and I
arned my lesson."

A nerve twitched near Victor's right eye. The world seemed
stop turning for a beat.

"I hope so, James. I would hate to think that you could
ing yet more shame on your mother's head. You've disap-
inted us enough over the years, don't you agree?"

"Yes, Father."

"You've not been fit to be called son, have you?"

"No, Father."

Victor blew out a considering breath before, finally, pick-
g up his knife and fork. "I'm sure you're keen to read to us
hen we've enjoyed the Lord's offering."

Jamie longed to scream *Fuck you!* but, although he'd grown
and learned to take care of himself, he couldn't bear to
e the bruises that would appear on his mother's face if any
sagreements raised their ugly head. "I am, Father."

"Then let us eat."

To get the food past the wedge of anger lodged in his
roat, Jamie lost himself in his imagination. By the time
e apple pie and custard appeared in front of him, he'd al-
ady seen his father smashed to a pulp by a speeding train
d drowned in a bubbling bath of acid.

Die, he silently urged him. *Just fucking die.*

Nothing happened, of course. Jamie was more likely to
t struck by lightning or win the lottery than watch the
stard die.

He often thought his birth must have been the only thing
his father's life that didn't come under the God's Will cat-
ory of events. Jamie must have been a mistake. Unplanned.
s arrival in the world must have occurred at an inconvenient
me because never once had it been attributed to God's will.

Pete, on the other hand, had come along five years later

and been hailed a gift, a blessing from God. None had we
comed his arrival more than Jamie. He'd loved his broth
dearly and his death was still a raw wound that wouldn't hea

The pain was almost as raw as that of losing his belove
Ben. Pete's death he could accept. The dog's he couldn't.

Jamie helped his mother tidy up and, when the table wa
clear, he took the old Bible from his father and sat to rea
After half an hour or so, his voice grew a little croaky. A
least he didn't stutter though. He spoke slowly, forming eac
word in his head before daring to give it sound.

"That will do, James. I'm sure we all feel better." Much
Jamie's surprise, Victor rose to his feet. "If you'll excuse m
I have business to attend to. Goodbye, James. I trust we'll se
you more often in future. And, please—" his expression wa
pained, "—think about the shame your mother has to bea
before you act unwisely."

"Yes, Father."

He was going out. Jamie couldn't believe it. His father wa
actually leaving the house. There should be drum rolls an
fanfares. Birds should sing out and rejoice.

Jamie heard the garage door being opened and the old c
being reversed onto the drive before chugging off.

"Where's he going?" he asked.

"Church. He and several of the elders have a meetin
today." His mother patted his arm. "Let's go into the gar
den. The sun's shining and it would be a shame to waste it

"Good idea." Jamie followed her into the kitchen,
warmer, sunnier room, and out into the back garden. "Lunc
was lovely, Mum. Thank you."

"I just wish you came more often," she said.

"I can't."

She stopped walking to look at him. "I know. I know yo
can't."

Jamie would have liked to hold her, to comfort her, to tal

...er away from this sad, dreary place. It would make her even more nervous, though. This was the only life she knew.

She sat on the wooden bench that had been there for decades. "Sit yourself down," she said, patting the space beside her, "and tell me what you've been doing. I know you're working hard, but what about everything else? Haven't you met a nice young girl yet?"

"One that I could bring here? No." He watched her eyes cloud and wished he hadn't spoken so harshly. "Actually, there is someone. Susan. Sue. She runs an animal sanctuary in Dawson's Clough. She's nice."

"Really?" Her face became animated once more. "And does she feel the same about you?"

"I hope so. I like to think so."

He was about to tell her about how the dog had been dumped at Sue's gate, but changed his mind. They never spoke of Ben. The reminder was always there, though. Off to Jamie's right, too painful to look at, was the shed where the loyal sleek-coated pet, the best friend Jamie had ever known, had crawled to die.

"Peter was the one who would have been bringing young women home," he said instead. He knew how much she longed to talk about Pete and how she wasn't allowed to. "The girls all loved him."

"Of course they did. He was so handsome, wasn't he?"

"He was. Especially in uniform. They would have formed a very lengthy queue."

She smiled, her expression dreamy as if she were picturing her dashing son leading beautiful debutantes across a vast ballroom. "He was clever, too, wasn't he?"

"Very clever."

Not clever enough to get the exam results Jamie had. Not clever enough for university as Jamie had been. But he'd been bright, funny and lovely.

"I write to him." Her voice was almost a whisper.

"Sorry?"

"Peter. I write to him." She wasn't looking at him. "You father doesn't know, of course, but sometimes, when I can't sleep, I come downstairs and write him a letter. I can't talk to him so I—I write to him. I keep the letters at the back o the airing cupboard."

Unsure what to say, and too filled with hatred for his father to speak anyway, Jamie patted her hand.

"I suppose it sounds crazy," she said.

"Of course not. It's all part of the grieving process."

"Yes. I don't think your father would understand though."

Jamie was damn sure he wouldn't. Victor Tinsley didn't grieve. "Probably not. It'll be our little secret, eh?"

"Yes, that would be best." Her expression changed. "You must always remember that you were the son born out of love, James."

"How do you mean?"

"Just that. Nothing more." She held his hand and he could feel her trembling.

"But what—?"

"Hush now."

The way she'd spoken, he, Jamie, had been born out o love whereas Pete hadn't. That was madness, surely. Pete had been the favourite son.

Something jolted in Jamie's stomach. "He didn't rape—"

"Hush!"

"Oh, no."

She shook her head in denial. It was clear she would say no more on the subject.

"Is that to be another of our secrets?" he asked.

Her throat worked, but her lips trembled and her face wa ashen. "You're a good boy, James."

So good that he allowed his own mother to live like this

Soon, he would return to his own home. Normality. He would see normal people. Talk to normal people. She couldn't even do that.

Despite his longings and fantasies, Jamie knew his father wouldn't die for years yet. Not from natural causes, at least. The man enjoyed remarkably good health and didn't take risks. Besides, it was a well-known fact that the devil looked after his own.

God wasn't planning on putting an end to Victor Tinsley's overbearing, bullying tactics so someone else would have to. Jamie would have to.

He patted his mother's hand. "It won't always be like this. I promise."

It was a promise he intended to keep.

NINE

"I'LL GO." THE dim red light on the alarm clock showed 3:21 a.m. Unfortunately, Dylan's daughter hadn't yet learned to distinguish between social and unsocial hours. And this was definitely unsocial.

"She probably wants feeding." Bev's voice was muffled by bedclothes.

"She was only fed an hour ago." Dylan had been awake ever since Bev had crawled back to bed and put ice-cold feet on him. "I'll see what I can do."

Dylan groped around in the dark for his jeans, pulled them on and crept out of the bedroom. He closed the door behind him, switched on the landing light and padded into the nursery.

Nursery was a grand name for the spare room, the one that had been piled high with junk until they'd had the shock news of Freya's imminent arrival. Dylan had been given the task, just before Christmas, of putting up wallpaper. Instead of tasteful pastel shades, the room was now a riot of scarlet giraffes, sky-blue monkeys and yellow elephants. It was no wonder the poor kid couldn't sleep.

"Okay, Trouble, what's the problem?" The light on the landing allowed him to see his daughter in a tangle of bedclothes. He lifted her out of the crib. "What you need is a tot of fine whisky. A wee dram of Lagavulin would have you asleep in seconds. She'd smell it on your breath though, and then we'd both be up a certain creek without a paddle."

Freya, as if pondering his words, fell silent. She could keep this up all night. She'd scream for all she was worth until someone lifted her out of her crib. Behaviour would then be exemplary until someone tried to put her back.

"Tell you what," he said, carrying her down the stairs, "I'll have the Lagavulin and you inhale deeply. Maybe that'll do the trick."

It was cold in the kitchen and he flicked the switch on the boiler and listened to the satisfying clicks as pipes and radiators warmed up. It was amazing, he thought as he poured himself a drink, how quickly man could adapt to operating with one hand. There were few things you couldn't do with a baby in the crook of your arm.

He pulled a chair close to the radiator and settled himself down. There were worse ways to pass the small hours than enjoying a drink in the company of a beautiful girl.

A creak on the stairs made him think Bev hadn't gone back to sleep after all, but Luke came into the kitchen.

"Have I reared raging insomniacs?" Dylan asked.

Luke grinned and helped himself to a glass of milk and a piece of cake. "She's great, isn't she?"

"She's beautiful. But why are you still awake?"

"I've got the room next to hers. Vicky—Vicky says she'd wake the dead."

The hesitation made Dylan smile. His mother thought the title "Gran" made her sound old so she insisted that Luke call her Vicky. The poor kid still couldn't get used to the idea.

"She's probably right," Dylan said.

"When do you think she'll fit into her pyjamas, Dad?"

"Sooner than you think."

Dylan had taken Luke shopping to buy a present for his new sister and all Luke had wanted to buy was a baby pair of Arsenal FC pyjamas. Even Dylan had to admit she'd look pretty cute in them. In another nine months or so.

Freya, little angel that she was, was fast asleep. Perhaps

he'd bored her sufficiently. Dylan wasn't about to risk lowering her into her crib yet, though.

"So how's it going, Luke? Are you and your mum all right?"

"I suppose so. It's better when Gran's here though. Vicky, I mean. Mum's pretty snappy."

Dylan knew it. "She'll soon be back to normal. Babies are tiring. She was the same when you were born."

That was an out-and-out lie. When Luke had been born, Bev had been blessed with more energy than was decent for one woman. She'd raced everywhere, desperate to be the perfect mother, eager to show off her beautiful boy to everyone who stopped to look. Now, she had no energy whatsoever and even less enthusiasm. She was quiet, moody and irritable. In fact, Dylan had mentioned his concerns to his mother.

"My God," she'd said, "you've actually noticed that your wife has problems. Wonders will never cease."

"How long did it take to perfect your personal brand of sarcasm, Mum?"

She'd laughed. "It comes naturally, love. And don't worry about Bev. I'll do as much as I can to help. I expect she's just tired. She might even have a touch of postnatal depression. It's early days. Goodness, my granddaughter's not even a fortnight old yet. It'll be fine, don't worry."

Dylan *was* worried. This was unlike Bev.

"Imagine what it's like, Luke, having no sleep. One night without sleep is bad enough but when it goes on for a week or more—"

"I know, Dad. It's cool. Everything's cool."

Dylan knew it wasn't but Luke shared his own what-can't-be-changed-must-be-endured philosophy on life. There was nothing either of them could do about the situation so they'd have to put up with it until things changed.

"What time are you leaving in the morning?" Luke asked

"Not too early." He felt guilty now. While Bev was depressed or tired or whatever she was, and while Luke had to cope with it, Dylan was swanning off to Lancashire. He'd had a long weekend at home, and that had been good, but tomorrow was a bank holiday. He felt he should be at home. "I wish I didn't have to go, Luke, but I really need to."

"I know. Gran—Vicky told me all about it. Did he kill her, Dad?"

Dylan groaned inwardly. Was it normal for a woman to tell her grandson grisly murder stories? Of course it wasn't, but while Dylan's mother was a lot of things, sadly, normal wasn't one of them. He could picture her, high on dope, embellishing the story too. Not that he supposed she smoked suspicious substances in front of Luke. That wasn't the point though.

"I don't know," he said. "Possibly. Probably. I don't know and that's the whole point, Luke. If there's even a slim possibility that he's in prison when he should be at home with his family, then I have to do all I can to help. Can you understand that?"

"Yeah. No worries. I think it's cool, Dad. I just wish I was old enough to be your sidekick. I will be soon though."

"I thought you were going to play for Arsenal."

"Well, yeah. That too."

"Footballers get paid more. A lot more. I'd concentrate on that if I were you."

"We'll see." Luke nodded at his sister. "She's great when she's asleep, isn't she?"

"She is." He ruffled Luke's hair. "And so are you. Time you were back in bed."

"I'm out of here." Luke had one more long look at his sister, then went back to his room.

Long after he'd gone, Dylan was still debating whether or not to go to Lancashire in the morning. Sue Kaminski was holding an open day to raise funds for her animal sanctuary and he'd like to look round and see who turned up.

And if he stayed here, what could he do? Bev didn't trust him to do anything properly so no matter how many times he offered to help, he'd end up twiddling his thumbs while she grew more and more stressed. In any case, his mother had promised to help out.

He was pleased his Easter offering had won approval. The huge egg with its bright yellow ribbon sat on the counter, and the flowers, very carefully arranged, adorned the table. Dylan had even spotted a telltale sign of moisture in Bev's eyes as she'd opened the card. Later, he'd read it again but he had no idea what had brought that on.

"I forgot yours," she'd said.

"You always forget mine."

Still looking close to tears, she'd smiled at that. "I do, don't I?"

Dylan finished his whisky and stood up very slowly. Freya was fast asleep and he wanted her to stay that way.

Hardly daring to breathe, he carried her up the stairs to her room. He lowered her gently into her crib, covered her with the sheet and stood watching her for a moment. She didn't stir.

Breath still held, he went back to their bedroom, took off his jeans, and slid in beside Bev. All was quiet. He hoped it stayed that way till morning.

TEN

Sᴜᴇ ᴡᴀɪᴛᴇᴅ ꜰᴏʀ the day to dawn. Another day without Alek. It was a little after six and wouldn't be light for almost an hour yet.

Three dogs of various shapes and sizes snoozed in baskets, enjoying the unexpected early warmth of the kitchen. They didn't stir. It was too early even for Alek's dog, Charlie.

She'd worried about Charlie, thought he might not settle without Alek, but dogs could be fickle. Charlie didn't seem to miss his master's voice, the early morning walks or trips out in the van. So long as he was well fed, Charlie was happy.

Sue read through her letter. So far, she'd managed four pages and had made her words upbeat and lighthearted. As she'd written them, the tears had trickled down her cheeks, but Alek didn't need to know that.

She longed for him. Ached for him.

It was an age since she'd seen him and, although she was grateful to Dylan Scott for agreeing to visit him, it meant that one of Alek's precious visits had been used up. She wished, too, that Dylan had sounded more convinced of Alek's innocence. When she'd phoned him after his trip to Strangeways, he hadn't even been sure he was taking the case.

She picked up her pen again.

I'll send you photos from the fundraiser, she wrote. *It's going to be good, even if I do say so myself.*

It was no use. If she wrote to Alek in this mood, she'd simply sound pathetic. Maybe later, when the day was over and they'd raised a lot of money, she'd feel better. She must keep reminding herself that at least she had the animals and a purpose in life. When Keith had been killed in that motorway pileup, she'd had nothing.

"You're young, love," her dad had tried to console her then. "You'll be okay. One day, you'll meet someone else and fall in love..."

She hadn't believed him but, amazingly, he'd been right. It saddened her that he hadn't been able to meet Alek but she knew her dad was up there somewhere, watching over her, watching over Alek.

What Sue hadn't known when she was grieving for Keith was that, in under two years, she would have lost her dad as well. Ever since she was nine years old, when her mother ran off with an Italian waiter, Sue and her dad had been everything to each other.

Her mother's fancy man hadn't really been Italian. He'd worked in an Italian restaurant and called himself Giuseppe, but that was as close to Italy as he'd ever been.

From then on, it had been Sue and her dad. Sue hadn't minded. In fact, she'd rarely wasted a thought on her mother. Life was good and, when Sue took Keith home for the first time, her dad said he felt as if he'd gained a son.

But now—Sue often thought her life was a long procession of loss. She'd lost Keith, she'd lost her dad and now she'd lost Alek. Everyone she loved went away.

Feeling sorry for herself would achieve nothing. Besides, Alek wasn't dead. He'd been taken away from her, locked up like an unwanted animal, but she hadn't lost him. One day, and she would wait as long as it took, he'd come home to her. Maybe, if Dylan Scott was as good as everyone claimed, it would be sooner rather than later.

Meanwhile, Sue would cope. She always had and always would.

She had plenty of friends. Anne was always inviting her out and Jamie was someone she could rely on. It was fine.

Having talked herself into a more positive frame of mind, she carried on with her letter to Alek. Maybe tomorrow, she'd get a letter or two from him. Not today, it was a bank holiday, but maybe tomorrow.

ELEVEN

IT WAS ALMOST two o'clock when Dylan arrived at the Pennine View Animal Sanctuary, and he was surprised to see so many people braving the weather.

A family of three blocked his way to the front gate. The parents were trying, with little success, to explain to their inconsolable daughter that they couldn't take a dog home.

"We're out of the house all day, sweetheart," the father said. "It wouldn't be fair on an animal."

Dylan gave them a sympathetic smile as he inched past. It was difficult, if not impossible, to say no a child.

Sue Kaminski and her helpers had transformed the centre from drab to colourful. Red, white and blue bunting fluttered from everything that stood still. Brightly painted signs, dotted with cute pictures of animals, showed the way to the kennels and the cattery. Other signs pointed to a long, low barn and promised cut-price pet supplies, secondhand books and freshly baked goods.

The sun was doing little more than peep out from behind the clouds now and again. Rain was holding off for now, but people wore waterproof coats to be on the safe side.

A lot of children were in fancy dress. Dylan spotted a couple of ghosts, a pirate and an astronaut.

A young woman headed his way with Trudy, the enormous Rottweiler, trotting at her side. The dog carried a wicker basket filled with small chocolate Easter eggs in its mouth.

"For the children," the woman said, nodding at the eggs. "But can I sell you a raffle ticket? You'll see the prizes in the barn. There's wine, a basket of fruit, a voucher for a meal at a local restaurant—all sorts of things."

"Yes, of course." He exchanged a five-pound note for a strip of tickets. "Hello, Trudy." He patted the enormous head.

"Have you two met?"

"Yes. When I came to see Sue on Monday."

"Oh. So you'll be—"

"Dylan. Dylan Scott. And you are?"

"I'm Anne. I've been working here for four years now." She cocked her head on one side to appraise him. "You're the private investigator then."

"That's right."

"I couldn't believe it when she said you were going to try and get Alek released. Do you think there's any real hope of that?"

"I don't know, Anne. You obviously know Alek?"

"Yes. I used to quite like him, too. He was always a bit quiet, but Sue doted on him and he made her happy so I thought he was okay. Now, though, I don't know what to think. I still can't believe he could cheat on Sue like that. What a rat. Not that she sees him like that. She still dotes on him, despite everything. The bloke can do no wrong in her eyes. Sue's very…" she sought for the right word "…trusting. She sees good in everyone. She'll never believe he killed that woman. Never in a million years."

"Do you believe it?"

She was a long time answering. "Yes. I mean, he must have, mustn't he? The police said he did it and they'd know, wouldn't they?"

Such faith in the country's police force was touching. "They might have made a mistake."

"They might." She sounded doubtful. Trudy tugged on the leash. "I'd better get moving. I need to sell raffle tickets."

"Perhaps I'll see you later." He nodded at Trudy. "That's a good trick with the basket."

Anne smiled. "One she hasn't been taught. I don't know what it is with her but she has to pick up things and carry them around."

"I know. She took a fancy to my briefcase when I first met her."

"It's a nuisance at times. If someone puts their handbag down, Trudy takes off with it. Anyway, go and spend some money, Dylan. I'll see you later."

He headed for the barn and saw someone he recognised. The vet. Jamie, was it? He, too, had a dog, a shaggy black-and-white one, on a leash.

"Hello, I'm Dylan Scott. We met briefly on Monday. You're the vet, aren't you? Jamie, is it?"

"It is. I remember you. You're the private investigator."

"That's it." Dylan gave the dog a stroke. "Is this one yours?"

"As from today, yes. Someone abandoned him at the gate. People do that all the time. We had a cat and seven kittens dumped here last week."

"Better here than on the motorway, I suppose," Dylan said.

"Marginally." Jamie ran a hand over the dog's head. "I used to have one like him as a child and I thought it was time I had another. He's eight or nine, I'd guess, but he's a good dog and there are still a few years left in him."

"It's lucky you can take him. It must be a nightmare finding homes for them all."

"It is."

Jamie's trousers still weren't speaking to his shoes. He was wearing the same green wax coat but today his jumper was red, green and yellow striped.

"Are you on duty today?" Dylan asked.

"No. I've only come to offer Sue some moral support. She works hard on these fundraisers."

"So I see. It must be hellish expensive keeping these animals, what with food bills, wages, vet's bills."

"It is. People have to make a donation when they re-home a dog or cat," Jamie said, "but it's a small token gesture and doesn't go far. Other than that, and a small profit from the sale of pet supplies, Sue relies on other people's generosity."

Jamie's attention was caught by a mobile rainbow. "Here he is."

Around fifty brightly coloured balloons moved in their direction. A gust of wind dragged them sideways, allowing Dylan to see Sue Kaminski.

"Dylan, what a lovely surprise." She was breathless from trying to hang on to her balloons. "I wasn't expecting you to be here."

They'd spoken on the phone since he'd seen Alek, but he hadn't told her he was coming today in case something cropped up and kept him away. Or in case he couldn't be bothered.

"I thought I'd stop by and see what was happening," he said. "It's going well, isn't it?"

"I hope so. There are plenty of people here. I just hope they dig deep in their pockets or fall in love with one of the animals." She bent to stroke Jamie's dog's head. "I've been telling Jamie for ages that he could take a dog. I'm so pleased he's fallen for this one."

"I'm calling him Monty."

"Aw, that's a lovely name. Isn't it, Dylan?"

"Perfect."

"I need to go and judge the fancy dress competition," Sue said. "I'll catch you later."

The balloons tugged her across to the barn and it took her a couple of minutes to drag them inside. Two children—one

dressed as a Roman centurion, and the other, a girl of abou
five, wearing a black cat's outfit—quickly followed.

"I hope you're not raising Sue's hopes unnecessarily,
Jamie said.

Dylan had no evidence to back it up, and they'd only sper
a couple of minutes in each other's company, but he had th
impression Jamie didn't like him. Perhaps it was because Su
was his friend and he didn't want to see her let down.

"I hope not, too."

"But you think you can get him out of jail?" Jamie's gaze
behind those rimless glasses, was intense.

"I don't know." It was unlikely and Dylan didn't want t
raise anyone's hopes. "Alek swears he's innocent, Sue believe
he's innocent, Alek's parents believe he's innocent. There's
possibility, a slim one perhaps, that they're right. If that's th
case, Alek deserves every chance, don't you think?"

"He isn't likely to confess to murder, is he?" His tone wa
scoffing.

"In his situation, I would have," Dylan said. "I expec
some sort of deal could have been struck and he would hav
received a shorter sentence."

Jamie shrugged as if that was neither here nor there. "Hi
family believes him, that's all. It doesn't make him innocent.

"It doesn't," Dylan agreed.

"I don't think it's fair for you to convince Sue that Ale
will come home—"

"I've told her it's unlikely."

"She hasn't listened, though, has she?"

Dylan had the uncomfortable feeling he was right. As fa
as Sue was concerned, Alek was innocent and it was only
matter of time before the rest of the world knew it.

"Is that why you don't want me investigating it?" Dyla
asked. "You're worried that what I find out could hurt Sue?

Jamie rocked back on his heels. "Who said I didn't want you investigating it? I've never said a word about it."

This guy was touchy. Very touchy.

"It's just an impression I get," Dylan said. "And it's understandable. Sue's a friend of yours and you don't want to see her hurt."

"Yes, well, that's right."

"And you think her husband's guilty of murder?"

"Yes, I do. It stands to reason he is." Jamie looked around, presumably to make sure Sue hadn't materialised beside him. "I don't say as much to Sue because I don't want to hurt her feelings, but the truth is, he was sleeping with that woman. He made threatening phone calls to her, or so it said in the papers. Someone saw him leaving the house too. And his fingerprints were all over the place. It's obvious to a blind man that he's guilty. The man's a killer and Sue's better off—we're all better off—without him."

"I can see your point." Dylan could also see that Jamie was no fan of Alek's. "But if there's the slightest chance he's innocent, he deserves help. Don't you agree?"

Jamie clearly didn't, although he managed a reluctant nod. "I suppose so."

"But you'd rather see Sue settled down with a nice young man who deserved her?"

Preferably you.

"She deserves that much so, yes, I would. Is that wrong?"

"Not at all."

Jamie was as tense as a tightly coiled spring. He also looked as if he was hoping for an argument, but he merely nodded. "I need to see if there's anything I can do to help. Goodbye, Mr. Scott."

"Be seeing you."

Jamie, with the dog trotting meekly at his side, strode over to the kennels and disappeared from view.

Dylan walked into the barn just in time to see the winner of the fancy dress competition announced. The astronaut look-alike accepted his prize of several activity books and an Easter egg with suitable pride. Other contestants happily accepted small eggs as consolation. Sue's balloons were safely tied to a table leg.

Dylan spent a few pounds in the barn, bought yet more raffle tickets, then wandered outside. A lot of people—volunteers, he soon realised—were walking dogs.

"I've been coming every weekend and bank holiday," one lady told him. "My husband's allergic to pets so I can't have one at home. This is the best I can do. It's nice for the dogs and it gives me a bit of exercise."

Sue wasn't short of helpers. Dylan wondered if people volunteered for the animals' benefit or if they simply liked Sue.

He chatted with as many people as he could. Everyone commended Sue's hard work for the centre. No one really knew anything about her private life, though, or about her husband.

He met a woman in her sixties who was being dragged along by a young German Shepherd.

"I'm thinking of adopting him," she told Dylan, "but I don't know. He's a bit headstrong."

She was obviously well versed in the art of understatement.

"I rescued an old dog from here four years ago," she said, "but sadly, he died just before Christmas. I don't know. Sometimes I think it's too soon to think about another dog. Then I see all their sad faces and I know I have a good home going begging."

"It's difficult." Dylan sympathised but he was pleased to have met someone who'd known Sue, or the sanctuary at least, for so long. "I expect Sue will persuade you to take him."

"Yes. She's cunning like that, isn't she?" She laughed a little ruefully. "And she knows I'm a soft touch."

"She certainly works hard, doesn't she? Still, I suppose it takes her mind off things."

"Exactly." She lowered her voice a little. "Hopefully, she'll be able to put it all behind her and move on."

"Let's hope so. Do you know her husband?"

"Don't." She put a hand to her chest. "He did some work for me. It was about a year before—you know. I wanted a kitchen extension and, because I knew Sue, I thought he'd be the ideal person for the job. God, to think I had him in my house. I was alone with him a lot of the time, too." She shook her head and shuddered as she imagined what might have been.

The young dog hadn't learned the meaning of patience and was eager to be moving.

"I'll have to go. Nice talking to you."

Dylan watched her being pulled along and wondered if the dog would win itself a new home.

He looked around him. The place was still busy. Across the grass, Jamie was watching him. Their eyes met. Jamie lowered his and went on his way.

Sue was holding the balloons once more but she'd obviously off-loaded a few. She was drinking from a plastic cup and Dylan wandered over.

"It seems to be a roaring success," he said.

"It's busy, and that's good, but I'll wait until I've added up the takings. Fingers crossed."

"I was talking to Jamie earlier and he was telling me how expensive it is to keep the animals."

"It's all outgoings." She took a sip of what looked like weak tea. "People give a donation when they take an animal, we insist on that, but otherwise we rely on fundraisers like this. Having said that, a lady remembered the centre in her will last year. She left us five thousand pounds so that was an enormous help."

"It must be a worry for you."

"It is." She gazed across at the house. "When my dad died
I sold his house and my flat, and bought this place. It's what
I'd always longed to do." She smiled suddenly. "But just when
I start to panic, something turns up. Like the lady leaving us
that money in her will."

"Yes, life's like that. And you have good friends. Like
Anne. And Jamie, of course."

"Anne's a star," she said. "She can't do enough to help.
Jamie's a good vet, too. Very thorough. We're lucky to have
him."

Jamie would like to be more than the centre's vet, Dylan
was sure of it. Jamie wanted Sue.

"You don't see Jamie socially?" he asked.

"Good God, no." The idea amazed her. "To tell the truth,
this place doesn't leave much time for a social life. I visit
Aunt Joyce, of course. Well, she has no one else now. When
I'm not with her, or working with the animals, I'm writing
to Alek. He's brave and doesn't complain, but I can't bear to
think of him locked up in that place. At least my letters are
a way for him to not feel so left out."

"Of course."

She put her hand on his sleeve. "You will get him out of
there, won't you, Dylan?"

What could he say? For all he knew, Kaminski could deserve to end his days in Strangeways.

"I'll do my best to find out what happened that day, Sue.
You have my word on that."

She nodded, satisfied. "That's all we ask."

TWELVE

DYLAN SPENT SO long pounding the streets on Tuesday morning, he felt like a bobby back on the beat. He walked from Hilltop Avenue, where Kaminski claimed he parked his car when visiting Carly Walsingham's bed, to number two, Lakeside Drive. He passed a hairdresser's, a fish and chip shop and the newsagent's where Kaminski stopped for cigarettes on the day of the murder.

A gale whipped occasional spots of rain into his eyes and he walked with his hands deep in the pockets of his overcoat. He looked for cameras but there was a surprising lack of CCTV in this area. Perhaps the wealthy side of town didn't need it.

He walked up to the front door of number two, Lakeside Drive and rang the bell. There was no response.

The schools were closed for the Easter holidays, but if Walsingham was working and unable to spend time with his sons, he'd probably take them to a grandparent or a favourite aunt.

He moved to the side of the house and looked around. Only someone in a light aircraft or hot air balloon would be able to see him.

The back garden was secluded and private.

He strode the length of the garden to the gate in the rear fence and turned to look at the property. Anyone in Walsingham's house would be able to see him clearly. To the neighbours, however, he would be invisible unless they happened to be paragliding. Or clearing leaves off their conservatory's roof.

This had to be one of the best properties in the country fo coming and going without being observed.

He went through the gate, closed it behind him and walke along Peebles Road. The first shop he came to, about a hun dred yards from the Walsinghams' home, was the Sandwic Box. Offering tasty sandwiches and hot pies, it would be godsend for anyone taking a quick break from work on Lake side Drive. Next to that was a newsagent's.

If Kaminski really did leave via the back garden, as th police believed, presumably he would have entered the prop erty the same way. Therefore, he would have bought his cig arettes from the shop on Peebles Road and not the one hal a mile away.

And would a man with murder on his mind stop to bu cigarettes? Well, yes, he might. But it was unlikely he'd bu them from a man who knew him.

Dylan walked on to Hilltop Avenue where Kaminsk claimed he parked his car that afternoon. There were no cam eras to prove or disprove that.

As he was mentally cursing the strength of the wind an wondering what to do next, a familiar blue Mercedes swep round the corner. In the passenger seat, sitting next to Ne Walsingham, was a young woman with red hair.

Dylan had left his car at the hotel so there was no hope catching the Mercedes. He began walking in the opposite di rection, took his mobile from his pocket and called the hos pital. He wasn't surprised when it rang and rang.

Eventually, it was answered by a bored-sounding woma who asked if she could help.

"I'd like to talk to Dr. Walsingham, please," Dylan said.

"Hold the line, please."

An unfamiliar and irritating sample of classical music kep Dylan company.

"I'm sorry, but he's at lunch at the moment. Perhaps you'd like to call back after two o'clock."

Dylan thanked her, and said he would.

It was a quarter to one, which would indicate that the doctor had at least an hour and a half's lunch break.

He used up more shoe leather to walk back through the centre of town and on to Dawson's Clough General Hospital. Visitors weren't welcomed until two o'clock so the car park was almost empty, and benches dotted here and there were vacant. He chose to sit where he could see the access road to the staff parking area. His collar was turned up but the wind still tried to claw its way inside his coat.

If he'd had a less conspicuous car, he would have used it, but something more eye-catching than a Daytona Yellow Morgan would be hard to find. He wasn't parting with it, though, and he certainly wasn't leaving it at home where Bev might be tempted to reverse it into a wheelie bin. For now, despite the howling wind, he was happy enough with his bench. If it rained, he'd seek out the hospital's cafeteria and hope it had a view of the car park.

Visitors began arriving around one-thirty. They grabbed parking spaces, queued at the ticket machine, and headed inside to wait for wards to open their doors.

Dylan stayed on his bench.

At one-fifty, the blue Mercedes drove through the barrier, along the front of the building and turned for the staff car park. The driver, Neil Walsingham, was alone.

Dylan was about to head inside, find the cafeteria and get a hot coffee, when a redhead wearing a nurse's uniform walked smartly into the car park. Interesting. Walsingham must have dropped her off nearby, something he'd only do if he didn't want colleagues knowing he'd been with her.

Dylan strode to the main entrance and collided with her.

"Sorry," he said, striving for breathlessness. "More haste,

less speed, eh? Oh, it's—wait a minute, I'm sure I recognise you. I wonder, do you work on my uncle's ward?"

"Not unless he's given birth to a premature baby." Attractive dimples appeared as she smiled.

"You work in the maternity department? What a terrific job." Eager to keep her talking, Dylan took out his wallet and showed off the photograph of Freya. "My daughter. She'll be a fortnight old tomorrow."

"Congratulations." She was about to walk away.

"Do you have children? No, you're too young, aren't you?"

"I wish. But no, I don't have any. I'm too busy caring for other people's." She moved forward and the automatic doors slid open. "Thanks for the compliment though."

She carried on walking.

"Megan!" The receptionist waved her arms to attract her attention. "A couple of messages for you."

Dylan wandered off before the receptionist recognised him. He found the cafeteria, decided he didn't fancy a coffee in a hospital after all, and strode back to the town centre.

When he was sitting in Costa's, with a coffee and a muffin in front of him, he took his phone from his pocket and called the hospital. Amazingly, his call was answered immediately.

"Oh, hello, there," he said, "I wonder if you can help me. I was told to call someone this afternoon and I can't remember her name. My son was born prematurely and she said to call her before—oh, wait, it was Megan something."

"Megan Cole. Do you want me to—?"

"Hang on a minute." Dylan covered his phone with his hand, and made rustling noises with a serviette. "Apparently my wife's already made the call. I'm sorry to have bothered you. Thanks for your help."

"You're welcome. Bye."

Dylan walked back to his hotel and spent the next hour sitting on his bed, his computer whirring as he searched the

nternet for anything on Megan Cole. Apart from a photo of
her at a hospital fundraising ball, and a mention of her running a half-marathon for a breast cancer charity, she lived a
quiet life.

He then did a little research on scalpels and soon lost the
will to live. One could read more than enough about the
blades most suited to different applications involved in surgical, dental and veterinary procedures.

Outside, the wind was becoming increasingly angry. It rattled his window and roared around the old walls as it sought
a way inside.

It was four o'clock. Time to return to the hospital.

This time he took his car and parked on a side street where,
courtesy of the rearview mirror, he was able to see the car
park's exit fairly easily.

Minutes passed slowly. Eventually sixty had passed. An
eternity later, sixty more had passed.

Half a dozen women, wrapped in thick coats to ward off
the wind, walked out of the main gates to the road. He recognised one as Megan Cole. They chatted for a few minutes,
then went their separate ways. Three went one way, one
crossed the road toward him and Megan Cole headed for the
bus stop that he could just see.

He watched her as she waited with a couple of other people.

A bus trundled into view. Her companions got on the bus.
Megan continued to wait.

A little over ten minutes later, her patience—and Dylan's—
was rewarded. A blue Mercedes exited the hospital car park,
drove slowly to the bus stop and pulled up. Megan, coat belted
tight, jumped in.

Dylan put the Morgan into gear and drove off slowly. He
didn't want to lose them. Nor did he want to attract their attention.

He followed the Mercedes for just under a mile, until it pulled up outside a row of small stone-built terraced houses.

It wasn't dark yet and Dylan's car was the only splash of colour in the street. He had to park some distance behind the Mercedes and hope Walsingham's mind was too preoccupied with other things—like taking Megan Cole to bed—to notice.

Megan was first out of the car. She dashed up to the front door, keys in her hand, and only when the door was open did Neil Walsingham follow her.

It was at times like this that Dylan wished he had a side kick as Luke suggested. His assistant could sit, wait and watch and Dylan could head for the nearest pub.

Only residents used this quiet road. It was a tidy area and the houses, although small, were well cared for. They would be sought-after and cherished by first-time buyers and newly-weds.

An hour passed and Dylan left his car to stretch his legs and walk the length of the street. It was dark now. Lights shone inside number seventeen, Peel Avenue but Dylan couldn't see the occupants.

What had Walsingham said? *We're slowly starting to move on and get our lives back together.* Progress in that department seemed to be going along very well indeed.

Dylan returned to his car. It was almost eight o'clock. Maybe Walsingham was spending the night with her. Given the long and probably unsociable hours he worked at the hospital, it was fair to assume he had reliable babysitters. His parents perhaps.

Dylan was starving. He toyed with the idea of phoning the nearest pizza delivery house and giving his address as the yellow Morgan parked on Peel Avenue. He could buy himself—

The front door of number seventeen opened, putting paid to his salt and vinegar laden fantasies. Walsingham ran down the path and jumped into his car.

Dylan had the Morgan's engine fired and first gear engaged when the Mercedes pulled away, but changed his mind. He knew what he'd get from Walsingham, more of the "too distressing to talk about" crap.

He killed the engine, left his car and walked to the house. He had a brief glimpse of Megan Cole through the ground floor window as she pulled the curtains closed to shut out the night.

He walked up the path and rang the bell, and a light came on in the hall before the door was pulled open.

"Yes?" She gave a start as recognition dawned, as if trying to decide if he was an axe murderer or rapist. Her anxious gaze darted up and down the street but there was no one to hear any cries for help. "What do you want?"

"I wondered if I might have a quick word." He gave her his best smile. "Sorry, we haven't been introduced, have we? I'm Dylan Scott. Private investigator. I'm working on a case up here."

There was a brief flicker of understanding, which meant Walsingham had mentioned him. "Why do you want to talk to me? It has nothing to do with me."

She was jittery. Her chest was rising and falling rapidly.

"It's about Dr. Walsingham's movements on the day his wife was murdered." Dylan kept his smile in place. "I understand you told police he was at the hospital—"

"So?" Arms were folded tight across her midriff. She was hugging her fear close.

So she *had* been the one to provide Walsingham with an alibi. How convenient. As Kaminski had said, life was full of surprises.

"I wonder if you could tell me what you told them," Dylan said.

He wanted to suggest they go inside, but he wasn't going to push his luck. He'd stumbled across the woman, or one of

them, who'd provided the doctor with his alibi, and that wa
enough for now.

"I was working alongside him that day, that's all."

"Really? I thought you worked in different departments.

"We do, but there had been an accident on the motorwa
that day." Her teeth started to chatter. Cold or nerves?

"Would you rather go inside?" Dylan asked. "The neigh
bours will miss the show, but you'll be warmer."

Dylan doubted the neighbours were watching, but he wa
pleased to see her look at the houses opposite.

She nodded and stood back to let him enter. When she
closed the door behind them, her arms crossed her midri
again.

She walked into the centre of a living room that was taste
fully if sparsely furnished. Two tan sofas were piled high wit
red and gold cushions. Light came from three art deco lamp
There were no photos, no books, no CDs, no magazines.

"There's nothing I can tell you." Her eyes were wide. Sh
couldn't have looked more terrified if he'd been wieldin
an axe. "There was an accident that day. A coach had ove
turned. It wasn't too serious but it was filled with Boy Scou
and Girl Guides going on a camping trip. They came in t
be checked out. Apart from a broken arm, it was mainly cut
and bruises. There were about forty children, though, so
was all hands to the deck and I ended up spending the day i
Accident and Emergency."

Dylan nodded his understanding. "You were with D
Walsingham all day?"

"Yes."

Why did she look so nervous?

"You were with him when he received the phone call?
Dylan asked.

"Phone call?" Her eyes narrowed as if she suspected hin
of trying to trap her.

"I thought the school called him at work to say his children hadn't been collected."

"Oh, that. Yes, I was."

"What time was that?"

"The time?" She licked dry lips. "About three-thirty. Four
o'clock perhaps. How can I be sure? It was busy. That department always is. All you do is race round treating people
and it's difficult to know who's there, who isn't, what time
it is—anything."

"So you're saying he may not have been there after all?"

"Of course I'm not saying that. You're twisting my words.
I'm saying it was difficult to remember the time. He was
here. I was working alongside him. I'm simply saying that it
was busy so no one else could have known for sure if either
of us were there or not."

"Ah, I see. So you were the only one who saw him there?"

"Yes. No. Teresa Simmons was with us so she knew we
were there. Anyway," she said, "why does it matter where
he was? What does any of it matter? The man who killed her
is behind bars."

"There seems to be some doubt about that. Tell me, how
long have you been having an affair with Dr. Walsingham?"

"What? Now look here—" Her face was the same shade
as the cushions. "Who's spreading lies about me? I'm not
having an affair with anyone." She paused briefly, guessing
perhaps that Dylan had seen Walsingham leave. "He sometimes gives me a lift home after work, that's all. He's a colleague. Nothing more."

And I'm the King of Siam.

"Not good enough." Dylan thought of giving her the old
it's-none-of-my-business line, but he wanted answers now.
While you're standing here throwing out your lies, a man is
locked up in Strangeways. Ever been to Strangeways, have
you? No? Then count yourself lucky. You're a member of

the so-called caring profession so I would have thought that you, of all people, would do all you could to make sure no one, and I mean no one, was locked up in that place unless they deserved to be."

"I—but he does."

"Says who? Not me. And not the people paying me to get justice for him." Dylan was surprised to hear himself speaking with such conviction. He had no idea if Kaminski was innocent or guilty.

"But he is." She was visibly shaking. "His fingerprints were there."

Dylan shrugged. "So were the cleaner's."

"Well, yes, but—"

Dylan stepped closer to her. "If I murdered you tonight, Neil Walsingham's fingerprints would be all over this house. It wouldn't mean he'd killed you though, would it?"

Her skin was a ghostly hue, dominated by green eyes. She couldn't have looked more terrified if she'd tried.

"She—she was sleeping with that Kaminski man."

"So? You're sleeping with that Walsingham man." He took another step closer until she must be able to feel his breath on her face. "If Kaminski didn't kill her, someone else did. And that someone else is still at large. Who knows? Maybe he's posing as a private investigator."

She jerked back from him.

"A word of advice, love," he said, "never invite strangers into your home without checking their ID."

A rush of scarlet flooded her face then ebbed away to leave it that sickly grey colour once more.

He snapped his fingers, startling her. She was still shaking. He didn't care.

"Can you guarantee," he said, "that Neil Walsingham was at the hospital on the afternoon his wife was murdered?"

"He—he was. Of course he was."

Dylan didn't know whether to believe her or not. He didn't now who he could believe.

"How did he feel when he found out his wife was having affair with Kaminski?"

"What? How should I know?"

"You were sleeping with him. Surely he mentioned it to ou?"

"What does it matter?" she asked. "When we first—when e first started seeing each other, he said he didn't mind. hey had one of those open relationships. Both were free to o as they pleased."

So Walsingham *had* known about his wife's affair before e was killed.

"When did you first start seeing him?"

"About two months before—before she was killed."

"Thank you. One more thing, the other person who said was at hospital that afternoon, who did you say that was? eresa...?"

"Teresa Simmons. She no longer works there. Her husand got a job in Coventry so they've moved down there."

"Thank you." He smiled at her as if they were the best of iends. "You've been most helpful. It's okay, I'll see myself ut. Oh and remember, don't let strangers into your house ithout checking their ID, okay?"

Her expression was one of shock and relief. Relief that was going, and shock at having shared her home, albeit it iefly, with a madman.

Dylan stood for a moment on the pavement watching the ouse. A light came on in another room, the kitchen perhaps, give him a shadowy glimpse of Megan Cole bending to ck something up, holding it to her ear and speaking.

THIRTEEN

JAMIE WONDERED IF it was a mistake bringing the dog with him. He hadn't been given much choice though. He'd been on a farm inspecting a valuable herd of cattle, with Monty waiting patiently in the car, when the call came from his mother.

"I don't want to worry you, James, but your father's been rushed into hospital. They think it's appendicitis. I'm here now, but they haven't told me much."

The call was so unexpected, and the news so shocking, that he'd simply promised to get to the house as soon as he could. House, not hospital. He had no wish to see his father. Besides, if it was appendicitis, they'd be operating and visitors wouldn't be allowed.

But the dog—

The house was locked so his mother must be still at the hospital. He'd always had his own key and, when he let himself in, Monty raced the length of the hall and into the sitting room where he stopped to sniff everything. It was the first time a dog had been in these rooms since Ben. Even now, all these years later, the walls echoed with Ben's memory.

"Settle down, Monty."

He couldn't blame the dog though. It was natural to check out any strange surroundings.

Jamie paced from room to room. He went to the kitchen, switched on the kettle, decided he didn't want coffee after all, and switched it off before it boiled.

The possibility, albeit slim, refused to go away. His father might die.

Few people died of appendicitis, of course, but his mother had said they weren't a hundred percent sure of their diagnosis. Perhaps it was something more serious. Maybe there would be complications. His father could be dead at this very moment.

Monty stretched out in front of the hearth. Years ago, Ben had warmed himself in that same spot. In those days, coals had sparked and flames had danced up the chimney. A gas fire with fake logs was considered cleaner and easier now.

Monty looked a lot like Ben. They were similar in temperament, too, although Monty, despite being abandoned to his fate at the sanctuary's gates, had an easier life and was more confident and outgoing.

Jamie never knew why he'd been allowed to keep Ben. He'd been a quiet child—it had paid to be, in this house—but he'd been insistent about wanting a dog. He'd nagged and nagged his mother. Of course, his father had put his foot down.

But one day, Jamie had walked home from school with Ben following him.

"You'd better go home," Jamie had said, but Ben had simply wagged his feathered tail and continued to walk beside him.

Jamie, not knowing what else to do, had taken the dog into the house and fed him some bread.

Miraculously, the dog had been allowed to stay and Jamie had no idea why.

It was almost ten o'clock when he heard a car pull up outside. He pulled back the curtain and, courtesy of a streetlight that had flickered outside the house for years, saw his mother paying a taxi driver.

He went to open the front door for her.

Her tired face broke into a smile when she saw him. "Aw, James, I knew you'd come. Thank you, dear."

"Of course I came. How are you, Mother?"

"All right. He's—" She broke off, and anxious shadows flitted across her face as she spotted Monty.

"He won't know, will he?" Jamie said. "How is he anyway?"

"Not too bad."

Jamie had almost convinced himself that his father was dead, and it was a bitter disappointment to learn that he was still breathing.

"He's sleeping now," she said. "They've run some tests and will see what the morning brings."

They walked into the sitting room, where she took off her coat and put it on the back of the armchair before bending to switch on the fire. Monty was following her, swishing his tail, but she acted as if he wasn't there.

She warmed her hands. "Will you stay tonight, James?"

"Stay?" Jamie hadn't spent a night under this roof since he'd graduated from university. He hadn't wanted to. Didn't want to now. Besides, he had Monty to think about now.

"He won't know about the dog," she said as if she'd read his mind. "Please stay."

"Of course I will." It wouldn't be too bad. As soon as they had news from the hospital in the morning, he and Monty would leave.

Happy to have company, his mother fussed around him. Did he want something to eat or drink? The bed was aired, but would he want extra blankets? She'd cook a full breakfast in the morning so what time would he like it?

"Your father won't like being in hospital," she said.

"No one does."

His father would dislike it more than most, though. Instead of barking out orders to his wife, he'd be confined to a crisp white bed where he'd be at the mercy of busy doctors and nurses. They'd soon put a stop to his bullying tactics.

"No, but you know what he's like," she said.

"I do. He's a—"

"James, stop it." She put a finger to his lips to silence him. 'He's your father. You can't say bad things about him." She made a hasty sign of the cross and looked heavenward, as f hunting out the thunderbolt that must surely strike Jamie down.

Jamie remained silent. He often wondered how she'd react f her husband died. Would she smile again? Would she ever admit that he was a vindictive, bullying bastard? He sometimes thought she'd been so brainwashed into thinking the man must be worshipped that she'd be unable to believe anything else.

"I'll take Monty for a quick walk round the block," he said, 'and then I'll turn in for the night. You should too, Mother. You'll be worn out."

She patted his arm, relieved that there would be no further discussion on his father. "Good idea. Everything will look better in the morning."

Only if his father died, but if the medical staff were correct in their diagnosis, that was unlikely. He'd have an appendectomy and return home expecting to be waited on hand and foot.

Jamie set off with Monty trotting beside him. They walked along roads, deserted and mainly unlit, that Jamie had once walked with Ben. Ben used to carry a stick in his mouth, waiting until they reached the park, at which point he'd drop it at Jamie's feet and wait for it to be thrown. Jamie wasn't going to the park now. It was too late.

Twenty minutes later, they were back and in time to see Jamie's mother heading up the stairs.

"Goodnight," she said. "Sleep well, James."

"Night, Mother."

Jamie wasn't ready for sleep. He went to the kitchen and

made himself a coffee. Monty settled down under the table head on paws, and went to sleep. The dog was happy to sleep anywhere.

Ben had been the same. That dog would have run all day but, if he wasn't racing around with sticks, he was asleep.

Jamie had owned Ben for five years. In one way, he was amazed that he'd been allowed to keep a dog for so long. In another, it seemed unfair that they'd only had those five short years together.

They'd been good years, the best Jamie could remember. At last he'd had a friend, a real friend of his own. Ben had had to stay in the shed when Jamie had been at school, although sometimes Jamie's mother would let him out into the garden but when Jamie was home, and throughout the long school holidays, Jamie spent every spare moment with his dog.

Church was another occasion when Ben had to be locked in the shed. The family went twice on Sundays and Jamie's father always insisted on long Bible reading sessions in the afternoon.

At night, on condition Ben didn't make a noise, Jamie was allowed to have Ben sleeping in his bedroom. They were happy times.

It was a Sunday evening during the summer holiday that Ben wandered off. He'd never done it before and Jamie panicked. He raced to the park to see if his dog was there. He walked the streets calling Ben's name. He ran home, hoping the dog had returned, but there was no sign of him.

"It's time for church, James," his father said. "You need to put the animal from your mind, don't you?"

"Yes, Father."

Jamie changed into his best suit for the second time that day and set off for church with his parents and Pete. On that short walk, he'd looked for the dog. All the while, his mind was a Technicolor horror show. His dog could be trapped in a shed or perhaps he'd been hit by a car.

"I can't go in," he whispered to Pete as they approached the church.

"He'll kill you if you don't. Get inside." Pete, only nine years old to Jamie's fourteen, had been the wiser.

"I can't," Jamie said.

Had he been able to see the future, Jamie would have stepped inside that church. All would have been well, and Ben would have lived for his allotted span.

Jamie hadn't possessed a crystal ball, though, so, frightened for his dog, he'd taken off at a run and continued the search. A beating would follow, he knew that, but it was a beating he was prepared to take. So long as Ben was safe, he'd suffer anything.

A little over an hour later, his family was back from church. Ben was still missing.

His father didn't ask after Ben. Instead, he slammed Jamie against a wall and pinned him there. Words and spittle landed on Jamie's face. *Disobedient…brought shame on your mother's head…not fit to be called son…will not tolerate your defiance…*

When the words ran out, Jamie was beaten. Pete tried to pull his father away but the boy was only nine. He was no match for their enraged father.

Jamie was bending over the table in the kitchen being lashed by his father's leather belt when Ben, wondering what was amiss, sauntered into the kitchen as if he'd only been gone five seconds.

Jamie could have shouted with joy. Ben was home and safe so what was a beating? It was nothing. The pain would subside.

Victor Tinsley saw the dog and snapped. He kicked the

animal around the kitchen, oblivious to Ben's terrified yelps or Jamie's screams.

When Victor had finished, Ben was barely able to stand. Victor opened the door and Ben limped out to the garden.

There was no escape for the dog. If Ben had been able to get out through a hole in the fence, he might have wandered into the street. Someone would have seen him and perhaps taken him to a vet. But there was no escape.

Jamie, watching from the window, saw his dog crawl under the shed.

"You've hurt him. He needs help." Jamie rained punches on his father's chest, not caring about further beatings, but he wasn't allowed to go to his friend.

Instead, he was made to remove his clothes. He was then locked in the cupboard under the stairs. His mother was sobbing and Pete was shouting, but Victor Tinsley was beyond all reason.

It wasn't the first, or last, time Jamie spent the night in that cupboard. It was small and dark, and his father dragged a chest in front of it to prevent escape.

So Jamie spent the night in that cupboard and Ben spent the night under the shed.

Victor Tinsley was an early riser. He didn't say a word when he finally released Jamie. Not a word.

Jamie pulled on his clothes and raced into the garden.

It was too late.

With tears rolling down his cheeks and a knot of anger that would stay forever in his heart, Jamie dragged the cold, stiff body from beneath the shed and began to dig a grave for the best friend he would ever know.

Time was supposed to heal, but Jamie had no experience of that. The pain of losing Ben in such a way was as raw now as it had been then.

"It's time for bed," he said and Monty cocked his head.

Jamie walked up the stairs, the dog following, and wondered what had persuaded him to stay in this house. Not even for his mother should he have to tolerate a night under Victor Tinsley's roof.

The bedroom was just as he'd left it years ago. Wallpaper and curtains in an identical blue-and-yellow pattern still had the power to make him shudder. The single bed still sat beneath the window. Wardrobe and drawers probably held his long outgrown clothes.

He pulled open the bottom drawer of a set of three just to check. There were no clothes. Instead, the drawer was crammed with books. Pete's books. He delved further. Everything was Pete's.

It made sense. Pete's bedroom, never to be used by Pete again, would be—

No, wait. It wouldn't be placed at the disposal as guests as they didn't have guests. No one was welcomed into this house.

More likely was that Victor Tinsley had ordered Pete's room to be emptied and Jamie's mother had been unable to throw out her son's belongings. She wrote to Pete. Maybe she hoarded his possessions too.

Monty finally gave up sniffing every item that was taken out of the drawer and lay down, head on paws, to watch the process.

As well as books, there were school reports, photos, Pete's camera and a few CDs. It was strange to touch things that Pete had held. It brought his brother closer. Perhaps that was why the items were still in the house. Perhaps his mother felt the same.

Jamie pulled out well-thumbed programs and tickets for various games Manchester United played. Earphones dangled from an old iPod. A heavy-duty torch needed new batteries.

A box had been pushed right to the back of the drawer, and he dragged it out. Even as he opened it, he remembered

Pete telling him how he'd brought a pistol home from an army training exercise in Germany.

Jamie's heart raced. Everything was in its place. The Glock, speed loader, magazine, even the cleaning kit. Jamie removed the Glock and turned it over and over in his hand. It was beautifully crafted and amazingly lightweight. Small but deadly. He'd bet it had never been fired.

Slowly, Jamie returned everything to the drawer. Everything but the Glock.

He dragged the old chair close to the window, sat down and gazed into the darkness. A pool of light from that stuttering streetlight fell on a short stretch of pavement but, other than that, it was completely dark. There were no lights shining from the houses opposite. The world was asleep.

His old room even smelled familiar. He couldn't say what the smell was exactly. Fear probably. That was all he'd known as a child. Fear.

No more, though. He'd grown up and was past all that nonsense. He could take care of himself.

He turned in his chair to look at the Glock lying on the dresser. Was this God's will? Had God sent his father to hospital and brought him to this house, this bedroom?

Or was it Pete's doing? Was Pete watching over him, telling him to put an end to it all?

Jamie had no idea. He did know, however, that he'd be taking the gun home. Finally, he had the means. If his father returned from hospital, Jamie could make sure he never lifted a finger to his wife again.

There was the private investigator, too. So long as there was breath in Jamie's body, Dylan Scott wouldn't learn the truth behind Carly Walsingham's murder. And Jamie had the means to stop him.

FOURTEEN

TERESA SIMMONS'S HOME was a semi-detached house on a new estate on the outskirts of Coventry. A child's cycle, complete with stabilisers and pink ribbons dangling from the handlebars, had been abandoned on the small patch of lawn at the front. Bird feeders, crammed with nuts or seeds, hung from a small tree.

Dylan rarely phoned ahead as he preferred to speak to people *before* they could concoct works of fiction. It meant Teresa might not be home though.

She'd been surprisingly easy to find. When living in Dawson's Clough, she'd been a keen beekeeper and it seemed she'd taken her bees with her to Coventry. She was a member of the British Beekeepers' Association and had written pamphlets on beekeeping and the health benefits of honey. Copies of the pamphlets could be obtained by sending a stamped addressed envelope to her home address.

Giving the world your address was an open invitation to fraudsters and worse, but Dylan knew that few people heeded the warning. He was glad Teresa Simmons hadn't. Her rash behaviour had saved him a great deal of work.

It was five o'clock and the ferocious wind hadn't dropped all day. It tried to take the Morgan's door off and Dylan rocked on his feet as he closed it.

He was bent almost double as he walked up the path and to the front door. His ring was answered almost immediately by a woman clutching a small kitten.

"Yes?"

He recognised her from a photo he'd seen on the internet showing her being presented with some beekeeping award or other. In the picture, she'd been smiling. Now she looked wary, as if she suspected him of trying to sell her something outlandishly expensive and useless.

"Mrs. Simmons?"

"Yes?" The frown deepened.

"My name's Dylan Scott." He smiled, trying to win her over. "Don't worry, I'm not selling anything. I'm a private investigator and I'm working for Aleksander Kaminski. You may remember—"

"But of course I remember. He killed Neil Walsingham's wife."

"I wondered if I might have a quick word. Could you spare two minutes, please?"

He showed her his card which was worth less than the cost of the printing. Anyone could print something similar and claim to be a member of the Association of British Investigators. She studied it closely though.

"Yes. Yes, of course. You'd better come inside," she said. "We've only had the kitten a couple of days and I don't want her getting out."

"Thank you. I appreciate your time."

She was mid-thirties, Dylan supposed, and was several pounds overweight. Dark hair was long and lank around a face that already boasted a couple of spare chins.

Once the door was closed, she put the kitten, a ball of grey-and-white fluff, on the floor. It raced along the hall and into the kitchen, skidded on the floor and crashed into a cupboard.

"So what do you want with me?" she asked. "What's going on? Has something happened?"

This woman was a joy to investigators. She was eager for any gossip that might be going spare.

"I really want confirmation that you were working with

Dr. Walsingham on the afternoon his wife was murdered," he said.

"But I've already told the police that."

"I know, I know. It's just that new evidence has come to light." If only it had. "I've spoken to Megan Cole and she said that you and she were working with Dr. Walsingham all day. Is that right?"

"Yes."

"She also said it was so busy that day—"

"It was. There was an accident. A coach carrying a load of kids was involved. That's why Megan was working there. She didn't usually work anywhere near A&E but we needed every spare pair of hands." She nodded at the sitting room. "Sorry. Would you like to sit down?"

Dylan wasn't bothered one way or the other, but she looked eager to talk and he was more than happy to listen. "Thanks."

All the furniture was cheap but serviceable and Dylan chose to sit on a tan sofa. A low coffee table in front of him was hidden by glossy magazines. Curtains were fraying at the hem and he wondered if the kitten was responsible.

"What do you mean, new evidence?" she asked.

"It's possible that Kaminski may be innocent."

"No. Really? Then who—?"

"No one knows," he said. "The problem is that no one seems sure of people's movements. That's why I'm here, Mrs. Simmons. I'm hoping you can tell me exactly what time Dr. Walsingham and—or—Megan Cole went home that day."

"Dr. Walsingham? Neil? You surely don't think—I mean, he can't have anything to do with it, can he?"

"I wouldn't think so, but you never know, do you?" Dylan wasn't in a position to point fingers at anyone. Yet.

"Well, well." She leaned forward and said in a low voice, "Mind you, I wouldn't be a bit surprised."

"Really? What makes you say that?"

"Rumour has it that his marriage wasn't happy. Well, it's obvious, isn't it? He was—and still is, I shouldn't wonder—a terrible one with the ladies. An out-and-out flirt. We had to warn all the new staff members about him. The young female new staff members, that is."

"Ah."

"Everyone felt sorry for his wife. We thought, well, there's him, carrying on behind her back and she doesn't have a clue. It makes you wonder, doesn't it?"

It certainly made Dylan wonder. "So can you let me know the times you can say for certain that he was at the hospital? For instance, were you there when he received the phone call? The one from the school asking him to collect the children?"

"I was in the building, yes."

"So you saw him leave? You knew of the call?"

"No." She leaned forward, elbows on her knees. "Blimey. Who would have thought it?"

"I'm sure Dr. Walsingham had nothing to do with his wife's murder," Dylan said. The expression on her face already had Walsingham proved guilty and charged.

"I always thought there was more to him than met the eye," she said.

Dylan suspected he was being served a generous helping of sour grapes. Perhaps the ladies' man that was Walsingham had never made advances to the overweight and not particularly attractive Teresa.

"Did you say as much to the police?" he asked, already guessing the answer.

"No, but they never really asked me much. They spoke to us at the hospital, that would have been the following morning. News had broken of Carly's murder by then, of course, and three or four of us were talking about it when the police came. There was me, Megan Cole, Bruce Taylor who worked as a porter and Daisy who worked on the main switchboard. Everyone was shocked. Well, who wouldn't be?"

"Quite."

"The police wanted to know if we'd seen anyone unusual coming to or leaving the hospital. Daisy would have, if there'd been anyone to see, but she noticed nothing or no one out of the ordinary. It was Megan who told them that me and her had been working with Neil all day. The police asked me later, when they were taking statements, if I'd been in the emergency department with Neil all day and I—well, I said yes."

"But you were too busy to notice if he was there or not?"

"I just assumed, because Megan said he'd been there, that he was. It's possible he wasn't. I mean, perhaps Megan just assumed too." Her eyes widened as a new thought struck her. "I can't even say for sure what time Megan was there. You know about Neil and Megan, do you? You know they're having, or were having, an affair?"

"I suspected as much, yes."

"You wouldn't think Megan would be so stupid, would you? Before her it was Sonia and what a mess he left her in."

"How do you mean?"

The kitten raced into the room and, without pausing, scaled the curtains. Realising it was stuck at the top, it clung to the rail and meowed pitifully until Teresa lifted it down.

"There were rumours going around the hospital that Neil and Sonia were having an affair." Teresa was too eager to gossip to be distracted by a kitten with a death wish. "No one knew for certain, but there's no smoke without fire, is there? Then one day, Sonia came to work and she was in a right state. You could tell she'd been crying all night. Then, along comes Neil. Well, he totally ignores her, doesn't he? She burst into tears and told everyone how he'd led her on, promised her the earth, said he'd divorce Carly and everything."

"Really?"

"Yes, and it was difficult to tell who was the more furious, Neil because she'd told everyone or Sonia because he'd treated her so badly. She was in a right state, threatening to make him pay and everything."

Who needed TV soaps when all you had to do was wander down to your local hospital?

"What happened?" Dylan asked.

"It all blew over." She sounded disappointed about that. "Sonia left the hospital about a month before Carly was killed. Actually, she left quite suddenly, now I come to think of it."

"Oh? What reason did she give?"

"Her husband had his own business—I can't think what it was now—and she left to help him with that. I bet there was more to it than that though."

"What's her name?" Dylan asked.

"Sonia Trueman. They live on Peebles Road—ah, that's it. I remember now. Her husband set up his own taxi business. She preferred to call it private hire though. You had to book him in advance and he did trips to the airport, stuff like that."

"Peebles Road? That's the road behind Lakeside Drive where Dr. Walsingham lives?"

"Yes, that was handy, wasn't it? It's a long road. At one end, the end that backs onto Lakeside Drive, there are shops. The houses are at the other end. They're big old terraced houses. Quite nice if you like that sort of thing. I prefer something modern but we can't all be the same, can we?"

"The world would be a dull old place if we were."

They talked, or rather Teresa gossiped about hospital staff and Dylan listened, for another half hour.

"Thanks so much, Mrs. Simmons," Dylan said, standing up. "You've been very helpful."

"What do you think will happen?"

"I don't know. Probably nothing. It may be that justice was

done and Aleksander Kaminski is where he deserves to be. We'll have to wait and see."

"You'll let me know, won't you? And if you want to know about anyone else who worked at the hospital, you only have to ask. I sometimes think I could write a book about the goings-on in that place."

The kitten had worn itself out and was stretched out, fast asleep, in the middle of the hall. She picked it up, presumably so it didn't escape when she opened the front door.

"Thanks again," Dylan said. "I appreciate your help."

"Any time. Bye."

Dylan was blown to his car and, once inside, wondered whether he should turn around and drive north, back to Dawson's Clough for a chat with Sonia Trueman. But no, it would have to wait. He was driving south. Going home for another long weekend.

He'd promised Bev he'd be home early to take care of the children while she and her friend Lucy had a night out.

Of course, if Dylan was late, or couldn't make it, then his mother would be more than happy to babysit. Bev wouldn't be too pleased with him though.

He fired the engine and drove off. It would be more than his life was worth to upset Bev right now.

FIFTEEN

"I CAN'T BELIEVE I'm doing this," Bev said. "Who in their right mind pays to feel this bad?"

Lucy was pounding out miles on the adjacent treadmill. "Nonsense, it'll do you good. Do us both good."

"Speak for yourself. I need sleep not exercise."

Lucy grinned across at her. "You'll sleep well after this. Anyway, Dylan's home so he can deal with everything. It's not as if you're breastfeeding so there's nothing he can't do."

Bev had decided against breastfeeding simply because she'd hated the experience so much with Luke. She'd come to realise that she hated feeling like A Bad Mother just as much, though.

She checked the timer on her treadmill. Only ten more minutes of this torture.

Buying a gym membership had seemed like a good idea at the time, but she'd forgotten just how boring exercise was. Thankfully, she had an excuse. As she'd had a baby, she was on the gentle program. Lucy, in a moment of madness, had opted for the moderate exercise plan and was battling with a steep incline.

Still, it was good to get out of the house and even better to spend time with Lucy. Once they got their breath back, they'd have a few laughs.

About a dozen people were making use of the weights or machines and Bev didn't think any of them were good advertisements for the gym. Lucy was tall and slim, but the rest

of them, including Bev, who hadn't yet got her figure back,
looked podgy and out of condition.

A man on one of the rowing machines had sweat pouring
off him and looked a breath away from a heart attack. Two
women on static cycles were debating whether five minutes
on the machines was enough.

Above them, silent but mesmerising TV screens were
tuned to BBC News 24.

"You ought to take out a membership for Dylan," Lucy
said. "They've got a special offer on and you'd get him in
for half price."

"He hates gyms." Bev was beginning to think he had a
point. "He keeps threatening to take up running again though.
Mind you, he went for a run a couple of weeks back and it
almost killed him."

"Yeah? How far did he go?"

"Three miles. Before he ended up in prison, he did that
most mornings." She smiled at the memory of his last run.
'He reckoned his shoes weren't right. I thought it had more
to do with all the cooked breakfasts he eats. He spends so
much time in hotels that he'll soon look like a full English."

"God, I could just eat a good fry-up."

"Me too. Sausage, bacon, fried egg."

"Mushrooms, tomatoes and—yum—fried bread."

"Which would rather defeat the object of this," Bev said.

"True. We'll take some liquid calories when we've finished."

"Oh yes, because liquid calories don't weigh as heavy,
do they?"

"Of course they don't. Not much longer now."

They carried on. To take her mind off her boredom, Bev
tried to guess what the newsreader was saying on the silent
screen. It was impossible.

A few minutes later, it was over. And not a second too soon.

Bev was feeling okay, quite smug in fact, until she'd showered and dressed. At that point, her legs resembled jelly rather than muscle and bone.

"The wine bar?" Lucy suggested.

"Lead on."

Unlike the gym, the wine bar was packed with people enjoying themselves. Drinkers talked and joked, laughter rang out. Eighties music was playing.

"This is more like it," Bev said.

They handed over a ridiculous amount of money for a not particularly large glass of white wine each and grabbed one of the vacant tables and benches.

"A seat and a glass of wine." Lucy lifted her glass. "Cheers."

Oh yes, this was much more like it.

"So how are things?" Lucy asked.

"Great." Bev didn't stop to think before answering. She rarely did at the moment. "I'm gradually getting into a routine. Yes, things are great. What about you?"

While Lucy updated her on her own life, Bev wondered if this was the first time she'd lied to Lucy. Over the years they'd shared everything. Not now.

Bev supposed she was too ashamed to tell it how it really was. She trusted Lucy, of course she did, but she couldn't tell her how she'd longed to escape the house and how she dreaded walking back into it.

It wasn't Dylan, she'd love to spend some time with him. It was Freya. Her heart still dropped like a stone every time her baby so much as whimpered.

Other mums she knew, all of them younger than her, couldn't get enough of their children. Bev wouldn't much care if she never saw Freya again.

Dylan melted when he saw his daughter. It wouldn't be long before he was hers to command. But Dylan was different

He took life in his stride and accepted what the gods threw at him. Bev longed to put back the clock a few years. She'd love to go back to the time before Freya, before Dylan lost his job and served his prison sentence, before Luke even—

"You haven't heard a word I've said, have you?"

"What? Oh, sorry, Luce. I was miles away."

"Where?"

Bev took a swallow of wine. It was crisp and cool. "I think was about to walk down the aisle."

"Wow. Who with?"

"Dylan."

Bev expected a witty retort that involved Brad Pitt or Hugh Jackman, but Lucy simply looked at her, expression serious.

"What's wrong, Bev?"

"Wrong? Nothing. I was daydreaming about marrying my husband all over again. What could possibly be wrong?"

Lucy didn't look convinced. "Everything's okay, isn't it? You and Dylan, I mean?"

"Everything's great. Come on, let's get these glasses re-filled."

It was far easier to drink, joke and pretend than it was to admit the truth. Bev couldn't tell Lucy that she couldn't find in herself to love her daughter.

And she certainly couldn't tell Dylan.

The taxi dropped her outside the house just before eleven. The driver was long gone when she finally walked down the path and opened the front door. Silence met her. She couldn't believe it.

She crept along the hall—this was what she was reduced to, sneaking around her own home like a thief.

Dylan was alone in the sitting room. He'd been stretched out on the sofa, hands linked behind his head, but he got up. "You survived it then? How did it go?"

"It was okay. More boring than anything. Why is it s
quiet?"

"Luke's asleep and Freya might be asleep. She's been qui
for, oh, about two minutes now." He gave her a quick kis.
"Coffee? Wine?"

It was so rare that she didn't have a screaming baby t
deal with that she couldn't decide. She'd already had win
and ought to have a coffee. It would keep her awake thoug

"Get me a glass of wine, Dylan. Be quiet, though, won
you?"

While he went to the kitchen, she sat on the sofa, put he
feet on the stool and closed her eyes. This had to be too goo
to last.

Perhaps Dylan was better with Freya. Perhaps she like
her dad more and felt calmer with him.

"Thanks." She took the wine from him. "So has Freya be
haved herself?"

"She's given her lungs a bit of exercise. Hopefully, she
worn herself out."

"Hopefully." She sighed. "Wouldn't it be lovely to just s
and relax."

"You can. We are."

But she wasn't. Couldn't. She was on edge, waiting for th
first whimper that would escalate into full-scale screamin
She knew she'd be awake most of the night just as she kne
she'd feel like death tomorrow.

She couldn't sit and pretend that life was great because
wasn't. Nor could she tell the truth, that she wished to Go
she'd never had this baby.

SIXTEEN

DYLAN HAD DRIVEN less than half a mile when his mother lit a joint.

"What the—for God's sake, Mum, you can't smoke that stuff in my car."

She opened the window fully and a sneaky gust of wind almost lifted the car from the road. With her hand shielding her precious tobacco, she closed it to leave just an inch gap.

"Who's to know?" she said.

"Me, that's who." A normal mother, one who'd spent the previous night in her son and daughter-in-law's home, would have been up early cooking breakfast. His mother had overslept and was now smoking marijuana. "Isn't it a bit early for that?"

"I always have my first smoke of the day around now."

"Tell me, is there ever a time when you're *not* stoned?"

She inhaled. "Good grief, Dylan, if you're going to fuss all way to Birmingham, it's going to be a long, tedious journey."

Long and tedious wouldn't even come close to describing it.

When she'd first suggested coming with him and catching up with her ex-neighbours, the Kaminskis, he'd thought a good idea. She'd kept in touch with them via Christmas cards and phone calls, which is how his name had cropped up in conversation and prompted the Kaminskis to ask Dylan to investigate their son's case. She hadn't actually seen them for years though.

He wondered what she'd think of them, if she'd see change.

On Dylan's one and only meeting with them, he hadn been able to fathom how these quietly spoken people cou be friends with his mother. They'd been neighbours, and h mother was always saying that good neighbours were mo precious than gold so she would have gone out of her way be pleasant to them. Even so, it seemed an unlikely friendshi

"I hope Bev has a good day," she said.

So did Dylan. "She's not right, is she, Mum?"

"She's never been right, as you put it." She chuckled. " she had been, she wouldn't have married you." She patt his arm. "She'll be fine, love. I expect it's taking her long than she thought, than any of us thought, to get used to ha ing a baby around the place again. Luke's thirteen. It's be a long time since she had to face all the sleepless nights, t teething and all the rest of it. She'll be fine."

Dylan hoped so, and his mother had a point. A baby i volved a major change in lifestyle.

It was worth it, though. Freya was adorable. During the d at least. In daylight hours, she was quiet, happy and placi At night, she was the devil incarnate and would kick and y until everyone was wide awake.

"She's a bit Jekyll and Hyde," he said. "Freya, I mean. N Bev." Although thinking about it—

"She is, which would make you think she'd been bo under the sign of Gemini rather than Taurus. But Tauru let me think. Taureans are easygoing and they love securit Persistent and determined, a bit like you, love. Warm a loving. Reliable."

Dylan rolled his eyes at such nonsense. "If only there we more Taureans in the world, eh?"

"Oh, there's always a dark side. She'll be jealous, posse sive, resentful and inflexible. Quite a handful, in fact."

"You do talk some rubbish, Mum." But he had to smile.

"Aleksander Kaminski—hmm, I'm pretty sure he's Taurus, too."

Jealous and possessive? Resentful? Dylan stopped his thoughts short before he ended up as crazy as his mother.

Traffic was usually at a crawl on Monday mornings but, so far, they were making good progress. He'd pay the Kaminskis a short visit and leave his mother to entertain them while he headed north to Dawson's Clough. He was impatient to meet Dr. Walsingham's ex-lover, Sonia Trueman.

He didn't have much to tell the Kaminskis, but he'd promised to update them.

They reached Birmingham a little before ten o'clock and ended up circling a one-way route twice.

"In three hundred yards, turn left." His all-singing, ridiculously expensive sat nav was determined to take him round it a third time.

"You haven't been able to take a left here since Adam was a lad," his mother said.

Dylan didn't know this area well because he'd been brought up on the other side of the city, and his mother was no help because she didn't drive. Buses had their own rules and took a completely different route.

A couple of streets looked vaguely familiar because he'd visited his mother a few times when she'd lived here. If memory served him correctly, he'd got lost then as well.

"I think you take a left here," she said. "Yes, you do. There's Asif's shop. I must have told you about Asif. A marvellous chap. You only had to mention an item and it would be in stock ready for your next visit."

Dylan took a left, carried on to the end of the road and then, on his mother's instructions, took a right.

"Here we are." She looked at the tall houses, most converted to flats, with a wistful expression.

Dylan wondered if she wished she still lived next door to the Kaminskis. She'd spent six years here, and then moved to a more upmarket place closer to the city centre.

When Bev threw her wobbly and evicted Dylan from the marital home, his mother had raced to London to be by his side and hadn't come back to Birmingham. Later, when Dylan was welcomed back home, Vicky Scott had decided she liked being in London, promptly sold her Birmingham flat and was currently renting Dylan's old home while she looked for something more permanent in London.

He'd spent his time wishing she'd return to Birmingham. Now, though, he wasn't so sure. He liked her being there for Bev. While he was working away from home, it was reassuring to know that she was a short bus ride away.

He hadn't even switched off the engine before Mrs. Kaminski ran down the path and waited, somewhat impatiently, for his mother to grab her cavernous bag and get out.

Given the greeting she received, one would think his mother had been exploring foreign countries for the past forty years. She was hugged, held at arm's length to be inspected and hugged again before being led into the building.

Dylan was treated to an effusive greeting, too.

He gave them a few minutes to catch up with each other. His mother told them how well they were looking, and he couldn't decide if she was lying or if they'd always looked so haggard. He'd assumed that having a son locked up on a murder charge was responsible for their tired, drawn faces, but maybe they'd always looked this bad.

It was easy to see the resemblance between Aleksander Kaminski and his father, Frederyk, but Agata looked too tiny, too birdlike, to have given birth to such a boy. Both were in their seventies and both wore worried expressions. Even when enthusing about seeing "our lovely Vicky again," they looked tense and anxious.

The flats boasted large rooms and high ceilings, and the four of them sat around a dining table that would easily have seated ten.

On the sideboard was a framed photo of Aleksander and Carly on their wedding day that Dylan hadn't seen on his first visit. He hadn't been inside this room then, though.

"Ah, happy days," Agata said, noticing him staring at the photo.

"Yes." Everyone looked happy on their wedding day, but this couple would outshine most.

"They made an attractive couple, Aggie," Vicky said.

"Better than—" Agata stopped. "Sue's a really nice girl. It's just that we don't see her much. Carly used to visit us often. Sue never has time."

Sue didn't have time for much at all other than tending Lancashire's stray cats and dogs. And maybe she thought the flat and its occupants, still exhibiting a gleaming photo of Aleksander and his first wife, didn't welcome her.

"It was never Sue's fault," Frederyk said. "It was just that Aleksander never seemed happy with her. Not happy like he'd been with Carly."

"He was about as happy with Sue as Carly was with Neil," Agata said.

"How often did you see Carly after the divorce?" Dylan asked.

Agata thought for a moment. "Three or four times a year, I suppose. Every time she came home to see her mum and dad. It was good of her to visit us because I'm sure she found it difficult."

"And you don't think she was happy with Doctor—with Neil?"

"Not really, no." Agata was knotting a small lace handkerchief. "She enjoyed the lifestyle, and she loved the twins, of

course, but I think she sometimes longed to be with peopl
who knew her, knew her from way back, I mean."

"And you had no idea she and Aleksander were seein
each other?"

"None." Frederyk wasn't happy about that. He hadn
wanted them to divorce, but he clearly didn't approve of thei
relationship.

"What about Neil?" Dylan asked. "Was anything ever sai
that made you think he might be seeing someone else?"

Agata looked at Frederyk before answering. "No. Noth
ing."

"Was he?" Frederyk asked.

"He was, yes."

"Are you saying he could have wanted Carly dead?"

"I'm saying nothing, Frederyk. Other than the fact that h
was seeing someone else. Oh, and he may not have been a
the hospital the day she was killed."

"Then why did the police say he was?"

"They were told he was there." They believed they ha
the killer, one Aleksander Kaminski, behind bars, so the
wouldn't have bothered too much with Walsingham's alib
"Indeed, he may have been there. It's just that there's som
doubt."

"But he's a doctor," Agata said. "He saves lives. He wouldn
take a life. He wouldn't rob those poor children of their mother.

Frederyk reached for his wife's hand and gave it a reas
suring squeeze. "Someone did."

"Yes, and it wasn't Alek." Agata looked imploringly a
Dylan. "He wouldn't have harmed a hair on that girl's head.

Which is exactly what Dylan's mother would have sai
if *her* son had been accused of murdering his wife. She'd b
right though. No matter what, there was no way on God's eart
that Dylan could harm his wife, the mother of his children.

"I need to go," he said. "If I learn anything interesting, 'll be in touch."

With Agata fussing around him, thanking him for his help, :lling him again that Kaminski was innocent, reassuring him 1at they'd make sure his mother caught the London train, it as another twenty minutes before he reached his car.

Damn it, he could still smell marijuana.

He switched on his sat nav and instructed it to take him) Kirsten Madeley's address.

He'd phoned her over the weekend and finally persuaded er to talk to him. She wasn't a fan of Kaminski. Far from . "For all the hell I care," she'd said, "Aleksander Kamin-ki can rot in hell."

It seemed to Dylan that Kaminski was doing exactly that.)ylan didn't need to talk to a member of the Kaminski fan lub though. He wanted some insight into the woman who as Carly Walsingham, and her best friend was probably is best bet.

"Destination in one hundred yards," his sat nav informed im.

Much to Dylan's surprise, there was Kirsten's house. It was small drab semi in the middle of fifty identical properties. Most had a small square of lawn at the front. The Madeleys referred oil-stained concrete and a couple of patio pots in vhich weeds thrived.

Dylan crossed the concrete and rang the doorbell.

A tall, rangy boy, about the same age as Luke, answered he door. He stared at Dylan, a frown tugging at his eyebrows s he waited for him to speak.

"Hi, I'm looking for Mrs. Madeley."

"Mum?" The boy hollered into the house. "There's some loke to see you."

Without waiting for a response, the teenager walked to the ide of his house for his cycle and pedalled off along the road.

The woman who finally came to the still open door wa
nothing like the person he'd envisaged as Carly Walsingham
best friend. Carly had been slim and fashion conscious. Thi
woman was neither.

She was clad in black jeans that struggled to stretch then
selves around treelike thighs, and a pink top that sported a
least two stains from something that could have been tea c
beer.

"Mrs. Madeley? Dylan Scott. We spoke on the phone."

"You'd better come in. Although as I said, I don't hav
anything to tell you. Alek can rot in hell, the bastard."

"You're assuming he's guilty," Dylan said as he followe
her into the room that overlooked that square of oily concret

The room looked as stained and uncared for as its owne
An overflowing ashtray had been dumped on top of severa
women's magazines spread across a square table. A coal
effect electric fire, covered with dust, offered warmth. /
sofa in imitation leather had been scuffed and scratched ove
the years.

She stood, flabby arms folded beneath huge breasts, an
looked at him. "What makes you think he isn't?"

"He claims he's innocent. His parents say he is."

She rolled her eyes. "There's a bloke hangs around Mc
Donald's who swears he's Jesus, but that doesn't mean he i
does it?"

"No."

She sat down and reached for a pack of cigarettes and
lighter. "Shove those out the way." She nodded at a pile c
clothes on the chair opposite.

The clothes, mainly jeans, were possibly waiting to b
ironed. They'd reek of smoke before she got round to it. H
found space for them on a sideboard covered in various knicl
knacks and sat down.

"What can you tell me about Carly's relationship with Aleksander?" he asked.

"I can tell you she could have done a lot better for herself." Her cigarette lit, she inhaled deeply. "He was obsessed with her, even when we were at school."

"You were at school with Carly?"

"Yeah. We only lived eight houses from each other in those days. We met on the first day at secondary school and we were mates all through. I was bridesmaid at her wedding."

"When she married Aleksander?"

"Yeah."

"You presumably kept in touch after she moved to Dawson's Clough because you'd planned to meet up, hadn't you?"

"Yeah. We didn't see much of each other, but we spoke on the phone most weeks. Sometimes we'd go six months or a year between get-togethers. We usually met up when she came down here to see her mum and dad." She wagged her cigarette at him. "They won't speak to you, you know."

The Kaminskis had already told him that. Carly's parents were too upset, they said. Distraught even. Dylan wasn't going to bother them unless he absolutely had to.

"When was the last time you saw Carly?" he asked.

"February last year," Kirsten said. "She came to her mum and dad's for the weekend, and we went round the pubs and to a couple of clubs. It was like old times. We had a good laugh. Her kids stayed up in Lancashire with their dad, so she was free to go out and get legless."

"Neil didn't visit Birmingham with her?"

If Dylan struggled to see Carly in this environment, he certainly couldn't picture her husband here.

"No. I only ever met him once."

"Oh?"

"He was too much of a snob for my liking. Thought he was a cut above everyone else."

"Carly was happy with him though, wasn't she?"

"She was happy with the money he gave her. And she was happy with her kids." Kirsten stubbed out her cigarette. "She'd have been as happy with anyone though."

"How do you mean?"

"Like I said, she was eleven when I first met her and, even then, she was obsessed with kids. You know how most kids want a puppy or a kitten? Carly wanted a baby of her own. Anyway, as soon as they found out Alek couldn't have kids, that was that. She didn't care about anything but having one of her own. If she couldn't have them with Alek, she'd have them with someone else. I tell you, anyone would have done. She didn't care who it was."

Kirsten lit another cigarette.

"She never loved the snobby doctor," she said. "It was only ever Alek."

Interesting.

"Didn't she consider adopting a child?"

"Nope. She had to go through the whole childbirth thing. She said she didn't want someone else's." She blew a cloud of smoke into Dylan's face.

"But if you say she loved Alek—"

"She did, but it didn't matter. She had to have kids of her own. Said she couldn't feel like a complete woman without them. I'll tell you something else, too. Now, I couldn't swear to this, but I think she was seeing someone else before she was killed."

"Oh?" he asked. Kirsten might not have wanted to talk to him but, now she'd started, she was keen to gossip. "What makes you say that?"

"She phoned me the day before—the day before that bastard killed her. She wanted to see me the next day, but I still had my job then and couldn't get the time off work. I managed to do a swap for the Thursday, though, and I phoned

er back to see if that was any good to her. She was laugh-
ng and messing around, said she was busy on Thursdays
nd couldn't miss her afternoon fix. She didn't tell me, but
omething in the way she spoke made me think she was see-
ng someone, a man."

"And you've no idea who that might have been?"

"No. I would have asked her when we met up on the Thurs-
ay but, of course—" She left the sentence unfinished.

They never had met up on that Thursday. A person or per-
ons unknown had seen to that.

"Could she have been seeing Alek, do you think?" Dylan
sked.

"Eh?" She gazed at him through a cloud of smoke.

"Carly's husband claims Alek used to pester her a lot, that
e refused to accept their marriage was over. Alek, on the
ther hand, claims he'd been seeing Carly for a while."

"Bloody hell." Kirsten shook her head and scowled. "I
vouldn't believe either of them. Carly never said anything
o me about Alek pestering her, as you put it. She didn't say
nything about seeing him either."

"But do you think she could have been?" Dylan asked.
That way, she'd have had everything, wouldn't she? She'd
ave had the children she longed for and the man you claim
he still loved."

"Bloody hell," Kirsten said again.

"Did you attend the trial?" he asked.

"No."

It was all well and good blaming judge and jury for Ka-
ninski's predicament, but what the hell had his lawyer been
hinking? Surely, a defence lawyer worthy of the name would
ave called Kirsten as a character witness. He would have
nade her tell the jury how Carly had only ever loved Ka-
ninski, how it was possible she'd been seeing another man.

"How did you find out what had happened to her, Kirsten?"

"Bloody coppers. And bloody Neil sodding Walsingham come to that. You'd think he could have phoned me, wouldn' you? He knew damn well she was coming down here so i wouldn't have hurt the pompous shit to let me know what ha happened. But oh, no. I was waiting for her on the Thursday. kept phoning her mobile and thought she was stuck in traffi on the motorway or something. It was about seven o'clock tha night when a copper turned up asking me if I was supposed t have spent the day with her. He told me what had happened."

"Then what?"

"The next day another copper came. He asked me loads o questions about her state of mind, how often we spoke, wher we'd planned to go, what we were going to do and stuff lik that. That was the last I heard from anyone. My mum saw Carly's mum and it was her who told us what was happen ing. Her who told us that Alek had killed her. I never hear a word from the pompous shit of a doctor."

"What was your reaction?" Dylan asked. "Did you believ him capable of such a thing?"

"Not at first, no, because they'd been friends forever. Bu he was locked up so we soon knew he'd done it."

Kirsten's faith in the judicial system was touching. An frightening.

She looked at him. "Don't you reckon he did it?"

Dylan didn't know what to think. "I think it's possibl he's innocent."

"Perhaps he didn't then," she said.

So much for her conviction that Kaminski should ro in hell. She had doubts. She was thinking that maybe, jus maybe, the man was innocent.

"So if he didn't do it, who did?" she asked.

"That's what I'm trying to find out."

They talked for another ten minutes, but there was noth ing Kirsten could tell him that he didn't already know. Lik almost everyone else, she'd assumed that, because Kaminski had been tried and found guilty, he'd killed her best friend.

Perhaps he had.

SEVENTEEN

DYLAN SOON FOUND the house he was looking for. Outside a large terraced house on Peebles Road was a sign: Trueman's Private Hire for all your travel needs. Dylan jotted down the phone number, just in case.

He parked on the road outside and was getting out of the Morgan when a woman, late thirties or maybe early forties, came out of the house. She checked that the door was locked and walked down the path.

She was all smiles when she spotted him. "Hello, did you want me? Are you hoping to make a booking?"

"Not a booking, no. I'm looking for a Mrs. Sonia Trueman. Would that be you?"

The smile became curious. "Yes. What can I do for you?"

"Ah, good. My name's Dylan Scott." He put out a hand which, after transferring a shopping bag to her left hand, she shook. "I'm a private investigator working for Aleksander Kaminski."

Her hand fluttered in his. "Oh?"

"Yes, I'd like to ask you a couple of questions, if I may. It's about your relationship with Neil Walsingham."

She snatched her hand back. "My—well, I'm sorry, but you'll have to come back another time. I'm going out now." She nodded at her shopping bag. "I need to get to the bank. Sorry."

There was no car in sight so she had to be walking.

"It won't take long and I don't want to bother you again. It's okay, I'll walk with you. I've been sitting in a car for hours so I could do with stretching my legs." He gave her his most charming smile.

"But—" She broke off, and he could see her searching for inspiration, a way of getting rid of him. "It's quite a walk. Listen, if you come back this afternoon, I can see you then."

"I don't want to put you out," he said. "Besides, a trip to the bank will be safer with two. You can never be too careful these days, can you?"

He had no idea what she was going to the bank for but, as she didn't argue, it was safe to assume she was paying in cash.

"Let's go," he said. "You're in a hurry."

She gave in, although not gracefully. Dylan wouldn't have been surprised to see her stamp her feet and throw a tantrum worthy of a five-year-old. She resisted the temptation and merely strode off with her teeth gritted.

Without the frown, she would have been beautiful. Even with it, she was attractive enough for the ladies' man that, allegedly, was Dr. Walsingham. Her hair was well cut, and makeup had been carefully applied. Slim ankles balanced on heels that were high enough to stretch her calf muscles. Her grey knee-length coat was of good quality.

"At least it's stopped raining," he said as they walked.

"Yes. So what do you want to know? Has someone from the hospital been tittle-tattling?"

"I wondered what you could tell me about Neil Walsingham." He ignored her last question.

"I can tell you he's a good doctor and a crap painter. He likes to think he's a bit of an artist but my five-year-old nephew has more talent. He's a social climber, a two-faced liar and he believes he's God's personal gift to the female population. Anything else?"

"You're not a fan, I take it?" He decided to state the obvious.

"No, Mr.—"

"Dylan. Dylan Scott."

"No. I'm not a fan." She sighed. "But I'm probably on my own. His patients think he's wonderful, as do his colleagues. I doubt you'll find anyone who has a bad word to say about him."

She slowed her pace slightly. Perhaps she felt better for having given her opinion of the doctor.

"You worked with him until quite recently, I gather," Dylan said.

She stopped abruptly to look at him. "Someone has obviously been talking about me so you know we had an affair."

"I heard a rumour."

She laughed, a bitter sound, and carried on walking. "The whole hospital knows about it. That's my fault, obviously, because I created a scene. And do you want to know something else? I'm glad I did. It embarrassed him and showed people he wasn't the goody-goody doctor and family man he liked people to see. They found out he'd been living a lie. And I'm glad."

Sonia's steps were fast and angry, and her breathing was becoming laboured. *Hell hath no fury...*

"Of course," she said, "I've only myself to blame. I was the stupid one who fell for his lies in the first place. He's good, I'll give him that. He can be utterly charming and make you believe you're the only person who matters in his universe. Ha."

"You weren't working at the hospital when his wife was killed, were you?"

"No. I couldn't bear to be anywhere near him. Being in the same town was bad enough, and I still live too close to him, but I was damned if I could work in the same building. Fortunately, Terry's business took off so I was able to leave the hospital and help him with that."

"When did you leave?"

"Last July."

A month before Carly Walsingham was murdered.

"When I discovered I wasn't important to him," she said, "I decided to try and get my marriage back on an even keel. We'd been having problems before Neil. I suppose that's why I fell for his lies. So I left the hospital, helped Terry with the business and tried to sort out my marriage."

She gave another sour laugh. "But people love to gossip, don't they? In a town like this, where everyone has to know everyone else's business, I knew it wouldn't be long before someone told Terry."

"Ah." Dylan didn't know what else to say. He had little sympathy. If people opted to jeopardise their marriages, they had to take the flak. Their choice.

"You're still together?" he asked. "You and Terry?"

"Yes, we're still together. Just. When your husband discovers you've cheated on him, you reach rock bottom. The only way is up, I suppose, but, believe me, it's a long, slow, painful climb."

They'd reached the bank, a small building crafted from local stone a century or more ago.

"I'll wait outside for you," Dylan said.

She nodded and strode inside.

Earlier, a small square of blue sky had been visible. All Dylan could see now were heavy dark clouds. So much for spring. He just hoped the rain held off until he was back at his car. It was cold too. Despite the brisk walking pace, Dylan was frozen and he stamped his feet while he waited.

There were few people about today. Those who didn't have to be in shops, offices or factories would stay at home on this miserable Monday. It wasn't the weather for strolling round the town.

Sonia came down the steps and, without saying anything, began walking. Dylan fell into step with her.

"Anyway," she said after a minute or two, "what does any of this have to do with that Kaminski bloke?"

Dylan was wondering when she'd get round to asking that. "He claims he's innocent."

She rolled her eyes at that. "Well, he would, wouldn't he?"

"Not necessarily. If he'd pleaded guilty, he might have been given a shorter sentence."

"And you think he could be telling the truth?"

"It's possible, yes." Dylan shoved his hands in his jeans pockets for warmth. "There's also some doubt about Dr. Walsingham's movements on the afternoon of his wife's murder. Some say he was at the hospital. Some say he wasn't." That wasn't strictly accurate.

"What do you mean? Where do people say he was? Has someone said he was with me that day?"

Her questions surprised him. "Was he?"

There was a pause before she answered. "No."

They put a yard of space between them as they avoided a woman walking toward them pushing a stroller. Sonia went right, Dylan went left.

"Of course he wasn't with me," Sonia said when they were side by side again. "I told you, I had nothing to do with him by then."

They walked on in silence for several yards. How Dylan wished he could read minds.

"What can you tell me about his relationship with his wife?" he asked.

"His marriage?" She dragged the words out, speaking slowly as if choosing her words with care. "Well, it wasn't very good, was it? If someone has an affair, well, it speaks for itself, doesn't it?"

"I suppose it does."

"I mean," she said, "you can't believe a word he said to me, but—"

"But what?"

"As I said, you can't believe a word he says. When I was with him though, he sounded convincing. He said he couldn't stand living with her, that marrying her had been a mistake, that he wished she hadn't been born."

"He said that?"

"And a whole lot worse. He promised me the moon. It was all talk, I know that now, but even when I was falling for it, I wondered if it was me he wanted or just an escape from his marriage. He told me he was going to divorce her as soon as he'd moved his money round a bit. He reckoned she'd take him for every penny he had."

They turned the corner and there was Dylan's Morgan.

"Where do people think he was when she was killed?" she asked.

"No one seems to know. He claims he was at the hospital but there's some doubt about it."

"Really? Well, who knows? A word of advice from me though. Don't take anything that man says as gospel."

Dylan didn't take anything *anyone* said as gospel.

They stopped by the Morgan and both looked up as a black Mercedes Viano turned the corner.

"Oh, no." Sonia's voice shook.

Trueman's Private Hire was emblazoned across the vehicle. The Viano would take seven or eight passengers and loads of luggage. It was ideal for driving people to airports.

"Your husband, I take it," Dylan said.

"Please, don't—"

She wasn't given time to finish the sentence as a huge man lumbered out of the car and put himself two inches from Dylan's face.

"Who the fuck are you?"

Dylan had always found northern people to be warm and friendly. Unlike their southern counterparts, they were happy to chat to strangers. Terry Trueman—he was sure she'd said his name was Terry—was obviously the exception. He was so close that Dylan could smell garlic on his breath.

"I'm Dylan Scott, a private investigator. I called for a couple of words with your wife about the murder of Carly Walsingham."

"A couple of words? Well, you've had your couple of words so you can fuck off." He leaned in even closer to Dylan's face.

"I was just going."

"Lucky for you." Trueman flexed his muscles. "And keep away. Walsingham has nothing to do with us, do you hear me?"

"I hear you. I just thought that maybe your wife, having worked at the hospital, might be able to provide some information about Dr. Walsingham."

"Well you thought wrong, didn't you? Now clear off."

"Terry—"

Sonia's pleading was cut off as Trueman grabbed his wife by the shoulder and frog-marched her toward the house. Dylan felt guilty. Trueman was good and ready to pick a fight and Sonia was the one about to suffer.

And there wasn't a thing Dylan could do about it.

EIGHTEEN

NEIL WALSINGHAM CURSED as the wind carried his ball into the bunker for the third time. Dawson's Clough's Golf Course offered stunning views but its vantage point, high above the town, brought its setbacks. The main being that one always had to compensate for the wind.

"Looks like I'm about to beat you for the second time this month," Tony said.

"Don't count on it."

Neil shouldn't blame the wind for his poor game. It was the same for both of them and Tony was doing okay.

No, the problem was Dylan Scott. What the hell was he up to? On the drive here, Neil had spotted Scott's distinctive yellow car parked outside Sonia Trueman's house.

Megan had been adamant that she'd told Scott nothing but, if that was true, what the hell was he doing at Sonia's? How else could he have found out about her? Megan had been close to hysterics when she'd phoned him to say Scott had been in her home asking questions so there was no knowing what she'd told him.

Confound the blasted man. Neil shuddered to think what venom Sonia would inject into their conversation.

"At least it looks as if we'll get back to the clubhouse before the rain comes," Tony said.

"Let's hope so." Neil tried to forget Scott for a while. He enjoyed playing golf with Tony on the rare occasions their free time coincided. It was peaceful on the greens, the scenery was breathtaking and the exercise did him good. The contrast between busy hospital and tranquil course pleased him.

He couldn't enjoy himself today, though, and he wasn't sorry when they were back at the clubhouse. The place was quiet on Mondays and, thankfully, they had the bar to themselves for the moment. Neil wasn't in the mood for small talk. He'd have a quick drink with Tony and then go home.

To do what?

"You okay, mate?" Tony asked. "You're miles away today."

"Sorry. Thanks." Neil took his drink and they walked to the easy chairs with a view of the course and sat down. "Yes, I'm fine. Busy at work, you know."

"Aren't we all."

Tony was a GP at the town's new medical centre, and there were times when Neil envied him the regular hours, the appointments system and the dragons on the reception desk who made life as difficult as possible for people wanting consultations.

"How long is it before you jet off to Thailand?" Neil asked.

"Four weeks on Wednesday. And I can't wait."

Neil wished he was jetting off to foreign climes. Unlike Tony, however, he didn't enjoy an uncomplicated GP's life. Nor did he have an adoring wife who cared for husband, son and daughter, held the family together and arranged holidays. All Neil had was a mess.

He didn't begrudge Tony his good fortune. He and his wife were good friends. Some would call Tony dull, and perhaps he was, but he was also loyal and dependable. He didn't gossip, he ignored rumours and could understand both sides of any argument.

"What's new then?" Tony asked.

"Not a lot." Neil took a swallow of his drink, a long, cold gin and tonic. "Well, actually, yes, there is something. A private investigator is working on Kaminski's case."

"Kaminski? But why? Has something happened?"

"Not that I know of. I imagine Kaminski's still protesting his innocence. Name me a case that doesn't go to appeal."

Tony shook his head in despair. "That's plain crazy. There was more than enough evidence to put him away. I'm sorry, mate. The last thing you need is that dragging up again."

Neil gave him a careless shrug. "Unless some crack lawyer can get him off on a technicality, I expect it will soon blow over."

"Let's hope so. You can't have this cropping up every year or so."

"Don't even think it. Anyway, on a lighter note, I've applied for a job in Cornwall."

"Cornwall? Why?"

Four golfers, all talking loudly or laughing at their own jokes, came in and took up residence on stools around the bar. Each was trying to be funnier and heartier than his neighbour. Neil hated people like that.

"I think it's time for a change of scene," he said. "A new start for us all. I think it's time."

Tony nodded slowly. "I can see why you might feel that way. Especially now that some prick's trying to get Kaminski out of jail."

"I haven't got the job yet and there are sure to be a lot of applicants. Jobs in the south are more sought-after than they are up here."

Neil would miss Tony, but he really hoped he was offered the job. Although they wouldn't even be considering applicants for interview for a fortnight, he couldn't stop imagining a new life on the south coast. He pictured himself teaching the boys to play cricket or showing them the magic of flying kites on a sunny beach.

He needed to get away from Dawson's Clough. From the hospital, too. And yes, from Megan.

She wouldn't be happy if he was lucky enough to land the job, but that was something else that had run its course. At the start, he'd been grateful to her and it had been a pleasure to be with her. The hints had changed to demands though, and he wasn't ready or willing to have anyone influencing his life.

He wanted a new start. Just him and the boys.

"I'll wish you well, of course," Tony said, "but we'll miss you."

"I'll miss you and Amy, too."

"Still, holidays will be cheaper." Tony always looked on the bright side. "Far easier to visit you in Cornwall than fly to Thailand."

"True. Oh, and keep it to yourself for a while, will you?"

Neil immediately wished he hadn't said that. Tony didn't talk out of turn, never had and never would. He didn't gossip, he wasn't one of those who had to spread the latest rumour. He was a good, honest, decent man, a man Neil was lucky to call friend.

He didn't deserve such a friend. Some would say he didn't deserve any friends, but, over the years, Neil had felt able to talk to Tony about anything. Well, anything except the women in his life or the state of his marriage.

He emptied his glass. "I've got things to do, so I'm going to run. I'll give you a ring about Thursday."

"Okay, mate. Oh, and don't forget you're invited to dinner on Saturday. Let us know."

Neil patted Tony's shoulder. "Will do and thank Amy for me, won't you? Be seeing you."

Traffic was clogged up at roadworks in the town centre, but Neil wasn't bothered. He felt aimless. He was driving home, but he wasn't sure what he'd do when he got there.

Refusing to speak to Scott had been a mistake. It made him look…uncooperative. Scott would believe he had something to hide.

What was Scott up to and why the hell was he speaking to Megan and Sonia? Neil had to be his chief suspect, that's why. He'd read the statistics, he knew that most murders were committed by people close to the victim, and it was difficult to be closer than a spouse.

As soon as he got home, he'd call Megan and ask her again exactly what she'd said to Scott. Then, much as it pained him, he might even speak to Sonia. He wasn't in the mood for a torrent of her verbal abuse, but he needed to know what Scott was doing.

The traffic started moving again.

"Shit!" The engine stalled and the driver behind tooted his horn.

Neil was so tense he couldn't even drive. He restarted the engine and pulled away. His heart was racing, and his throat was dry.

Damn and blast Scott.

Neil had looked up Scott on the internet and discovered that he was either the best private investigator ever or he wrote his own press. An ex-copper, as most of them were, he'd served time in prison for assaulting a member of the public. People said it was wrong, said he shouldn't have been locked up just because some piece of scum with a criminal record claimed he'd used excessive force when arresting him.

Scott didn't matter though. The police, judge and jury were who mattered, and they'd done their bit. A private investigator, no matter how clever he was, simply didn't matter.

Kaminski was behind bars and he could damn well stay there.

NINETEEN

DYLAN STOOD AND gazed up at a couple of cameras. They watched a large car park and, possibly, although he couldn't be sure, captured the comings and goings along Darwen Road.

If he was travelling from his hotel to Neil Walsingham's home on Lakeside Drive, Dylan would come along Darwen Road and turn left at the lights. It had to be said, however, that if he was going to a lot of places he'd come this way and turn left at the lights.

It was a reasonably direct route to Peebles Road too. Since their acrimonious encounter, Dylan had done a little research into Terry Trueman. Surprisingly, given his angry demeanour, he'd never been involved in so much as a brawl. He had a motive for killing Carly Walsingham though. Neil had tried to steal Sonia so maybe Trueman had decided to take away Walsingham's wife. Perhaps he'd even hoped that Walsingham would be found guilty.

What had Sonia said? *When your husband discovers you've cheated on him, you reach rock bottom. The only way is up, I suppose, but, believe me, it's a long, slow, painful climb.*

Dylan was still gazing up at the security cameras. They were set up to watch proceedings in a car park belonging to T&T Securities. Signs in the office's windows boasted unbeatable prices for all security needs including alarms, cameras, guards and dogs.

Dylan crossed the road and stepped inside the office. A man in his thirties was busy at a computer but he leapt to his feet. "Hi, there. What can I do for you?"

"Sorry, but I'm not a customer."

"I've forgotten what a customer is." He spoke with a wry smile but seemed undaunted.

"I'm a private investigator," Dylan said, "and I've just spotted your security cameras overlooking the car park. I was wondering if they record traffic on this road."

"They certainly do."

"I don't suppose you keep the recordings, do you?"

"We do, yes. They're cracking good video cameras. Great colour, you know, and a good range. They're not terrific in the dark, but if you can see the camera, it's odds on you'll be caught. We don't sell many for use outdoors, but the indoor version really comes into its own in shops. As I said, you get crystal clear videos and you'd easily catch thieves."

They sounded like must-haves, but no use to Dylan if images were only stored for a few hours. "And you keep the recordings for quite a while?"

"Not for any definite length of time. We put the cameras outside for security reasons, obviously, but mainly, they're demonstration models. We show people the results, you see. As I said, they're great cameras. You'd be hard pushed to find a better one for the job."

Dylan wondered if he ought to tell him again that he wasn't a customer.

The chap pointed to a small domed camera in the corner of the shop. "That does a good job, too, but only for an area this size. If you had a large store, you'd need something better."

"I see." He was getting nowhere fast. "How about last August? Is it likely you'd still have recordings for that far back?"

The chap sucked in a breath. "Oh, that's doubtful. I'll have a look for you, but that's a long time. Come with me."

He led the way into a large room at the back of the building, one crammed with boxes and where a wall was taken up completely by computers.

"It's good of you to check. I appreciate it, Mr.—?"

"Eddie." He pushed hair from his eyes and shook Dylan's hand.

"Dylan. And thanks for your help."

Eddie patted a box. "This is a good camera, probably the best model on the market. We sell quite a few of those."

"Really?" Dylan didn't want to encourage him, but he wanted to stay on the right side of him.

Eddie sat at a desk in front of a computer. "Let's see."

As he clicked open files, Dylan received a not so quick lesson in every type of camera available.

"But just look at these images." Yet more mouse clicks. "Ha. There we are."

Dylan was impressed. He was convinced he was taller than he looked on screen, but the clarity was stunning. As he was standing directly in front of the camera, albeit some distance away, and looking straight at the lens, he supposed he shouldn't have been surprised by the clear image of himself.

Cars passing him were equally clear. Impossible to see the vehicle's occupants, but thanks to the camera's angle, it was reasonably easy to read the registration plate of cars travelling north.

"What do you think?"

"Very impressive," Dylan said.

"Isn't it just? We don't sell so many of these, more's the pity." He gestured to the boxes of cameras piled up behind him. "Most people want cheap and cheerful. Of course, most people don't expect they're going to be targeted by thieves."

"I suppose they don't."

"What are you interested in particularly?" Eddie asked.

"I want to see who was using this road last August." As Eddie was being so helpful, Dylan knew he had to explain. "As I said, I'm a private investigator and, last August, a woman was murdered not far from here."

"Yes, I remember hearing about that. She was a doctor's wife, wasn't she?"

"That's right, and a man's currently serving a life sentence for her murder. However, there's a slim possibility that he might be innocent and I'm working on his behalf."

"Wow." It was Eddie's turn to be impressed. "Hmm, I wonder if we can help you. Let's see."

Dylan didn't know what amazed him most, the speed at which geeks like Eddie used computers or the speed at which his particular computer reacted. Dylan often thought he could drive to town, buy all he wanted and drive home in the time it took him to purchase something online.

"I don't suppose the police asked you about CCTV at the time of the murder?" Dylan asked.

"No."

Dylan wasn't surprised. As usual, he was clutching at straws. The killer could perform cartwheels in front of the cameras, but it wouldn't prove he'd been anywhere near the Walsinghams' property.

Dates flashed up on the screen so fast it was difficult to read them. October 21. October 3. September 19. This was looking promising.

"Here we go. It looks like you're in luck." Still the dates flashed past until the screen stilled with June 14 emblazoned across it. "Wow. Just look at that. The last time we deleted files was June the fourteenth. So, you want to look at August?"

"The victim was murdered on the third," Dylan said, "so I'd really like to look at images from the middle of July to the first week in August. Really, this is amazing."

"Isn't it just? But—"

Why did there always have to be a but?

"It's going to take you hours—make that days to look

through this lot." Eddie drummed his fingers on the desk. "What sort of computer do you have?"

"Just an ordinary laptop."

"Processor?"

"I don't know."

"Hmm." More finger drumming. "Tell you what, I can put the files you want on an external hard drive. If your laptop's a fairly new model, you should be able to cope okay."

"An external hard drive? What's that?"

Smiling, Eddie pointed at a slim silver box on his desk. A tiny *2TB* glowed blue. "It has a USB cable which you can attach to your laptop. You just use it as another storage device. Simple."

"I see." Dylan wasn't sure he did, but he'd muddle through somehow.

"Yes. As soon as you attach it, your laptop will show it as an extra device. Just click on it and hey presto."

"How much do I owe you?"

"Just bring the hard drive back when you're done," Eddie said. "There's no rush."

People's trusting natures surprised Dylan. There was nothing to stop him selling this hard drive to the first buyer. "You don't want a deposit or something?"

Eddie smile. "No. You've got an honest face."

Dylan smiled, but he knew better than most that Strangeways was heaving with honest faces.

He left the building clutching the external hard drive. Attaching it to his computer and managing to see the images would be a miracle in itself. That it would provide anything of interest was probably asking too much.

He was almost back at his hotel when his phone rang. He looked at the display. Neil Walsingham? That had to be a mistake, surely.

TWENTY

THE CONSERVATIVE CLUB struck Dylan as an odd choice of meeting place. He couldn't complain though. It was Neil Walsingham's choice and that was good enough.

Dylan had offered to call at Walsingham's home, but the doctor had declined.

"I've got something on this evening," he'd said, "so it will be easier for me to call at the Con Club for a quick chat. If that's okay with you, of course."

The building was a couple of hundred years old, solid and timeless, and only a very small blue sign gave any indication as to what it was. It was busy, even at seven o'clock on a Tuesday evening. A lot of young people clustered round the bar or gathered in a side room to play snooker or pool.

Dylan would have preferred to meet Walsingham on his own territory, but he could picture the doctor's home. It would be uncluttered, spotless and tidy thanks to a cleaner who was sure to be paid well to take good care of it, and there would be the obligatory photos of a happy, smiling Carly Walsingham with her husband.

He bought himself a pint of beer and discovered why the club was so busy. The drinks were much cheaper than in the local pubs. He couldn't imagine Walsingham choosing this place for financial reasons though.

Dylan sat in one of four comfortable blue armchairs that hugged a circular table. From his vantage point, he could see who came and went through the tall oak door.

He had twenty minutes to kill before Walsingham arrived

and he spent the time wondering why the doctor had had a change of heart about talking to him. Whatever the reason, Dylan would heed Sonia's advice. *Don't take anything that man says as gospel.*

The club was noisy and perhaps that's why Walsingham had chosen it. People were talking, laughing, shouting to each other. No one would notice two men having a quiet chat.

Or perhaps he was reading too much into the choice of venue.

Dylan was grateful to be away from the hotel, or at least from his computer screen. He'd spent all afternoon staring at it and had started to wonder if anyone had yet invented a more boring waste of time. Watching grass grow would be a thrill a minute by comparison.

At two minutes to seven, Walsingham dashed inside the club—smart suit, expensive shoes, silk tie and a smile—spotted Dylan and came over.

"Sorry I'm late, Dylan. What are you drinking?"

"That's generous. A pint of IPA, please."

"Won't be a second."

Dylan watched Walsingham at the bar. His smile didn't slip. He chatted to the barmaid and said something to make her laugh. She blushed, too. Walsingham was a handsome, charming man.

Was he also a killer?

There were smiles and handshakes when Walsingham returned to the table with drinks.

"Dylan—may I call you Dylan?"

"Please do. Neil, is it?"

"Yes, and let me say again how sorry I am about our first meeting." Walsingham sat in the chair next to Dylan's and pulled it closer, probably so he wouldn't have to shout to make himself heard above everyone else's chatter. "It was the shock I suppose. When you go through something like that—and believe me, I hope you never do—it takes much longer than you imagine to come to terms with it. You crave peace. You need the quiet. You have to heal, you see."

"I understand. Thanks, by the way." He lifted a glass and chinked it against Walsingham's. The doctor was drinking a large whisky with plenty of ice.

"My pleasure. And needless to say, if there's anything I can do to help, you only have to ask. I don't like the idea of it being raked over again, but nor do I like the idea of an innocent man being behind bars. You believe Kaminski's innocent of my wife's murder, I take it?"

Saint Neil. The sudden willingness to help and the belated worry about a man being wrongfully imprisoned were making Dylan cringe.

Or perhaps Sonia had tainted his views on the doctor. Maybe, after all, Walsingham was genuine.

"I believe it's possible," Dylan said. "He claims he is, and there are several discrepancies between the various stories."

"Really? Well, yes, I can understand that. Innocent people, as I'm sure you know only too well, don't assume they'll need to state their whereabouts for an alibi. People go about their daily business and, half the time, can't remember where they are at a specific time. Take us, for example. In a fortnight's time, if asked to tell police where we were at—" he paused to study his watch like a child who had only just learned to tell the time "—five past seven on the evening of Tuesday, seventeenth April, I bet we wouldn't be able to."

Given the way he'd immediately felt obliged to discuss alibis, Megan Cole must have told Walsingham that she wasn't terribly convincing when confirming his whereabouts on the day in question.

"Probably not." Dylan gave him an understanding smile, but he resented being treated like an idiot. He knew how innocent people struggled to remember where they'd been at a given time. Just as he knew the way guilty people concocte the most elaborate to-the-second alibis.

"On the day my poor wife was—murdered—"

He broke off and Dylan wished he had an Oscar in his bac pocket. He would present the award with a flourish.

"On the day Carly was taken from me," Walsingham sai on a long, suffering breath, "I was asked to tell the polic where I was. Well, I knew where I was, of course. We'd a. had a long, gruelling shift at the hospital. But when it cam to telling them who I was with, well, I couldn't. Can yo believe that? It was so busy, so chaotic, that I couldn't hav said who was working alongside me and who wasn't. That' what happens. People get so wrapped up in dealing with th current emergency that they simply don't take these thing in. That day was exceptional, I know. There had been an ac cident on the motorway."

"So I believe," Dylan said. "A coach full of children, wasn it?"

"Yes. Girl Guides and Scouts heading off on a campin holiday. Thankfully there were no serious injuries, but yo have to check each one thoroughly. Children get easily frigh ened in such circumstances so you need to tread carefull too."

"I can imagine."

"You go from child to child. The nurses go from child t child. You check them over, you fill in paperwork. Everyon else is doing the same, but you're not aware of them."

Walsingham had long slender hands. On the third finge of the left hand was the shining gold wedding band that Carl would have placed there.

"So," he said. "Kaminski is still protesting his innocenc is he?"

Walsingham was nervous. As soon as there was a paus in the conversation, he felt obliged to fill it. Fill it with cra

oo. He knew damn well that the only reason Dylan was in
Dawson's Clough was because Kaminski was still protest-
ng his innocence.

"He is, yes. He's adamant he left your wife at three o'clock.
Almost an hour before your neighbour claimed to have seen
someone in the back garden." Dylan hadn't, as yet, spoken
to the neighbour. He couldn't see much point in doing so,
but it was on his list. "He also denies threatening your wife
during a phone conversation the previous evening. Or at any
time, come to that."

"He would, wouldn't he, but I know what I heard."

"His story is that she phoned him to say she was meeting
a friend on the Thursday and suggested he call round on the
Wednesday instead."

Walsingham shrugged and tried to conceal his frustration
by taking a slow drink of whisky.

"Your wife's friend confirmed that they'd made a spur-
of-the-moment arrangement to meet, I gather?" Dylan said.

"Carly had planned to meet Kirsten, yes." Walsingham
took a breath. He must have reminded himself he was supposed to be Laurence Olivier too. "If Kaminski really is innocent, then no one would be more pleased to see him freed than
me. But all I can tell you, Dylan, is what I know. I overheard
Carly's part of a phone call the evening before. She was upset
and distressed. She told the caller to stop threatening her."

"She didn't tell you who she was talking to?"

"No. To be honest, the mention of Kaminski's name used
to drive me crazy. The man simply refused to accept that his
marriage was over. He used to call her all the time. It was
embarrassing for her, and I found it infuriating. So no, she
wouldn't have told me who was calling. She wouldn't have
wanted to upset me. Besides—" he smiled a sad smile "—she
was a brave little thing. She would have believed she could
handle Kaminski."

"Who did she say the call was from?"

"Oh, she gave me some nonsense about it being a salesman. She said he was pushy. Well, they are, aren't they? They need to make sales to earn a living."

Dylan nodded at the truth of that.

"I didn't believe her," Walsingham said. "I even suspected it might have been Kaminski. But I didn't push it. It sounds silly now, but we were going out for a meal and I didn't want to spoil the evening." He put his elbows on the table and made a steeple of his fingers. "Of course, the next day she was gone."

"Indeed. So you told the police about the threatening phone call?"

"Yes. They checked with the phone company and found that the only call Carly made or received that day was from Kaminski."

Walsingham looked triumphant as he waited for Dylan to comment. Dylan merely took a swig of beer. He wanted Walsingham to do the talking.

"You see, Dylan, I really can't think of anyone else who could have done such a terrible thing. At first, I thought perhaps a burglar but—well, nothing was taken. Nothing had been disturbed."

Walsingham was desperate for Dylan's agreement, but Dylan still didn't speak.

"So what have you learned?" Walsingham asked. "Anything interesting? Anything that might help?"

"Not really. It's odd, though, don't you think?"

"What's odd?"

"All of it." Dylan took another swallow of beer. He was enjoying Walsingham's discomfort. "If your wife was being threatened by Kaminski, I can't understand why she'd let him into the house and—"

"She was kind. She would have tried to be nice to him,

to try and make him understand that he couldn't keep bothering her."

"—why she'd let him in the house and then have sex with him," Dylan finished. "There's no doubt that they had intercourse and there was nothing to suggest it was nonconsensual." He put up a hand to fend off Walsingham's interruption. "There was a bruise, I know, but Walsingham claims she enjoyed rough sex."

"That's an out-and-out lie." Walsingham laughed at the notion, a strangled sound. "My wife's sexual appetite was perfectly normal, I assure you."

"With you, maybe." Dylan felt like a cat batting a mouse around a room before going in for the kill. "But perhaps she had different preferences with her ex-husband. After all, she'd known him intimately for many years. She had intercourse with him when she was a teenager, and, as we know, youngsters like to experiment. It's the only way to learn what they like and dislike, isn't it?"

"Okay, so maybe as a teenager, she did like other things. The Carly I married, the Carly who was murdered, didn't experiment."

"She had a selection of sex toys, I understand."

Again that scoffing laugh. "Name me a woman who doesn't. They're just a joke. Silly presents given to her on her hen night."

"Yes. It's odd that Kaminski knew about them though, don't you think? I find it amazing that he can describe them in great detail. If, as you believe, she was trying to get him out of her life once and for all, showing him dildos and handcuffs was a very strange way to go about it."

Walsingham emptied his glass and Dylan stood up. "Let me get this round."

He strode off to the bar before Walsingham could claim he needed to keep another appointment. The club was still busy and he had to wait a couple of minutes to be served. At least twenty people were clustered round the pool table in the smaller side room. Two teenagers had cues in their hands. Four young girls wearing six inches of clothing between them drank something blue from bottles and wobbled on nail-like heels.

With the drinks paid for, a pint for himself and a double whisky for Walsingham, Dylan returned to their table.

"Thanks, Dylan. That's kind of you." Walsingham took a sip of whisky. "I'll have to be off in a minute though. I think I told you I had something on?"

"Yes. And I appreciate you taking time out to see me."

"I just wish I could help."

"I'm sure you do." Dylan leaned back in his chair, ankle resting on his knee, as relaxed as someone having a quick chat with his best friend. "Tell me something, Neil. Who were you having an affair with when your wife was killed? Was it Sonia or Megan? I'm getting confused."

Walsingham's eyes were like chips of polished steel.

"I wasn't having an affair with anyone," he said. "I had, I admit, been involved with Sonia Trueman. A silly mistake that I regretted immediately. When you work together, when you see life and death on a daily basis, relationships are formed. Dangerous relationships. I broke things off between us."

"A wise move," Dylan said. "I get the impression Sonia's husband isn't a man to upset."

"Him." Walsingham pulled a face. "He's all brawn and no brain."

"Did you ever have dealings with him? Did he make threats or—?"

Walsingham snorted. "Of course not. I can say with some relief that we don't mix in the same circles. I've never even spoken to him."

"I see." It seemed that Walsingham didn't see Trueman as
a possible suspect for his wife's murder. "So if you weren't
having an affair, who told me—? Ah, yes, it was Megan. She
said you'd known for some time that your wife was being un-
faithful with Aleksander Kaminski."

Anger flashed across Walsingham's face but was gone in
an instant. Blink and you'd have missed it. A smile, one that
looked as if its forming had caused actual physical pain, replaced it.

"I remember saying something of the sort to her. Kaminski had been bothering Carly, you see, and we'd had a silly
row. I'd offered to talk to him, but Carly would have none
of it. Believe me, if I'd had a couple of words with him, he
would have thought twice about making a nuisance of himself. Anyway, we had a row and I said some stupid things. I
even accused her of enjoying his attention."

"I see."

"So, needing someone to talk to, I ended up at Megan's.
I was still angry with Carly. My head was a mess and I al-
most believed I was right, that Carly *was* seeing Kaminski.
That's why I said those crazy things to Megan. God, I knew
Carly wasn't having anything to do with him. The idea was
ludicrous."

"Right."

"Megan was someone to talk to, that's all. She works at the
hospital. She understands. And after Carly—" He shrugged.
"A man needs someone to talk to after a tragedy like that."

"I'm sure he does."

"Is that why you were involved with Sonia Trueman? For
someone to talk to, I mean."

"Sonia." Walsingham rolled his eyes. "The way she carried on, you'd have thought we were Romeo and Juliet. It was
a silly, senseless fling, that's all. It meant nothing. Well, not
to me. And if I'd had any idea she was reading things into

it, I would have put her straight a lot sooner. The last thing, the very last thing, I wanted was to upset her, to give her the wrong impression."

He emptied his glass in one long swallow and rose to his impressive height. "Well, if there's nothing else you need to know, Dylan, I'll be off."

"There is one thing."

"Oh? And what's that?"

Dylan stood up too. Walsingham was a couple of inches taller.

"I'd very much like to know who killed your wife. Was it you?"

Every expression flitted across Walsingham's face. Dylan saw anger, shock and frustration. Anger was uppermost.

"Me? You think I could kill my own wife? You think I could murder the mother of my two sons?"

"You wouldn't be the first."

Walsingham surprised Dylan by sitting down again. Dylan sat next to him. Waiting.

For a moment, he thought the doctor was about to confess all.

"It's funny," Walsingham said, "but when the police came that day—the day I found Carly—I knew immediately that they had me down as chief suspect. Afterwards, I spoke to one of the detectives. He said a spouse is always looked at very closely. Something to do with the number of murderers who are close to their victims."

Dylan nodded at the truth of that.

"I couldn't believe it," Walsingham said. "I mean, not me. I save people's lives. All sorts are brought into the hospital, you know. We get drunks, wife-beaters, drug addicts, thieves. I expect we even get killers. They all have one thing in common and that is receiving the best medical attention we can provide. I took an oath, Dylan. I couldn't kill anyone. I just couldn't do it. And I certainly couldn't kill my sons' mother."

Dylan almost believed him. Almost.

Walsingham rose to his feet again. "And now, I really must go. Goodnight, Dylan."

"Goodnight."

Dylan quickly finished his drink and left the club. He was in time to see Walsingham jump in a cab parked on the nearby rank and be driven off to who knew where.

Dylan could jump in another and say "Follow that taxi" but there was little point. Walsingham would be on to that one.

One thing was certain, he wasn't going to be fooled by someone claiming that they'd taken the Hippocratic Oath and, therefore, couldn't harm anyone or anything. Harold Shipman had taken that same oath before hanging himself in a police cell after being found guilty of murdering over two hundred of his patients.

Dylan would head back to his hotel and stare at his computer screen until it put him to sleep. Within about ten minutes, he'd guess.

As he walked, he called home. Bev answered within three rings.

"Hi," he said. "How's it going?"

"Fine. Yes, it's okay." She sounded tired, as if she didn't care about anything. "Your mum's been here all day, so that was good."

"Yeah? So what have you been up to?"

"Not a lot. I went and sat in the garden for a bit. I thought I'd read, but I couldn't find anything I fancied. And I didn't want to listen to anything."

Bev was a bookaholic. He'd bought her a Kindle over a year ago and he dreaded to think how many ebooks she had on that. Plus the fact, whenever they went into town, she couldn't resist browsing in bookshops. No sooner had a cover caught

her eye than she'd read the blurb on the back and taken it to
the till. He'd bet any money on there being over a hundred
unread books at the house in one format or another.

Bev was the woman who sat in bed late at night, complaining that she had to be up early, and finished a book. So long
as it featured a hero and heroine who were going to fall in
love and live happily ever after, she didn't care.

"Oh, well," he said, feeling at a loss, "it's sometimes good
to just sit and do nothing."

"Yeah. How about you? How are you getting on?"

He told her about his security firm find and about his meeting with Neil Walsingham. He couldn't claim to be getting
on well, but at least he'd been doing something.

"How are Luke and Freya?"

"Luke's fine," she said. "Freya's Freya."

"Is she asleep?"

"Yes, for all of five minutes. Perhaps she's trying to beat
her own record."

He smiled, but he knew it wasn't funny. Bev was struggling.

"Why don't you get an early night?" he suggested.

"Because I have a hundred and one things to do. The house
is a tip, I have enough washing to set up my own laundry
business—"

"But nothing that can't wait."

"I suppose. Yes, I might. Or I might see if there's anything
on TV. I don't know, I can't be bothered to do a lot."

"Then do nothing. Sit and gaze at your navel. Or pour
yourself a glass of wine and have a long hot bath."

"I might. What are you doing now?"

"I'm going back to the hotel to sit and stare at CCTV pictures for an hour or so."

When he ended the call, he thought of phoning his mother
to find out her opinion of Bev. After all, she'd spent most of

the day with her. He couldn't face it though. Why do today what he could put off till next week?

It was almost dark when he reached the hotel. He was putting his card in the door's lock when his phone rang. The display showed a local number, one he didn't recognise.

"Hello?"

"I know who killed Mrs. Walsingham." The voice was muffled, distorted.

"Who is this?"

"Neil Walsingham. He killed his wife. He should be locked up."

"Who is this?"

The connection was cut. The line was dead.

TWENTY-ONE

DYLAN SHUT DOWN his computer. He'd wasted most of the morning staring at cars travelling along Darwen Road and had reached the stage when a bunch of strippers on an open-top bus wouldn't have registered.

He'd spotted Neil Walsingham's car, though, so that had been cause for a minor celebration. Not that Walsingham driving through Dawson's Clough a week before his wife was murdered proved anything.

He grabbed his jacket, wallet and car keys, and left the hotel.

Forecasters had threatened Lancashire with more gale-force winds and heavy rain but, so far, it was dry if a little breezy. He drove into the town centre, parked and walked through the pedestrianised shopping centre.

Last night's mysterious call had come from a local number, but Dylan's attempts to reach it had rung out unanswered. It was early this morning that he'd finally got a response.

"Er, yeah?"

"Who is that?" Dylan had asked.

"What do you mean?"

"The number I've reached, where is it? Who are you?"

"Well, it's a phone box, isn't it?"

"Where?"

"In Clough centre. Outside Smith's."

"Right. Okay, thanks for your help."

There it was. A few yards from WH Smith's was a public phone box.

Dylan stepped inside, lifted the receiver and tapped in his own number for confirmation that his anonymous caller has used this particular phone. They had.

As he headed back to his car, he tried to come up with answers to a dozen questions. First, was the caller male or female. The voice had been too muffled to even guess at the gender. Also, why would someone use a town centre phone box to call him? Why, if that person believed Neil Walsingham should be behind bars, didn't they give him a clue? Could they *know* Walsingham was responsible for his wife's murder or were they just guessing?

He had no answers and it was time he headed to the fun factory that was Strangeways. As the route took him half a mile from the Pennine View Rescue Centre, he decided he might as well pay Sue Kaminski a visit.

Her car, a battered, rusty Fiat, was the only vehicle in sight. Thankfully, there were no huge Rottweilers guarding the gate. None that Dylan could see at least.

He was about to risk opening that gate when Sue came out of the front door and spotted him.

"Dylan, what a lovely surprise. Are you on your way to see Alek?" She strode over and opened the gate. She was wearing clean black trousers, a blue jacket and shoes with small heels.

"I am, yes. I thought I'd call in here as I'm passing, but it looks like you're on your way out."

"It's my day to visit Aunt Joyce," she said. "Come inside and I'll make you a coffee."

"No, it doesn't matter. I don't want to delay you."

"Come on." She smiled. "Aunt Joyce won't mind."

"Okay then, thanks. Sorry, but I don't have anything new to tell you."

"You can tell me how you're managing to get all these visits to Alek."

"I'm sorry," he said again.

"Hey, I'm only teasing. In any case, when you get him out of that place, I'll have him back here where he belongs."

Dylan gave her a noncommittal smile.

She took him into the kitchen which, to Dylan's surprise, was empty of dogs. A cat was curled up in the windowsill, waiting for the sun to shine perhaps, but it was the lone four-legged occupant.

"Milk and two sugars, wasn't it?" She filled the kettle and switched it on.

"Please."

The Aga was throwing out heat, as it had been on Dylan's first visit. The extra warmth was still needed as Lancashire couldn't understand that spring was supposed to have arrived. The only sign of the new season that Dylan had seen was a couple of brave lambs being buffeted by the wind.

"I saw Alek's parents on Monday," he said.

She tried to stifle a groan and failed. "Agata phoned me last night. They're paying me a visit tomorrow."

"Oh? Any particular reason?" Strange that they hadn't mentioned it.

"It was a spur-of-the-moment decision, I gather. Agata said they hadn't seen me for a while. Which is true. I keep meaning to call them but time just vanishes. How are they?"

"They're fine." He took a seat at the table. "How do you get on with them?"

"Okay." The reply was automatic but her hand stilled on the kettle. "They'd known Alek's first wife for a long time so they were upset when he got divorced. I'm not sure anyone could measure up after that."

Dylan could believe that. He'd seen no framed photos of Sue with Alek.

"And she used to visit them more often because she still had family in Birmingham. She used to call on Alek's parents when she saw her own, you see." She put a mug of coffee in front of him. "There you go."

"Thanks."

She was waiting for Dylan to speak and it served as a reminder that he was getting nowhere. All he'd discovered was that Neil Walsingham had an affair more often than Dylan changed his shirt, and that he might not have been at the hospital when his wife was killed. Other than that, he had nothing.

"Do Alek's parents ever talk to you about Mrs. Walsingham?" he asked.

"Not really, no. Sometimes, they'd tell Alek that she'd called in. They'd say it was nice to see her, that's all."

"They never mentioned any problems she was having? Financial problems? Disputes with anyone?"

"No. Never. Why do you ask?"

"Someone wanted her dead, Sue, and I can't think of a single reason why anyone would."

"You know what I think? I think a burglar got in, thinking she was out and then, when he realised she wasn't, he killed her."

"An opportunist?"

Dylan didn't think so. Burglars tended to stick to their own craft. They might, if disturbed, hit out at someone, but they were unlikely to turn killer. It wasn't as if Carly had disturbed anyone as she was still lying in her bath.

"Do you know Kirsten? She was Carly's best friend and acted as bridesmaid when Alek married Carly."

Sue shook her head slowly. "Never heard of her. But I wouldn't expect to. Why? What's she been saying?"

Frederyk and Agata Kaminski were paying Dylan too well for him to worry about hurting people's feelings.

"She claims Carly was still in love with Alek," he said.

A nerve twitched at Sue's throat and she pulled a face,

as if she had a bad smell under her nose. "Well, she would, wouldn't she? Carly didn't want Alek, but she didn't like it when he married me. She couldn't have, could she? That's why she made him go round to her house. If he hadn't, if he'd kept away from her—" She broke off, preferring to chew on her bottom lip.

Sue could live to be a hundred and still not accept that her husband had enjoyed sex with his ex-wife. He was a grown man, not a child. He hadn't been forced into Carly's bed. He'd gone willingly.

"Well, I won't keep you from visiting your aunt, Sue. I'll go and see Alek."

"Give him my love, won't you? I hate to think of him stuck in that place when he should be at home. I know you're doing all you can, Dylan, but all the same—" She broke off. "Tell him I've written, and that I'll see him soon."

"I will."

TWENTY-TWO

DESPITE TELLING HIMSELF not to, Alek had looked forward to Dylan Scott's visit. He'd failed to quash the hope that maybe Scott was as good as everyone claimed. He'd dared to think that maybe, just maybe, the bloke really was capable of getting him out of this hellhole.

He was doing okay in here. It was possible to cope with Strangeways so long as you kept the right attitude. If you kept yourself to yourself and didn't upset anyone, you could get by.

At first, he'd thought he had nothing to get out for, but then he'd imagined taking Charlie for a long tramp across the hills. He'd discovered a longing to feel the wind on his face, and to sort out his fishing gear and spend a day on the riverbank.

As soon as he spotted Scott, he knew he'd been a damn fool to raise his hopes. He'd be better off putting his head down and accepting that this was as good as it got for the next decade or so. It was clear the bloke had no good news for him.

"Hi, Alek," Scott said. "How are you doing?"

"Okay."

They sat opposite each other on plastic chairs that were attached to the table.

"Sue sends her love," Scott said with a forced smile. "She's written to you and she says she'll see you soon."

Sue wrote every day. Every. Single. Day. It would only be newsworthy if she hadn't.

"I called to see her on my way here," Scott said. "She was on her way out. Off to see her great-aunt."

"Like the old lady will care whether she's there or not."

Scott shrugged. "I saw your parents on Monday."

"How are they?" He knew damn well how they were. It hurt to think of them having to go through this. They'd come to England years ago, when he was only three years old, but they were still outsiders. It wasn't England or the English, it was them. They considered themselves inferior, saw themselves as the unwanted guests at a party. Alek could have made them proud, made them feel as if they belonged in this country, but instead, he'd wound up in Strangeways, branded a killer.

"They're doing okay," Scott said. "They're paying Sue a visit tomorrow."

"Sue?"

Scott smiled. "You sound surprised."

"I am a bit." A lot. His parents had never taken to Sue and any meetings were always strained. "We don't see much of them."

"Yes, so Sue said. While I was in Birmingham—I think I told you Carly's parents have refused to see me? Well, I spoke to Kirsten."

"Oh, yes?" He hadn't seen her since he and Carly divorced. He'd never really liked or disliked her. In his eyes, she'd been Carly's best friend. Nothing more and nothing less. He'd always believed she'd been jealous of him though. She'd wanted Carly for herself.

"She's not your biggest fan," Scott said, "but, unlike everyone else, she did say that Carly still loved you. She didn't know you'd been seeing Carly, but she wasn't surprised to hear it."

Alek nodded again. Scott was telling him nothing he didn't know, and nothing that warranted his parents handing over a lot of cash.

"I had a chat with Neil Walsingham, too."

"Lying bastard."

"Yes." Scott drummed his fingers on the table. "The trouble is, I can't think why he'd kill Carly. His life seemed to be going okay, after all. He had his sons, a nice house, a job he enjoyed, a mistress. Why would he want her dead? It wasn't as if he'd taken out a huge life insurance policy so he didn't gain financially."

Alek had asked himself that same question countless times and, just like Scott, hadn't come up with a single answer. Walsingham had enjoyed playing the respectable doctor, meeting up with his golfing cronies and climbing the social ladder. A wife like Carly, an attractive one who any man would enjoy taking to functions, and one who didn't make demands, suited him. Carly might have been made for him. So why the hell would he risk everything by killing her?

"Perhaps he had nothing to do with it," Alek said.

The hopelessness of it all hit him in the stomach. Carly's killer could be long gone. Maybe a young thug had got into the house and been surprised to find Carly there. Perhaps he'd only intended to steal some cash. Drug addicts would kill their own grandmothers for a fiver. That thug would be long gone by now. Either that or he'd be living in Dawson's Clough and laughing with relief.

"In which case," Scott said, "why would he lie about the phone conversation he supposedly heard between you and her? Why would he claim you threatened her the night before?"

Alek wanted to scream. He had no fucking idea.

"According to him," Scott said, "he didn't push her for information because they were going out for a meal and he didn't want to spoil the occasion."

"He didn't want to spoil—fucking hell, that's rich. He picked a fight with her."

"A fight? What are you talking about?"

"He did it all the time. Image, his image, was everything

to him and, whenever they went out, he reckoned she didn't look pleased to be with him. He used to accuse her of chatting up blokes and stuff like that. He was right, she did. She used to do it to piss him off half the time."

"And you're saying they quarrelled about it that night?"

"Yes. Carly told me about it the next day, the day she was killed. She said he was in a foul mood all evening. He accused her of chatting up the waiter and then sulked like a child. Once he got her outside, he had a right go at her. She was laughing about it when she told me. The car was parked at the back of the restaurant, apparently, and he kept shouting at her and wouldn't unlock it."

"That's interesting. Did you mention any of this at the time?"

"Only about a dozen times. He denied all knowledge and, of course, they couldn't find any witnesses. They wouldn't. He was always careful to lose his temper in private. Besides, I expect they didn't try too hard."

"I'll have a word with him about that and see what he says. But he's lying about other things too," Scott said. "According to his current mistress, he knew his wife was seeing you."

Alek shrugged. "We always guessed he did."

"When I questioned him, he brushed it off. He claims he'd told her that when he was still angry with Carly. According to him, he and Carly used to argue about you. You kept phoning her, pestering her, refusing to accept your marriage was over and he accused her of enjoying your attention."

"If he *did* know about us, I'm surprised he didn't say something to Carly."

And yet—

Alek hadn't said as much to Scott because it was none of his business, none of anyone's business, but, on that last afternoon, Carly had said she was ending things between them. She'd been a little crazy. Crazier than usual.

"For good this time, Alek," she'd said.

"Yeah, yeah." He'd grinned at her, pulled her into his arms and kissed her.

"I mean it. I've got the boys to think about. They're growing up fast, and I can't have them finding out that their mother's—you know."

"I'll go now then, shall I?" He'd heard it too often. How many times had they, for one reason or another, decided to put an end to their relationship once and for all? He'd lost count. "I hope you'll be very happy, my love."

He'd been at the door before she'd called him back.

"Honestly, Alek, you always take things too literally. I didn't mean now, this minute, for God's sake."

"Ah. So when are we supposed to end this thing?"

"Stay for a while." She'd slipped her hands beneath his shirt and covered his face with kisses...

Alek hadn't taken her seriously. They'd both known for years that they had to get over each other, that they both had spouses, that Carly had children. They'd known that what they were doing was wrong. The truth of the matter was that they'd been powerless to do anything about it.

Perhaps this time, Carly would have done something about it. Maybe Walsingham had confronted her. Perhaps he'd threatened her with divorce. If she'd thought she was on the brink of losing her safe life as the doctor's wife and, far more important, her children, she might have ended things between them.

He'd never know the answer to that one. No one would.

"I'm a bit short of suspects," Scott said.

"So were the police." Alek knew he sounded bitter, but he couldn't help it. "That's why I'm here."

"You're here because one hell of a lot of evidence put you here."

"I had no motive though. If, as everyone wants to believe,

I couldn't accept our marriage was over, I wouldn't want her dead. If, as I know, she was the only woman I ever truly cared about, I wouldn't want her dead. Why in hell's name would I?"

Scott looked at him for long moments and finally shook his head. "I don't know. I don't know why anyone would."

Scott pulled at his tie to loosen it. The bloke always looked uncomfortable. Alek wondered if Strangeways was making his skin crawl or if Scott felt guilty about wasting his parents' money.

"You were close to her," Scott said. "If someone had wanted her dead, surely to God she would have said something, mentioned something odd, talked about someone who disliked her."

"She didn't."

Alek's heartbeat picked up pace and he tried to take a few steadying breaths. His panic attacks were becoming more frequent. His hands were cold and clammy, his throat was dry. He began tapping a tune with his foot, anything to take his mind off the panic.

Tap, tap, tap.

That bruise on her arm—Christ, he'd never bruised her before. He'd claimed she liked rough sex, but she hadn't. She liked to have fun in the bedroom, but she didn't like any rough stuff. She certainly wouldn't have liked anything that involved pain, so how the hell had he bruised her?

"You okay?" Scott asked.

"Yeah." He ran a hand over his face. "Yeah, I'm good."

"It's this sodding place," Scott said. "It gives me the creeps and I know I'll be walking out soon."

"Sue's the same." He sighed. "God, she must be having one hell of a time of it."

"She's doing okay."

"Financially she isn't. Without my income, she's had it. She's already sold her car. Not that it was worth anything.

All she's done is exchange one heap of rusting crap for another. She sold my van too and got a couple of grand for that, but she must be really struggling. And knowing her, she'll go without herself rather than give the animals less food."

"She has a lot of friends," Scott said. "I'm sure they'll help her out."

"It's not the same though, is it?"

"No, but they'll help. She has Jamie, and I get the impression he'd be more than happy to help her out."

Alek almost smiled. "Yes, I bet Jamie's loving every minute of this. Having me stuck here must make him feel as if all his birthdays have arrived at once."

"Yes, I suppose it must."

He saw a hundred questions in Scott's eyes. "Don't go getting ideas about him."

"Why not? If you didn't kill Carly Walsingham, someone else did. Until we know who that someone is, everyone is a suspect."

"But Jamie? Come off it. And even if he was a killer, he'd have gone for me, not Carly. One thing *is* certain, the killer couldn't have known I'd take the blame for any of it."

Scott shrugged. "He could if he'd known you were visiting Carly that afternoon."

"But no one did. Christ, I didn't even know myself until the night before."

They talked some more and, with every passing moment, Alek's heartbeat increased.

He'd been a fool to think that Scott might be able to work a miracle and get him out of this place. It would be far more sensible to accept what had happened and make the most of it. He'd been doing okay in here until Scott arrived on the scene. Since then, he'd started to fall apart. It wasn't just the panic attacks, it was those fucking awful nightmares.

TWENTY-THREE

MEGAN TOOK HER time locking her back door and steppin
out into the night. It had been dark for more than an hou
but the stretch of canal running past her house was close t
the dual carriageway, and lights from that made it possibl
to see the path. Just.

An icy wind whipped up the water. No one else was abou
Only the mentally challenged would be down by the canal ;
this time. A bubble of anger rose inside her. Only Neil woul
expect someone to meet him here.

He'd strolled into the ward after lunch, something he'
never done before. Usually, even if they met in the corrido
he wouldn't acknowledge her. But today, he'd been all smile;
holding doors open for staff. He'd been on show.

At first, she'd been pleased when he'd taken her aside. "I'
be out running this evening. About seven?"

She'd nodded eagerly, pathetically grateful for any crum
he threw her way.

The afternoon had dragged on, though, bringing with it th
knowledge that something had changed. Neil had changed i

She stood close to the stone bridge that straddled the dar
water, hands deep in the pockets of her coat. The wind guste
loud and angry. A duck splashed nearby, startling her.

Damn it, she shouldn't be standing here like a crimina
Or a prostitute.

It struck her as strange that this spot had once seemed s
romantic. It was where they'd shared their first kiss.

She'd seen him at the hospital before then, of course, an

hey'd exchanged smiles and a few words while they'd been
t the coffee machine or travelling in the lift together. There'd
been no hint of what was to come until, one June evening,
Megan had decided to walk along the towpath to enjoy some
are sunshine. Neil had been out for his usual run and they'd
topped to chat. One minute Megan had been telling him she
ived near the canal and the next he'd been kissing her. Ten
minutes later, he'd been in her shower. Eleven minutes later,
he carried her to bed.

Things had been good between them. Life had been an ex-
iting whirl of secretive smiles, note passing, sneaked meet-
ngs and hot sex.

The only problem had been Neil's wife. If not for her—

Surprisingly, given the strength of the wind, she heard
Neil's feet pounding along the towpath before she saw the
man himself.

He stopped in front of her and put his hands on his knees
s he got his breath back.

"Hi," he said, still breathless.

She wanted him to take her in his arms, to lead her back
o her house, to take a shower with her, to make love to her.

This deserted spot felt anything but romantic now. It was
oo dark to see the litter, but she guessed there would be
mpty beer cans under the bridge and maybe a syringe or two.
t was where the town's drunks and drug addicts came to get
igh. There was a nasty smell too. Probably urine.

"So," she said. "To what do I owe this unexpected—plea-
ure."

He'd been brushing hair back from his face, smile in place,
ut he stopped. Her tone had him frowning at her. "Sorry?"

"Why do you want to see me?"

She could guess. He was moving on to pastures new. He'd
eft Linda for Sonia, and he'd left Sonia for her. She'd been
aive to believe she was The One. Neil liked the thrill of the

chase, the newness and excitement of it all. He didn't like re
lationships. They were too difficult for him.

"Oh, I bet I know." Outwardly, she was calm. Inside sh
was seething. "I haven't seen her, but I've heard about the new
temporary addition to your staff. A young blonde, isn't she?

Even as she spoke, a tiny spark of hope refused to die. I
he'd just take her in his arms and tell her he loved her, she
forgive him anything.

"What are you talking about, Megan?"

"You've obviously got something to tell me. It's nothin
short of a miracle that you came into the ward and spoke t
me. Usually, you treat me like slug slime, something to b
avoided in case, God forbid, anyone should see us and pu
two and two together."

"Megan, sweetheart."

"Don't sweetheart me. Just say what you have to, Neil."

He didn't speak, he looked at her in an odd sort of way, a
if he couldn't make up his mind.

She guessed he'd talk about his children, how they wer
growing up and how he needed to be there for them. He'
promise to meet her for a coffee now and again, maybe tak
her out for a drink one evening. She could almost hear hir
telling her they'd always be friends.

He didn't say a word and that in itself unnerved her.

"Come on, then," she said. "You want to tell me it's ove
don't you?"

"Megan, I don't know what's got into you," he said at las
"Of course I don't want to tell you it's over. God, you're th
only thing that makes sense at the moment. You know that.
He ran his hands through his hair in a gesture that had alway
turned her on. Now it left her cold. "We haven't seen much o
each other because I've had things to deal with. That blaste
investigator for one."

Of course!

"I swear to God, Neil, I didn't tell him anything." She was still reeling from the shock of having the man in her home. "I told him about Teresa, said that she knew we were at the hospital, that's all. He must have spoken to her and she must have mentioned Sonia. I swear to God I never mentioned Sonia's name."

"I know that, sweetheart. I know." He grabbed her wrist. "Come here."

She stood in front of him and she was frightened. It wasn't the temperature making her shiver. She'd been crazy to think he'd come here to end things. How could he? He was angry with her for talking to Dylan Scott, for not sounding sure about their movements on the day of Carly's murder. It hadn't been like that though. Scott had taken her by surprise.

"There's no harm done," Neil said. "I can vouch for you being at the hospital and you can vouch for me. So long as we both swear we were there—"

"But we weren't, were we? Neither of us was at the bloody hospital that afternoon. That investigator will find out, he'll tell the police—"

"Of course he won't. For God's sake, Megan, get a grip." His scowl was menacing in the dim, almost nonexistent light. "Don't you dare go falling apart on me now."

He was strong and held her wrist firm. No more than six inches away from her, the deep dark water swirled to the beat of the wind. No one could see them. There was no one in earshot. He could do as he wished with her and no one would hear her cries. If he pushed her—

"You'll speak to no one," he said. "Got that?"

"I can't stand this, Neil. That investigator will—"

"He'll do nothing, you stupid bitch." He lifted his hand to slap her. It was difficult to tell who was more surprised, him or her. She didn't stop to find out.

She ran.

It wasn't far to her house, but he was fitter. He was wearing running shoes, she had on low heels. It was madness to think she could outrun him.

She could hear a pounding, but didn't know if it was Neil gaining on her or if it was the blood pumping in her ears.

TWENTY-FOUR

SUE WOULD BE thankful when the day was over. She'd been up early, cleaning the place for Alek's parents. They wouldn't say anything, conversation would be as polite and strained as usual, but she knew she'd fall well short of their expectations. When your house was filled with animals, it was difficult to assume the role of domestic goddess.

She had no idea what had prompted this visit but she wished it hadn't. They could only talk about Alek's plight for so long and, other than that, they had little to say to each other. She knew nothing of their life or their friends, and they were ignorant of hers.

On her way back from her great-aunt's nursing home yesterday, she'd bought supplies. Given the awful weather, hot stew and dumplings might have been more appropriate, but she was giving them salad with plenty of smoked ham for lunch. She wasn't the greatest cook in the world, and she didn't want to risk giving them a meal that tasted of failure. She'd made a trifle for dessert and, if they stayed any longer, which she hoped they wouldn't, they'd have to make do with a sandwich or biscuits.

She looked at her gleaming kitchen and her clean jeans and decided she and the house were as ready as they were ever going to be.

Spice, an ancient tabby, wandered into the kitchen, stretched and scrambled onto a chair. Sue picked her up and gave her a stroke.

"They'll never like me," she told Spice. "They hate me

for not being Carly. And for marrying Alek. They probably hate me for not having a job that brings in some money too."

Spice purred her understanding and nuzzled Sue's chin.

The Kaminskis had hoped to arrive by ten o'clock and, by ten-fifteen, Sue's hopes started to rise. Maybe they couldn't come after all. Perhaps the traffic was bad and they'd decided to turn around and go home.

At ten-twenty, a car horn tooted. Her spirits sinking, Sue peeped behind the curtain in time to see Agata climb out of the car and reach inside to retrieve a bulging shopping bag from the backseat. Frederyk joined her, took the bag and stood for a moment to look at the house. He said something to his wife and they began walking up the path.

Sue took a deep breath and went to open the door for them.

"Frederyk, Agata, how lovely to see you. Thank you so much for coming."

"You're looking well, dear." Agata gave her the customary hug. "We should have come before."

Agata took the bag from Frederyk and they walked along the hall and into the kitchen. "We've brought a few things for lunch. A pie—steak and kidney. I hope you don't mind. I thought we should contribute, but I'd hate you to think I was taking over. I know you're perfectly capable, but—"

"It's fine. Thank you very much."

Agata was nervous. They didn't have Alek to act as go-between and she was as nervous as Sue.

"Good." Agata gave a small, relieved smile. "I thought wine, too. Frederyk can't have any because he's driving, but you and me, Susan, we can have a drop."

The last person to call her Susan had been the vicar who'd christened her.

"You shouldn't have bothered," she said, "but thank you. And yes, Agata, we'll have a glass of wine. Let me take your coats and get you a drink after that long drive. Did you have a good journey?"

While they discussed the state of the UK's roads and the weather, Sue thought that Agata seemed to be shrinking with every passing month. Frederyk, too, looked beaten by life. The couple looked bewildered.

They had something in common, after all. Sue shared something with these people that Carly never had. The three of them were trying, and finding it difficult, to cope with seeing the person they loved most in the world caged like an animal. She felt herself unexpectedly warming to these people.

She wasn't sure of their exact ages, although she knew Frederyk was four years older than his wife. Agata was somewhere in her early seventies. Sue remembered Alek visiting her on her seventieth birthday. That meant Frederyk was probably closer to eighty than seventy. That they'd undertaken this long journey surprised her. She felt the burden of guilt pressing down.

To be polite, Sue supposed, Frederyk suggested they look round the kennels. Sue passed a pleasant hour explaining where the animals had come from and telling them how Alek had built the examination rooms.

Another surprise came when Agata fell in love with Friday, a pretty but unsociable smoke-grey cat.

"She's about twelve, we think," Sue said. "She was dumped here with her four kittens. We have a waiting list for kittens and puppies, so as soon as they'd been given a clean bill of health, we rehome them. Friday's been here for three years though. No one wants an old cat. Especially an unsociable one like Friday."

"Oh, the poor thing." Agata stroked the cat and, surprisingly, wasn't spat at or hissed at.

"She's taken to you," Sue said with a smile.

"Would she settle in a new home after so long?" Agata asked.

"I don't see why not. I think she'd love company and a bit of fuss. Once she got used to it, that is."

"Frederyk, look at her." Agata's voice was pleading.

Frederyk looked from the cat to his wife and gave her a smile that touched Sue. In that smile was all the love a woman could need.

"Would she mind being confined indoors?" Agata asked. "We don't have a garden. Well, you know what our flat's like. But if she wouldn't mind that, we could give her a home."

"You could? Oh, my goodness. Well, yes, of course she'd love it. I don't know her history, but she's been an indoor cat for the last three years. Are you sure, Agata?"

Agata looked at Frederyk and received that warm smile again.

"I'm sure," Agata said. "If she doesn't settle or if she hates life with us, can we bring her back?"

"Of course." Sue was delighted for Friday. She was a stroppy, unsociable cat but she deserved a chance of happiness. It would also be one less hungry mouth to feed. "Let's sort out her paperwork and a travelling box. She's healthy enough and all her vaccinations are up to date. If there are any problems, give me a ring."

Sue could understand Agata's delight. When there was something missing from your life, a cat was always willing to soak up any spare love. She knew that only too well. These days, it was the animals she confided in, the dogs who listened to her outpourings and mopped up her tears.

Preparing Friday for her departure took time and they were late sitting down to lunch. Agata helped prepare the food while Frederyk glanced through the local newspaper.

Sue opened the wine and poured a glass each for her and Agata.

"Cheers," she said, chinking her glass against Agata's. "Here's to the future. To Dylan Scott's success. To Alek's return."

"Hear, hear," Frederyk said.

"I phoned Dylan last night," Sue said, as they tucked in to pie and vegetables. "I wanted to know how Alek was when he saw him. He said he was doing well. Said he sounded cheerful enough."

Agata nodded. "He keeps himself cheerful."

He did, but Sue had no idea how. In his shoes, she'd go crazy. She couldn't bear the thought of being locked up in that place and knew she wouldn't be able to cope.

She'd been eight years old when two friends, Louise and Jenny, during a supposed game of hide-and-seek, had locked her in a cellar. The idea had been for Sue to wait in the cellar at Jenny's house while the two girls hid. After counting to a hundred, Sue would then race off and find them. Except, as a joke, the two girls had locked her in that cellar. All these years later, the memory still made Sue's heart race. She'd panicked, thought she wouldn't be able to breathe, and had screamed and kicked at that door until they released her. The idea of being locked in a room had terrified her ever since. No way could she survive in a prison cell.

"He's a nice young man, isn't he?" Agata said. "Dylan, I mean."

"He is. Very clever, too, by all accounts. I looked him up on the internet and he's been very successful in his other cases." Not that he'd had many cases. Only a couple of missing persons that had caught the headlines. His main claim to fame was being dismissed from the police force in disgrace. "If only he could prove Alek's innocence. If only people would accept that it was someone else, that a burglar had entered that house."

"We must put our faith in Dylan," Agata said. "His mother said he won't give up until he learns the truth."

"I'm sure he won't," Sue said. "One day, Alek will be home again. We have to believe that."

To add courage to her conviction, she poured them another glass of wine. She rarely drank wine, or anything else, because alcohol didn't agree with her. It didn't agree with her bank balance either. The first glass had made her a little light headed. She was a blink away from bursting into tears too.

"I always thought that temper of his would get him into trouble," Frederyk said. "He wouldn't have upset Carly, I know that, but I expect that temper raised its head when the police called on him."

Agata didn't comment and Sue wasn't sure what to say. She couldn't deny Alek had a temper. He'd flare up over the slightest thing if he was in one of his moods. A couple of years ago, someone had put a brick through his van's window. It was only the small window at the back so, even if there had been anything of value in the van, which there wasn't, no thief would have been able to gain access. That display of mindless vandalism had shown her the ugly side of Alek. He'd vowed vengeance on the person responsible and it had been a couple of days before Sue could speak to him without being on the receiving end of his anger.

Such events were rare, though. Sometimes, Alek could cloak himself in silence. On those occasions, Sue knew not to push him as experience had taught her he'd flare up. When he felt like talking, he would. She'd learned to wait until the anger passed.

"I made a trifle," she said, changing the subject. "Is anyone going to join me?"

Frederyk and Agata accepted a helping of trifle and both complimented her on it.

Agata helped with the washing up, Sue made them cof

ce and they were soon loading a boxed and not-too-happy
cat into the car.

"I'll let you know how she settles in," Agata said.

"Do that. Phone me this evening, just to let me know you
got home safely."

Frederyk looked surprised by the request. Pleased, too.
"We will, love," he promised.

The endearment, one that Carly would have grown used
to, touched Sue. "Speak soon," she said.

She stood by her gate, waving until the car was out of
sight. The day had been far better than she'd anticipated, the
ice had finally been broken, and a little warmth had seeped
into their relationship. Yet she still found herself wondering
what had prompted their visit.

Not finding an answer, she went inside, changed into more
suitable clothes and headed outside to check on the animals.

She had Misty, a young collie, on the leash when Jamie's
car pulled up. She was sure he wasn't due to visit today.

Monty was sitting in the passenger seat, looking as if he
owned the car. Sue hoped he'd stay there because Misty didn't
like other dogs. Or cats. Or horses, she'd discovered. Misty
loved people, and that was as far as it went.

Jamie got out of his car and locked it, leaving Monty to
watch proceedings from behind his window.

"Hi, Jamie. I wasn't expecting you today."

"I know. I was passing so I thought I'd call in and check
that all was well. I'll have a look at the staffie while I'm here,
if you like."

"That would be great, thanks. I'm pleased with her, though.
She's picked up a lot. You can find her yourself, can't you?
I'm about to take Misty out."

"Yes, of course. I'll see you when you get back."

She didn't want him to stay but couldn't say so. "Okay.
How's your father, by the way? Is he back home now?"

"Yes. He's fine, thanks. Almost back to normal."

He hadn't welcomed the enquiry. She'd noticed before how reluctant he was to talk about his family. His brother, a soldier, had been killed in Afghanistan. Things must be difficult for them all.

"That's good. It's a worry when our parents are ill, isn't it? They don't fight off things as easily."

"He's fine," Jamie said again. "I'll go and check out the staffie. I'll see you when you get back."

Sue set off with Misty but her cheery mood had darkened. It was Dylan Scott who'd put the idea in her head and, ever since, she'd noticed that Jamie called in far more often than necessary. Sometimes, even when Anne had told him all he needed to know, he'd hang around to see her. There was no reason for him to call today and, although he might want to check on their new resident, a Staffordshire Bull Terrier, there was no reason for him to linger and certainly no reason for him to wait to see her.

She didn't know what to do. She didn't want to say anything to Jamie because she might be imagining things, but nor did she want him getting any ideas. There was only one man for her and that man was currently locked up like an abandoned animal.

It seemed ridiculous that Jamie should be thinking of— well, she didn't know what he was thinking. Since Dylan Scott had commented, though, she'd noticed that Jamie spent far more time at the centre than was necessary. And he watched her.

It was beginning to unnerve her.

TWENTY-FIVE

DYLAN FELT AT home in the Dog and Fox these days. Last night he'd called in a couple of pubs within walking distance of his hotel, but neither had appealed to him. They'd both been dark, miserable places. Residents of Dawson's Clough must have shared his verdict because both were short on customers.

He was at the bar, ordering his drink, when ex-DCI Frank Willoughby came in.

"Frank, what are you having?"

"A pint of whatever you're having. IPA, is it? Thanks."

They carried their drinks to what Dylan now thought of as his table and sat down.

"Lewis is going to try and get here," Frank said. "He's got a lot of stuff on, though, and he's off to some conference or other in London in the morning. He said to apologise if he didn't make it."

Dylan didn't suppose it mattered one way or the other. Lewis had told him all he knew.

"He still looks like a copper, doesn't he?" Dylan said. "In fact, I couldn't help thinking that you both looked like coppers. Why's that?"

Frank grinned. "I know exactly what you mean. I've always thought Lewis will go to his grave looking like one. There's no way he could work undercover."

Dylan would have said the same about Frank, yet it was when Frank was on one of his many successful undercover jobs in London that they'd met.

"I'm quite happy to look like a copper," Frank said, "bu
I know I could disguise the fact if I tried."

Dylan nodded at the truth of that. "What about me? Do
look like a copper?"

"Nah. You don't even look like a disgraced one." Frank'
gaze was appraising. "You look more like a used-car salesman. Or perhaps one of those moody second-rate actors."

"Christ, you're hot with the compliments tonight."

Frank laughed. "Or maybe you look like a private investigator. How's it going?"

"Bloody badly."

"Of course," Frank said, "it could be that you're wasting
your time? There was no doubt in anyone's eyes that Kaminski is guilty."

Dylan took a long drink from his glass. Pure nectar.

"But the more I speak to people, the more convinced I an
that he's innocent." *Convinced* was pushing it a bit. Dylar
wouldn't bet his house on it. "The good doctor's lied for some
reason. According to his current mistress, he knew damn wel
his wife was having an affair with Kaminski."

Frank dried the bottom of his glass on a beer mat. "Maybe
he did, maybe he didn't. It means nothing."

"It means he's lying," Dylan said. "It's not conclusive,
agree, but if he's lied about that, who's to say he hasn't lie
about everything else? Also, his whereabouts on the after
noon in question, along with the whereabouts of the people
who gave him his alibi, are in doubt."

"What?"

Before Dylan could answer, ex-DI Cameron breezed in
side and to their table.

"I'm rushing about like a bloody lunatic, but I'll have
quick pint with you. It will be quick too." He was out o
breath. "What's anyone having?"

"Thanks, Lewis, but I've still got one," Dylan said.

"Me, too." Frank lifted his pint glass. "Don't worry, we'll remember it's your round next time."

They watched him ordering his drink at the bar. Even as he spoke to the barmaid, he was watching everyone.

"You're right," Frank said. "He might just as well be in uniform."

When Lewis was sitting at their table with his pint, Frank brought the conversation back to Dr. Walsingham.

"Dylan thinks there's some doubt about the doctor's whereabouts on the day in question," he told Lewis.

"How come?"

Dylan noted the tight lips and sensed a little hostility. He couldn't help that. Lewis should have done his job properly in the first place.

"Dig deep enough," he said, "and you find that no one can say for sure who was in the Accident and Emergency department that afternoon. It was so chaotic, no one knows who was there and who wasn't."

"That's interesting," Frank said.

"Yeah. Interesting but inconclusive."

"What you have to bear in mind," Lewis said, "is that Walsingham is a highly respected member of the community. If he *is* having an affair—"

"He's had more affairs than I've had good pints."

"Okay, but that's not against the law. At least, not in these parts." He smiled, but it clearly didn't come easily. "As I was saying, he's a highly respected member of the community and I imagine he likes his position. He's a bit of a social climber, I gather, so he'll probably tell the odd white lie to maintain that position."

"Hmm."

Dylan knew what he meant but he still wished he could pin something on the doctor. He didn't like him.

"His current mistress, Megan Cole, is a nurse at the hospital," Dylan said. "If she'd wanted the doctor for herself, she might have grabbed a scalpel from the cupboard and set off to kill Carly Walsingham."

Frank rolled his eyes. "Are you sure you're just not looking for someone to blame?"

"Exactly." Lewis had the superior expression of a respected copper indulging a rookie who'd been thrown off the force.

"I do want someone to blame, yes," Dylan said, "but there's something odd about those two. Maybe Walsingham killed his wife. Maybe Megan wanted to be the second Mrs. Walsingham and decided to get rid of the competition. Maybe they were both in it together."

That made sense to Dylan. They could cover for one another easily. Doctor and nurse. The lovers could give each other an alibi.

"Have you got any real proof of anything?" Frank asked.

"Nope."

"Ah."

"I have found some CCTV though." Dylan supped his pint.

"What?" Lewis didn't seem to like that idea.

"Yes. There's a security firm on Darwen Road and their cameras catch all the comings and goings along there. I've got all the footage from the end of July to the middle of August."

Frank looked at him as if he were mad. "Darwen Road?"

"Bloody hell, Dylan." Lewis looked as if that was the funniest thing he'd heard all year.

"People driving from the hospital or from Dawson's Clough centre might go along that road if they were visiting Lakeside Drive or Peebles Road."

"They might." Frank's tone was dry. "And they might not. Kaminski, by his own admission, didn't use that road."

Frank had a point.

"I've already spotted Neil Walsingham on the images."

"On the day of the murder?"

"Well, no." He'd gone over and over the footage from that afternoon and found nothing interesting. "I'm still working on that."

"Dylan," Frank said, "you could see him walking along that road on the day of the murder with a scalpel in his hand, and still not be able to prove anything."

He was painfully aware of that.

"I can understand how you want to make money out of this case," Lewis said, "but come off it, Dylan, there are limits. Have you ever wondered why you were considered unfit for police work?"

Dylan bristled at the insult, but ignored it.

"I tend to concentrate on people who don't like me delving into cases," he said. "Walsingham refused to talk to me at first. Now, having thought about it, he's apologised, said it's all too distressing to go over again and assures me that no one hates the thought of an innocent man behind bars more than him. Blah, blah."

He put up his hand to fend off Frank's interruption. "Yes, I know what you're going to say, and yes, that could well be how he feels. However, another who's very anti me being in Dawson's Clough is Jamie Tinsley."

"Who?" The name obviously wasn't familiar to Lewis.

"I don't suppose he figured in the original investigation, and there's no reason he should. He's a vet at a local practice and is the one used by Sue Kaminski for the animal shelter. That he's got the hots for Sue is obvious. That he doesn't want me investigating this case is equally obvious."

"Right." Lewis drew the word out. "And you're saying that makes him a suspect? I can't see that."

Dylan couldn't either.

"Oh, really. This is laughable," Lewis said.

"Not if your name's Aleksander Kaminski," Dylan replied.

The atmosphere at their table was becoming a little frosty, but there was nothing Dylan could do about that.

"Why would he want Carly Walsingham out of the way?" Frank asked. "If he *has* got the hots for Sue Kaminski, I expect it's far more likely that, with her husband behind bars, he's suddenly realised that, for the next twelve years, Sue is on her own and available. He wouldn't want Kaminski walking free, would he?"

Dylan enjoyed bouncing ideas around with Frank. Or, to be more accurate, he enjoyed giving Frank ideas only for Frank to return them with the harsh voice of reason.

Frank was right. For all Dylan knew, Jamie Tinsley probably hadn't looked at Sue twice before Kaminski was detained at Her Majesty's pleasure. Sue certainly had no idea that he was interested in her.

Dylan was drawing a blank. He had several half-baked ideas as to what might have happened that afternoon, but none that made any sense and certainly none that he had a hope in hell of proving.

"A motive would be good," he said.

"Christ, you're master of the understatement." Frank grinned.

Lewis finished his drink and got to his feet. "Sorry, but I have to dash. I can't sit here wasting time. And that's all you're doing, Dylan. Wasting everyone's time." He leaned down to add, "You're also wasting your client's money."

"Maybe."

There were smiles all round as Lewis said his goodbyes.

"He's getting a bit niggled," Frank said when Lewis had left them.

"I thought I was supposed to be master of the understatement."

"I'm just saying that it might not be wise to antagonise him."

"He should have done his job better then. There's a shoddiness to his investigation." Dylan emptied his glass. "I'll get the refills. You have a think about motive."

Dylan walked over to the bar where Zoe and Christine were dealing with a rush of customers. They worked well together and no matter how brisk trade became, no one was kept waiting too long.

"Same again, Dylan?"

"Please, Zoe." He was even on first-name terms with the barmaids in this pub. Yes, it felt very homely here.

He weaved his way through people wanting to be served and back to their table where Frank was sitting with the same blank expression.

"Cheers," he said as Dylan put a pint in front of him. "Remind me that I need to get the next two rounds."

"Don't worry. I will."

Before he could take a swallow, Dylan's phone vibrated in his pocket. He took it out and saw from the display that his mother was calling. In the past, he'd ignored her calls effortlessly. Now, he still ignored them, but they worried him.

"My mother," he said for Frank's benefit. "If it's important, she'll leave a message."

No message was left so he assumed she'd only been ringing for a chat. If there was anything wrong with Bev, she would have left a message. In any case, there was nothing he could do about it from nigh on three hundred miles away.

"Motive," he reminded Frank. "I can't think of a single person who might want Carly Walsingham dead."

"Someone did." They'd soon have a PhD each in stating the obvious.

"Let's take Kaminski," Dylan said. "He may or may not have been having an affair with her. We assume he was, and we assume it had been going on for a while. He may or may not have threatened her by phone the previous evening. It's possible that, if she wanted to end things between them, or even if *he* did, he could have decided to end it permanently. Possible. But highly unlikely."

Frank shrugged.

"Kaminski's a lot of things, but I don't think he's particularly stupid," Dylan said. "He doesn't seem to care about spending a dozen years in Strangeways so I doubt he'd be beside himself if Carly threatened to tell his wife about their affair. No, I can't find a solid motive for Kaminski."

"Okay, what about Neil Walsingham? Why in hell's name would he want rid of her? There was no great windfall coming to him on her death. She wasn't insured. She had no money of her own. They existed on his income."

"I know. If he'd wanted her out of his life, he would have employed a good solicitor and divorced her as quickly, quietly and cheaply as possible."

Dylan was aware of the sound of the wind. Logs had been crackling in the fireplace but now, the wind had increased and was roaring inside the chimney. It was difficult to say for sure, but he thought he heard a deep rumble of thunder too. He and Frank were in the best place.

"There's his mistress, Megan Cole." Dylan wasn't sure that a woman who tried to give premature babies the best welcome to the world could turn killer. Stranger things had happened though. "If she wanted Walsingham to herself, and if he wasn't rushing to divorce his wife, perhaps she lost patience and decided to hurry things on."

"Possible," Frank said.

"There's his ex-mistress, Sonia Trueman too. She loathes Walsingham with a passion. She believed they were about to sail into the sunset together and he made it clear it was just a fling. She dreams of him meeting a sticky end and, given very little incentive, I can imagine her killing *him*. I can't imagine she'd kill his wife."

"Jealousy maybe?" Frank said. "Maybe she believed that only his wife was preventing them sailing into the sunset."

Dylan couldn't see it. Sonia hated Walsingham. If she was planning to butcher anyone, it would be him. If she'd harboured even the tiniest hope that only Carly stood in her way, her hatred for the doctor wouldn't have been as great.

"There's her husband, Terry Trueman," Dylan said. "Walsingham was trying to steal his wife so maybe he decided to take Walsingham's wife. Maybe he even thought Walsingham would take the blame for her murder."

"What's he like?"

"Angry." Dylan sighed. "At least, he was when I saw him. He's got no previous form for anything. Even his driving licence is clean."

"So he's not your typical killer," Frank said.

"No." Dylan supped from his pint. "The only other person who raises question marks is Jamie Tinsley, the vet, and I can't see that, either. If he'd been planning to remove someone from the planet, it would have been Kaminski. And although he's got his wish, he couldn't possibly have known that Kaminski would take the rap for the murder."

"Did he have dealings with the Walsinghams?"

"Not as far as I know."

"I see. So, basically—"

"I don't have a clue. That's about the height of it, Frank."

A heart attack might have ended Frank's distinguished career with the police force, but it had done nothing to slow his brain. His hair was greying, his mind was as sharp as ever.

"Forget motive for the moment," he said. "Picture the murder scene."

"I've done little else," Dylan said, "and I still can't make sense of it. It's the pillow that confuses the issue."

"Forensics know it was used because they found fibres in her nose and mouth."

Dylan knew that. "I can see why a killer would be reluctant to look his victim in the eye but, if that were the case, he'd drown her. That he slashed her indicates he had no qualms about looking at her. That takes anger. The knife, yes. The pillow, yes. The knife and pillow? It doesn't add up."

"Exactly how I feel about it," Frank said. "And what about the knife? Was the killer skilled with a blade or did he just get lucky?"

Dylan hadn't the remotest idea.

Over a third pint, they talked about their plans for the weekend. Frank was aiming to spend a couple of days in his garden avoiding the advances of his amorous neighbour. He'd been married three times and, despite her best efforts, was determined not to make it four. Dylan was spending time with his family and had vowed to go out for a good run and see if that dragged his brain cells into action.

Over a fourth pint, they went through Dylan's painfully short list of suspects again.

Over a fifth, they tried to remember what conclusions they'd drawn during the fourth.

TWENTY-SIX

CHURCH BELLS RANG out, calling the faithful to worship, and Dylan realised it was a sound he hadn't heard for years. He stopped for a moment to listen. That was what he told himself anyway. The fact that it allowed him to get his breath back was an added bonus.

He couldn't decide if his lungs or his legs were hurting the most. As his entire body was screaming in pain, it was difficult to tell. He walked on, his body drenched in sweat, until he felt able to break into a run again.

A man who had to be in his seventies ran toward him and didn't even look breathless. Perhaps he was only in his fifties, and an excess of exercise had greyed his hair and wrinkled his skin. Either way, Dylan was at least ten and probably thirty years younger so he damn well ought to be able to run three miles without a problem.

Ignoring the way his lungs refused to take in enough air, he kept going, grateful that the last quarter of a mile to his home featured an incline in his favour.

He walked up his drive, let himself into the house and went straight to the kitchen to pour himself a glass of water.

Bev came through from the sitting room. "Do I need to call 999?"

He shook his head. "It was easier this time. Much easier."

"Yeah?" A knowing smile curved her lips. "Then you should have recovered by—what?—Wednesday?"

"Ha, ha." Deciding it probably would be Wednesday before he felt back to normal, he poured another glass of water and drank it in one.

The smile left her face and, with a long sigh, she took clothes, all Freya's, from the dryer.

"So what do you want to do today?" he asked. "Let's go out somewhere. All four of us."

She shook her head. "Luke's out at Tom's this morning and Freya's a bit fractious."

"We can go out later then."

"No."

"The sun's doing its best to shine," Dylan said. "We could have a wander round the park or something. It would do us good to get out of the house and take in some fresh air."

She shook her head but didn't bother to answer.

"Do you want me to take the kids out later? You can put your feet up?"

"Stop fussing, Dylan." She folded Freya's tiny clothes and put them in a pile on the table. "Whether I go out or stay in, it's all the same, isn't it? What does it matter what I do? In or out, I just do my motherly duties. I'm a mother. That's all I am."

Dylan was saved from answering that particular conundrum by the phone. Bev snatched at it and her face broke into a strained smile as she spoke to her best friend. While she chatted to Lucy, he decided to go and shower.

The mystery of Carly Walsingham's murder was nothing compared to the mystery that was women. Why they had to speak in riddles, Dylan had no idea. What was all that I'm-a-mother nonsense? He was a father. So what?

Something was wrong with Bev, had been since Freya was born, but he was damned if he knew what. Nor would he find out so long as she insisted on expecting him to understand the nonsense she came out with. God, it was like living with a walking crossword puzzle.

Ask a bloke what was wrong, and you'd be told in words of one syllable. Ask a woman and you'd be expected to solve Mensa's top challenge.

I'm a mother. That's all I am. What the hell was that supposed to mean? She was all sorts of things, the same as he was. She was a teacher, a reader, a shopper—she could shop for England.

By the time he'd showered and dressed, he decided he didn't feel too bad at all. Perhaps he was getting fitter and his recovery time was improving. Cheered, he went downstairs to the kitchen where Bev was staring gloomily out of the window.

"That was a short chat." Usually, she could chat to Lucy for over an hour, regardless of whether they'd seen each other the night before. "Lucy okay?"

"Lucy's fine." The way she spoke let him know that, although Lucy was fine, she most certainly wasn't.

"Right. Good."

"Of course Lucy's fine. She has a boyfriend who's wining and dining her in style this evening. What's not to be fine about?"

Four Across. Baffled.

"But you don't want wining and dining in style." Every word he spoke was taking him nearer an explosion. He could see it coming, but there was damn all he could do about it.

"I don't? Says who?"

"I offered to take you out last night."

"You *offered?* Well, forgive me if I don't drop down at your feet in gratitude."

Dylan had always believed he had good interviewing techniques. While on the police force, he'd had a great deal of success getting information from suspects, reading between the lines and dragging out the truth. It had to be said, though, that he'd interviewed very few women.

Luke was of an age when he was becoming all too aware of the differences between boys and girls, and Dylan vowed to impress upon him that the physical differences were as nothing compared to the mental differences. Female minds were a definite no-go area.

"Lucy's boyfriend doesn't *offer*," Bev said. "He *wants* to take Lucy out."

"I want to take you out."

"You do? And how would I know that? To hear you talk, people would think you were *offering* to take me out because I'm your personal bloody charity case."

"Of course I want to take you out. I can think of nothing better than having some quality time, away from house and kids, with the woman I love."

She grabbed Freya's clothes from the table, turned on her heel and strode from the room. He heard her putting stuff in the airing cupboard. Then all was silent.

It was a good five minutes before she returned. Her eyes were red and moist, and it looked for all the world as if she'd been crying.

"Okay," she said. "Ring your mum and see if she can babysit for the evening. We'll go out."

Still baffled.

"Right. Where do you fancy going? Do I need to book a table?"

"Ramone's."

"I'll book a table then." He'd book resuscitation for his credit card too.

RAMONE'S WAS AS busy as ever and Dylan couldn't understand why the restaurant was so popular. He'd never yet left the place feeling as if he'd had a decent meal because the ridiculously expensive food came in minuscule portions. Sprigs of parsley, or whatever the crap of the day was, were transformed into works of art. The chefs, he was sure, were failed artists.

When Bev was seated, she looked around with a satisfied smile. "It's lovely here, isn't it?"

"Very nice." He couldn't see the appeal and would have been as happy eating fish and chips out of the paper in the park. His credit card would have rejoiced at that too. There was no point disagreeing with her, though.

While they studied the menu, Dylan ran through the list of instructions he'd been given before leaving home.

"Don't talk work," his mother had whispered. "Or about the house or the children. Discuss something exciting like holidays. Make her laugh."

"She'll want champagne," Luke had said.

He'd ordered a bottle of wine but, as to conversation, he was at a loss. He hated making small talk at the best of times and if work, house and family were off topic, he was lost.

The waiter fussed around Bev and assured them all ingredients were English. And fresh.

"The fish is responsibly sourced," he said.

"That's good then," Dylan said. Responsibly sourced fish? What the hell was that about?

He oohed and aahed over his steamed asparagus but, really, it wouldn't have kept a sparrow alive. It was pleasant, and no doubt fresh and grown in England, but not worth mentioning.

"We should do this more often," Bev said.

"We should." If he won the lottery, he'd suggest it more often.

"Hey, let's have champagne to celebrate."

"Celebrate what?" There was already a decent bottle of white wine on the table.

"Well, Freya, I suppose," she said. "And we should drink to your mum. She's been such a help, hasn't she? We're lucky to have her."

Dylan declined to comment on that, and Bev laughed.

"You love her really."

He did, that was the crazy thing. He simply wished she were more grounded in reality. He wished, too, that she'd been a secretary during the sixties rather than a pot-smoking, peace-loving hippy.

"At least Freya's keeping her out of mischief," he said. "She can't coo over her granddaughter and book holidays at the same time."

"I wouldn't count on that."

Bev was right. Vicky Scott could easily nurse a baby and scan brochures for adventure holidays. For all Dylan knew, she was probably telling Freya right now that she wasn't too young for backpacking through darkest Africa.

"It was a good holiday, though, wasn't it?" Bev said. "I know there were a few problems, but we all had a good time in the end."

Last year he, Bev and Luke had accompanied his mother to the desert. Few people could boast they'd been camel trekking in the Sahara. Few people would want to.

Bev was right though. In its own way, it had been okay, and they'd all returned unscathed.

"It was," he said. "And Luke's still dining out on it."

Remembering his mother's instructions, he said, "We should think of going away in the summer. Somewhere less risky than the Sahara. Is there anywhere you fancy?"

"I'll have a think about it," she said. "Perhaps we do need a holiday."

She caught the waiter's attention and ordered a bottle of champagne. Dylan had thought he'd sidestepped that suggestion. Apparently not. The waiter scooted away, only too pleased to oblige.

Bev was looking more relaxed than she had for weeks though so Dylan knew he shouldn't complain.

Responsibly sourced or not, his duck, when it came, was
delicious. Bev's salmon was washed down with plenty of
champagne and she was smiling more with each swallow.

"I'm supposed to be on a diet," she said, looking wistfully
as the dessert menu.

"I don't suppose the portions you get here will pile on
many calories."

"Dylan, shush!"

She opted for lemon and goat's curd cheesecake. Dylan
decided that, as he was still hungry, he'd have plum and al-
mond tart with clotted cream.

"So how's work going?" she asked over coffee.

"Okay." He wasn't supposed to be talking work. "Yes,
it's fine."

"Have you almost solved it?"

"I wouldn't go that far."

She was slurring her words slightly, he noticed. Her eyes
were brighter than usual too. "But you're sure Aleksander
Kaminski is innocent?"

"I wouldn't even go that far," he said. "I'd like to believe
he's innocent, but I wouldn't put money on it."

"Who's your chief suspect then?"

"I don't know. Possibly her husband."

"Ooh." She giggled, a sign she'd had too much to drink.
"How would you kill me if you'd had enough of me?"

"That's just it, I wouldn't. I'd divorce you. It would be a lot
less messy. My finances would never recover, but the pay's
not so great in Strangeways."

"I'd hit you with your old cricket bat." She sounded as if
he'd given the matter a great deal of thought. "That wouldn't
be too messy, would it? A good thwack on the head with that
ought to do the trick."

"Maybe. You might just fracture my skull though."

"Then I'd hit you again. Harder."

"Where is my cricket bat?"

"I don't know. In the garage probably, along with all your other junk." With a satisfied sigh, she reached across the table for his hand. "Actually, I'd probably just divorce you too. I'd make a packet out of you."

"I'm relieved to hear it."

Dylan was prepared for the bill but, when it came, he still felt the blood drain from his face. That was the thing about Ramone's. One could mentally calculate the cost of the meal, double the figure for luck and still end up with the shock of a lifetime.

"Shall I get them to order a taxi?" he asked.

"No. Not yet. Let's go for a walk. I like walking at this time of night."

Unlike Dawson's Clough, a town that liked to call its curfew early, Shepherd's Bush was home to crowds of people dashing to pub, club or restaurant from underground station or bus stop. It was lively and noisy, and Dylan liked it.

The area wasn't famous for much. Queen's Park Rangers played football at the ground on Loftus Road, many of the Monty Python sketches had been filmed there because of the proximity to BBC Television Centre, and an old sitcom, *Steptoe and Son*, had been set in the fictional 24 Oil Drum Lane, Shepherd's Bush.

Bev linked her arm through his and soon proved that she was incapable of walking in a straight line. The fresh air might sober her a little. He hoped so as he didn't want her throwing up in a taxi.

"You do still love me, don't you, Dylan?"

Oh, God. She'd had more champagne than he'd realised. "Of course I do."

"Even though I'm a miserable cow?"

He smiled at that. "Yes."

"Even though I have nothing to talk about except baby sick?"

"Yup. I used to dream of a miserable cow who talked about nothing but baby sick."

"You wouldn't rather be with Angelina Jolie?"

"God, no. Far too cheerful."

They walked on until Bev spotted a pub that looked "cosy." It was a bad move, Dylan knew it, but they went inside and Bev ordered a coffee and a brandy. He hadn't the heart to remind her that she hated brandy.

At least she didn't throw up in the taxi on the way home. She did, however, pause for a long time before she'd walk into the house. It was if she expected all sorts of demons to be lurking there.

The reality was silence. Darkness and silence. Everyone was in bed and, amazingly, everyone was asleep. Even Freya.

"Do you want a coffee?" Dylan asked in the whisper he used if his daughter was sleeping.

"Please."

Dylan made coffee, and Bev swayed through to the sitting room. He wondered if she'd fall asleep and start snoring in her drunken haze or if she'd burst into tears about the hamster that died when she was seven.

When he carried their coffees through, she was sitting on the sofa with her shoeless feet resting on the coffee table. She patted the space beside her and, after putting their coffees where she was unlikely to kick them, he sat down.

"Are you sure you still love me?" she asked.

"Er, let me think." He put his arm round her and pulled her close. "Of course I do, idiot."

"I love you, too." And she promptly burst into tears.

TWENTY-SEVEN

MEGAN COLE COULDN'T find bananas in Tesco and it had already taken her a good ten minutes to choose a decent bottle of wine. The store was quiet at this time on a Monday night which was why she preferred it, but she was beginning to wish she hadn't bothered.

She gave up on bananas, put grapes and pears in her trolley and consulted her list. She needed coffee and that was on the far side of the store. Not wanting to face the morning without her caffeine, she set off, three wheels on her trolley going one way and one hampering progress by refusing to budge.

She rounded the corner to avoid the pet supplies and collided with another trolley.

"Sorry—oh, er, Sonia." Shock rendered her incapable of speech.

Sonia had put on a little weight since she'd left the hospital. Maybe it was the sign of a contented life. Or perhaps that's what happened when you stopped working long shifts. She was wearing black linen trousers, white shirt and wide red belt. Megan, in jeans and jacket, felt underdressed.

They struggled to disentangle their trolleys.

"Long time no see," Megan said. "How are things?"

"Hello, Megan." A cold smile ended a long way short of her eyes. "Things are good, thanks. How are you?"

"Fine. Overworked and underpaid. The usual." She hoped her own smile was more successful than Sonia's.

An awkward silence descended. Megan would like to tall

o Sonia, but Neil, the only subject they had in common, was off-limits.

"Good to see you. Must dash though." Sonia finally extricated her trolley and headed for the deli counter.

Megan continued in her quest for coffee. There were a couple of other things on her list but nothing she couldn't survive without for a week and she was soon in the queue for the checkout. She was aware, as she put her goods on the conveyor belt, that her hands were shaking. She'd been a wreck ever since her canal-side meeting with Neil on Wednesday night, and seeing Sonia hadn't helped.

She still wasn't sure what had happened down by the canal that evening. She'd fumbled in her pocket for her key as she raced away from Neil, and she'd been in the house with the door locked behind her before he hammered on her door.

"Megan, what the hell's got into you?" He'd tried the handle. "Megan, for Christ's sake, have you gone bloody mad?"

Crouched in the hallway, in complete darkness, she thought he probably had.

She'd called in sick on Thursday and Friday and, although she'd gone to work today, she'd more or less managed to avoid Neil. Their paths had only crossed once. She and a nurse had been getting coffee from the machine when Neil strode along the corridor.

He slowed his pace. "Hello, Megan. Are you feeling better?"

"Yes. Much better, thanks. Just a stomach bug."

"Good." With a nod to them both, he'd gone on his way.

As she'd watched him march off, confident and handsome, she'd thought she was probably losing her mind. She couldn't explain, even to herself, why she'd suddenly been so frightened of him. Yet she'd been terrified. The wind and the deep, dark water had seemed benevolent in comparison to Neil.

"Do you need any help with your packing, love?"

"Sorry?" While she'd been lost in her thoughts, the check‐
out operator had finished serving the customer in front of
Megan. "Oh, no. Thanks. Sorry, I was miles away."

"I know how you feel. I'm having one of those days myself
and I've only just started. It's going to be a long night." She
picked up Megan's grapes to scan. "These are good value,
aren't they?"

"Yes. Very good."

Megan threw her purchases in her bags and put her credit
card in the machine. She had the usual brief panic that she'd
forgotten her pin number, and the relief when she remem‐
bered it.

The cashier handed her the receipt. "There you go, love.
Have a good evening."

"Thanks. And you." Megan thought of dumping her trol‐
ley and carrying her bags to her car, but she had visions of
the thin bags giving way and discarding her purchases across
the tarmac.

She left the building and was surprised to see Sonia out‐
side. It looked as if she was waiting for her.

"Sorry, I must have sounded a bit abrupt back there." Sonia
jerked a thumb in the direction of the store.

"Not at all."

"So how's it going?" Sonia asked. "Is work still good?"

"The same as ever. You know how it is."

"I certainly do." Sonia grinned. "Still, they say sleep is
overrated, don't they?"

Megan smiled at the tired joke.

"And are you and Neil okay?" Sonia asked.

So she knew about their affair. What was the point in
sneaking around like thieves in the night when it was impos‐
sible to keep a secret in Dawson's Clough?

"We're fine, thanks."

Perhaps Dylan Scott had told Sonia about them.

"That's good," Sonia said. "I'm pleased for you. Truly. Are we to expect wedding bells?"

"Good grief, no. No, nothing like that."

"Oh, I thought with—well, you know. Neil's a free man now, isn't he? He can marry the woman he loves without all those divorce excuses."

So Sonia wanted to gloat. She was saying, in her roundabout way, that Neil would discard her, just as he'd discarded Sonia.

"I'm not the marrying type, Sonia. I never have been. I like to enjoy life, if you get my drift."

"I can't say I blame you." She gave a chuckle that was supposed to convey the message that they were both women of the world. "All things being equal though, I quite like being married. Only if it's going well, of course. There was a time, you'll know this, when my marriage hit a rocky patch. That's why I turned to Neil. He did me a favour really in showing me that I wanted my marriage to work. Thankfully, it did. It is."

It never failed to amaze Megan that Sonia had ended up with Terry Trueman. The bloke was big, not particularly fat perhaps, but broad and chunky in a repulsive way. He never smiled, and everyone within a fifty-mile radius of Dawson's Clough knew about his temper.

"I'm glad." Megan tried to push her trolley forward but that obstinate wheel must have drummed up support from the other three.

"It's funny, isn't it," Sonia said, "how this private investigator has come to the Clough asking questions? After all this time, I mean."

"I suppose it is. Has he spoken to you?"

"Oh, yes." Sonia shrugged. "I gather he's talking to everyone who works or used to work at the hospital. Everyone who knows Neil too."

Neil had assumed Sonia's name had come from her. Per
haps Sonia believed the same thing.

"How did he find out about you and Neil?" Megan asked
trying to sound casual.

"I've no idea."

Megan didn't believe her.

"What about you?" Sonia asked. "I suppose you've spo
ken to him?"

Megan nodded. "Yes."

"What did you tell him?"

"The truth. What else? That I was working alongside Nei
that day."

Sonia laughed. "Which one? The truth? Or that you wer
working alongside him?"

Megan wanted to slap the stupid smile from her face
"They're one and the same, Sonia. We were working togethe
that day. All day."

The smile was still there. "You don't have to lie to me
Megan. It doesn't matter to me what you told that private in
vestigator."

"I'm not lying, Sonia."

Sonia rolled her eyes. "I know where you were that day
Megan. Both of you. But don't worry, I didn't say a word."
She tapped the side of her nose. "Your secret's safe with me."

A woman struggling with a fully laden trolley and thre
toddlers was trying to get around them.

"I'd better be going," Sonia said. "Nice to see you, Megan."

Sonia strode off to her car. The lights flashed briefly a
she hit the remote to unlock it. She climbed inside, fastened
her seat belt and drove out of the car park.

"Fuck!" With a burst of strength she didn't know she pos
sessed, Megan forced her trolley forward. She wished she'
never heard of Sonia Trueman or Neil Bloody Walsingham
"Fuck, fuck, fuck!"

TWENTY-EIGHT

DYLAN NEEDED INSPIRATION, as he couldn't bear the thought of another wasted day, but he wasn't sure a cemetery was the place to find it.

He'd been late leaving London yesterday, thanks mainly to waiting for Bev to recover from her hangover, and had achieved little. Or perhaps nothing was a better description. An early night meant he'd been wide awake at six o'clock this morning. As it was too early for breakfast, he'd decided to take a walk and had ended up at the deserted cemetery.

Someone had provided a convenient bench almost opposite Carly Walsingham's headstone and he'd spent half an hour sitting on it. Thinking.

As graveyards went, this was pleasant enough. Sturdy old trees provided shelter in winter and shade in summer, the winding roads were smooth, and the grass was short and neat.

Many of the headstones had been erected centuries ago. Some only weeks ago. The newer graves had flowers. One had a selection of toys around it. Was there a sadder sight, he wondered, than a child's grave? One headstone read *Born asleep.*

Carly Walsingham's inscription was a simple one. *In Loving Memory of Carleen June Walsingham. Died 3rd August, 2011. Aged 44 years. Loving Wife, Mother and Daughter. Always in our thoughts.*

If he'd been hoping that his nearness to Carly's resting place would provide inspiration, he was disappointed.

To find her killer though, if indeed her killer wasn't currently banged up in Strangeways, he needed to know the woman. It was often the victim that led the way to the killer.

Although he'd seen plenty of photos of Carly, he didn't feel as if he knew her. She'd come from humble beginnings and could easily have stayed in Birmingham near her friend Kirsten. Instead, she'd worked hard to improve herself. Her job as a radiographer had introduced her to Neil Walsingham and given her the children she'd longed for.

There was no doubt in Dylan's mind that she'd loved her children with every breath in her body. Everyone agreed on that.

What about Kaminski? Had she loved him? Despite what Kaminski liked to believe and what Kirsten had said, Dylan wasn't convinced. If she had, would she have divorced him? If Bev had discovered that he'd been unable to father children, he couldn't imagine her going off with any bloke she could find. But Bev wasn't Carly, and he knew of many women who put themselves through a great deal of personal and physical agony to become mothers.

Maybe Carly really had loved Kaminski.

What else did he know about her? She was reckless. If Kaminski was to be believed, she'd enjoyed living dangerously. Having Kaminski in the marital bathroom and bedroom had given her some sort of thrill.

Maybe she'd been pushing Walsingham. Perhaps she'd wanted him to discover her unfaithfulness and divorce her. Would she have taken the children from their father? Probably. Her life would possibly have been perfect if she could have had her children *and* Kaminski.

If Walsingham had discovered she wanted a divorce and planned to take his children from him, what would he have done? What would Dylan do if, God forbid, Bev decided to up sticks and take Luke and Freya to live with another man?

He didn't know. He wouldn't go so far as to end Bev's life in a bath of blood, but he wouldn't like it.

Life would be so simple if couples married, had the obligatory two point four children and lived happily ever after. Their children, having been set the perfect example of the perfect life, would marry and have their two point four children. The world would revolve in complete harmony. Private investigators would be out of work, true, but that seemed a small price to pay.

Dylan's stomach grumbled as a reminder that a full English breakfast washed down with a couple of coffees awaited him.

He was about to surrender his bench when he realised he no longer had the cemetery to himself. He checked his watch. It was just after seven o'clock.

If a visitor to a cemetery at such an early hour surprised him, it was nothing to his shock on recognising the woman. She had her back to him and was carrying a container and a large bunch of yellow and white flowers.

Dylan wondered whether he should make himself known. Not wanting to intrude, he decided against it. Besides, he wasn't in the mood for chirpy conversation.

She knelt in front of a black headstone with gold lettering. Dylan was too far away to read the inscription, but close enough to hear her talking to herself. Or talking to the body six feet under the damp earth, which amounted to the same thing.

She spent fifteen minutes gathering up faded flowers and replacing them with the new blooms. All the while, she talked. Finally, she stood and took one final look at the grave before striding off in the direction she'd come.

When she was out of sight, Dylan crossed the grass to inspect the headstone. *Frank Arthur Blackman, a loving husband and father, who passed away 17th January, 2002 aged*

49. In our hearts you will always stay, loved and remem-bered every day.

Along with the flowers, Sue Kaminski had signed a small card that read, *Miss you, Dad.*

Her father had been too young to die. Her first husband had barely started out on life when a tragic accident cut his time on the earth short. Now, with a husband behind bars for a murder he possibly didn't commit, Sue must think the gods had something against her.

Making a mental note never to visit cemeteries at such an ungodly hour, Dylan set off. Breakfast called.

He was in time to see Sue driving out of the cemetery's small car park. Another vehicle had been parked under the tall trees and it followed. Coincidence? As far as Dylan was aware, the driver of that car hadn't been inside the cemetery.

Dylan didn't like coincidences. He took his phone from his pocket, searched through his list of contacts and hit the Call button. It rang twice before a familiar voice answered.

"Pikey, me old mate," Dylan said. "How are you?"

"Pissed off with people who only call when they want something. But never mind me, how does it feel to be a father again?"

Dylan was taken aback. "How do you know about that? I was calling to tell you."

"Liar. You're calling because you want something. Something to do with the case you're working on in Dawson's Clough, I imagine." Pikey laughed. "Your wife talks to mine now and again, you know. Congratulations, you old bastard."

"Thanks. We ought to get together and catch up." Dylan meant it. He'd spent most of his career in the police force working alongside DS Pike and he'd trust the bloke with his life. "What are you doing at the weekend?"

"I can probably make time for a couple of pints with you. What time?"

"Why don't you and your better half come round to our place on Saturday afternoon?" Dylan said. "The women can talk babies and we can escape to the pub."

"Sounds good to me. I'll ring you to confirm on Friday. Okay?"

"Great. I'll look forward to it." Dylan would mention it to Bev at the first opportunity. The mood she was in, he'd be in trouble for making arrangements without consulting her.

"So," Pikey said. "What are you wanting from me?"

"Who says I want anything?" Dylan wished they'd hurry up and get to the point because there was only so long he could repeat a car registration to himself.

"I do. What is it?"

"Well, if you could do me a quick vehicle check I'd be grateful. As much as you've got on the owner. And in a couple of days, I might ask about several more. Is that okay?"

"Fire away."

He gave Pikey the number and, while he waited for his friend to call him back, he walked slowly in the direction of his hotel. Thoughts of his breakfast were making his mouth water now.

He was almost there when Pikey called.

"Okay, your vehicle is registered to a James—"

"Bloody Tinsley. I should have known. I'm right, aren't I?"

"Well, his middle name is given as Matthew not Bloody, but yeah, ten out of ten, detective."

"Have you got anything interesting on him?" Dylan asked.

"Nope. He's as clean as a dog's bollocks. Why? What's he been up to?"

"Nothing, I suppose." The worst he'd done, as far as Dylan knew, was have a crush on a young woman and follow her. "Okay. Thanks, Pikey. All being well, I'll see you on Saturday."

"Great. And don't forget it's your round." Pikey was chuckling as he ended the call.

Dylan, in need of sustenance, walked on to his hotel.

Maybe, he thought, as he tucked in to bacon, sausage and egg, Tinsley had a family member buried in that cemetery. Just because Dylan hadn't noticed him putting flowers on a grave didn't mean he hadn't done so.

When his second coffee was finished, he went to his room, switched on his computer and searched for information on the Tinsleys. He soon found what he was looking for. Lance Corporal Peter Tinsley's funeral had been large, as befitted all dead heroes, and he'd been laid to rest in his parents' hometown of Blackburn.

That meant nothing, though. For all Dylan knew, Tinsley could have other family members buried in Dawson Clough's cemetery.

If Tinsley was following Sue Kaminski, it wasn't a crime. Perhaps he aimed to bump into her, strike up a conversation and ask her out on a date. Maybe his nerve kept failing him. He might be a good vet, but Dylan thought he lacked the usual social skills. There was something about Tinsley that Dylan didn't like. He couldn't put his finger on that something, but he'd be reluctant to leave his kids with him. Or a dog come to that.

He'd have a word with him. Or with Sue.

Meanwhile, he passed the morning staring at CCTV images. There was a kind of method to his madness. He was making a note of every vehicle that travelled along Darwen Road during the day, and trying to match them with cars that used the road on the day Carly Walsingham had her date with a small, sharp blade. There were probably worse ways to spend time but, offhand, Dylan couldn't think of any.

When he had a list of interesting vehicles, he'd pass it on to DS Pike and see what came of them.

In the afternoon, sick and tired of staring at a screen, he drove out to Pennine View Rescue Centre. Sue's battered heap of rust was outside the house and, as there were no dogs guarding the property, he decided it was safe to open the gate and venture to the front door.

Sue opened the door in an instant. Her hair, as short as it was, stuck up at every angle and her face was flushed.

"Dylan, what a nice surprise. Come in, come in."

He followed her into the kitchen where the table was completely covered in papers. Looking more closely, he guessed she was doing her accounts and, given the two final demands he could see, finances weren't a cheerful subject in this house. No wonder she looked as if she'd attempted to pull out her hair.

"Can I get you a tea or a coffee?" She was already reaching for the kettle.

"No, thanks. I was just passing so I thought I'd call in, but it's only a quick visit. And, sorry, but I don't have any news."

She nodded as if she'd expected nothing more.

On the table, almost hidden by final demands, cheque stubs and invoices for dog food, was a cheque for a hundred pounds signed by Frederyk Kaminski. It was made payable to the rescue centre rather than Sue.

She saw him looking at it. "Agata fell in love with a cat while she was here on Wednesday. She took it home and phoned me yesterday to say that all was well, the cat had settled, and she'd put a cheque in the post, a donation for the sanctuary. It arrived this morning."

"Ah." Dylan knew the Kaminskis had little money. They were paying him out of their savings, but a cheque payable to Sue might have been more useful than one for the animal sanctuary. Or perhaps giving her money would have embarrassed them. And her.

"I'm so pleased," Sue said. "It's wonderful that Friday, the cat, has a good home, and it'll be company for Agata, too. It's funny, but we had quite a nice day together. I got the impression she was lonely though. Or, if not lonely, struggling to cope with Alek being in prison." She sighed. "I know how she feels."

"Alek's parents are getting on a bit," Dylan said. "I expect they worry that they won't be around when he comes out of Strangeways."

Sue bit her lip. She nodded at the truth of that but looked as if she couldn't bear to agree with him.

She shoved some papers aside and pulled out a leaflet with Alzheimer's UK blazoned across it. "At least they don't have Alzheimer's."

"Well, no."

"Aunt Joyce," she said, and he thought she was a blink away from bursting into tears.

"Oh, I see. I'm sorry."

She took a deep breath. "She has good days and bad days. She's not too bad." She crumpled up the leaflet and aimed it at the waste bin.

"How are the accounts looking?" Dylan thought finances might be a safer if no less depressing subject. "Are you managing without Alek's income?"

"Barely. But we'll be fine. The Easter fundraiser did well so that should keep us going until the next one in July. Thankfully, I have plenty of people willing to volunteer. They enjoy feeding the dogs, exercising them and grooming them. I don't have to pay wages." She gave a rueful smile. "I couldn't afford to pay wages."

"What about vet's bills? They must be quite steep."

"They are. No animal leaves here without being spayed or neutered, wormed and microchipped. It's expensive, of course, but we're lucky to have Jamie. He does all he can to keep the expense to a minimum."

Dylan didn't doubt it. "Ah yes, Jamie. I meant to mention him, Sue. I think, although I could be wrong, that he might be following you."

She looked at Dylan as if he'd suddenly become fluent in Swahili.

"As I say, I could be wrong. I saw you when you were leaving the cemetery this morning," he said. "Jamie was there too. He followed you out of the car park."

She opened her mouth to speak but closed it. Her hands went into her pockets and then out again.

"I think I'll have a coffee," she said. "Are you sure you don't want one, Dylan?"

"Quite sure. Thanks."

She turned on the tap, and the sudden force sprayed water all over her and the kitchen window. "Damn."

Dylan watched her. To say his words had shocked her was putting it mildly.

"I expect," she said, "that Jamie worries about me now I'm alone here. He's such a sweetie, but I'm sure that's all there is to it. With Alek locked up, he'll be looking out for me. I like him, I like him a lot, of course I do, and if I didn't have Alek, well, who knows? But I'm sure he's just being a bit protective."

"Probably." Dylan gave her a reassuring smile. "And as I said, I could be wrong. I just thought you should know you have an admirer, that's all."

She blushed to the roots of her hair. "I'm sure that's nonsense."

"Well, you've been warned. I wouldn't be surprised if he didn't pluck up courage to ask you out very soon. At least you'll be ready for him."

"Good grief." She laughed at herself. "I don't think I'm Jamie's type. And anyway, he knows I'm waiting for Alek to come home, he knows there could be no one else for me."

"I'm sure he does, but I thought I should mention it."

They chatted some more, about safer subjects like the weather and the rubbish shown on TV these days.

"I'd better leave you to your accounts, Sue. It's time I was off."

TWENTY-NINE

MEGAN HAD BEEN staring at the phone for a full thirty minutes. If it rang, it would probably bring on a full cardiac arrest. It was unlikely to do that, though. She'd spoken to her parents, her sister and one of her brothers already today, and Neil, who had a habit of calling at odd times, had given up trying to speak to her. Ever since their encounter by the canal, she'd ignored him and his calls.

Since last night's meeting with Sonia, though, she knew she had to talk to him.

She mixed herself a gin and tonic that was heavy on gin and light on tonic and picked up the receiver. Before she could change her mind, she called his mobile. It was almost ten o'clock so, if he didn't answer, she'd assume he'd had a busy day or an early start and had gone to—

"Megan?"

"Hello, Neil." She took a big gulp of gin.

"Welcome back to the world of the sane," he said.

Beneath the sarcasm, she detected anger. It helped, but not a lot. He was expecting her to apologise for her childish behaviour, but she couldn't.

"You've been avoiding me," he said. "Any particular reason?"

"For Christ's sake, Neil, you were going to hit me."

"Nonsense."

"You were. You lifted your hand—"

"To touch your face. I've touched a lot more of you than that in the past. Why the hell would I hit you?"

She had no answer.

"And why didn't you answer your door?" he asked.

"I wanted to be alone."

Neil laughed. "In true Greta Garbo style."

She was slowly starting to hate him.

"I saw Sonia last night," she said.

Silence met her comment.

"You knew Dylan Scott had spoken to her, right? Do you know what she told him?"

"I've no idea. He didn't say and I couldn't ask, could I? Why?"

"She wouldn't tell me who put him on to her, but it must have been Teresa Simmons, mustn't it? It sure as hell wasn't me, Neil. That's what you thought, wasn't it? You blamed me, didn't you?"

"I had no idea how her name had come up. I certainly wasn't blaming you."

She didn't believe him. That was why he'd acted so strangely down by the canal, why she'd been so frightened of him. It wasn't what he'd said, it was the way he'd looked at her. Nothing would have convinced her he didn't intend to drown her in the canal. It was dark so no one would have seen, and the wind would have covered her screams.

She carried the phone to the window and pulled the curtains across to shut out the night.

"It must have been Teresa, mustn't it?" she said. "He must be doing a thorough job if he's going down to Coventry to speak to people who no longer even work at the hospital."

She realised, belatedly, that it was she who'd given him Teresa's name. She hadn't given him her address, though, as she didn't have it, and she hadn't believed for a second that Scott would follow it up.

"He lives in London," Neil said. "Shepherd's Bush to be precise."

"How do you know?"

"I've done a little digging of my own."

She shouldn't have been surprised. Neil was a control freak. He was the most charming man on the planet when things were running along to his satisfaction. To him, people were toys. He pulled the strings and they danced like puppets. That was his plan anyway.

"It wouldn't be far out of his way to call on Teresa," he said. "What else did the lovely Sonia have to say for herself?"

"She wanted to know what I'd told Scott." She brought to mind Sonia's cruel, knowing smile. "I said I'd told the truth, that I was working alongside you that day, and she knew I was lying. She asked again what I told him, whether I'd told the truth or said we were working together all day."

"What did you say to that?"

Megan emptied her glass and carried the phone to the kitchen to pour herself another. She'd wake up with a headache in the morning, she always did, but she was a long way past caring. "She just laughed and said she knew the truth. She also told me not to worry and assured me that our secret's safe with her."

"Bloody woman."

"What did she mean, Neil? Exactly what does she know?"

"She knows nothing, that's the whole point. She's just a vindictive little shit stirrer. Christ, it's no wonder that gruesome husband of hers knocks her about."

"If she knows nothing, why the hell is she so confident that she does?"

"Forget her. She's not worth the effort."

"Right." Megan wished she could. She wished she could forget she'd ever laid eyes on Neil Walsingham too. "That's all I rang for. I thought you should know that I had nothing to do with anything Sonia may or may not have told Scott."

"Fine. Thanks for calling. If you want to talk again, or to

see me, you know where I am. I won't offer to contact you
because I'd hate to bring on another bout of insanity."

Before she could reply, he cut the connection.

He wouldn't offer? *Offer?* If it had been anyone else, and
if she'd had more gin, she might have laughed at that. He was
so bloody conceited, so bloody sure of his own attraction, that
he thought he'd been doing her a favour by taking her to bed
on rare occasions. Did he think she was that desperate for
male company? *Was* she that desperate for male company?

No, she damn well wasn't.

THIRTY

By LUNCHTIME THE following day, having spent countless hours staring at recordings of the comings and goings on Darwen Road, Dylan had a grand total of four vehicles that appeared on film regularly enough to arouse his interest. It was depressingly pathetic but, thanks to a dearth of CCTV in the area, all he could do was clutch at straws.

He had registration details for a silver Rav4, an ancient Volkswagen Beetle, a blue Ford Mondeo, and a silver Ford Focus. He called DS Pike's private mobile but, as Pikey didn't answer, he left a message asking him to check out the cars.

With that done, and expecting nothing to come of it, he walked into the town centre for lunch. It was time for a spot of brainstorming.

Over scampi and chips, with his eye on a slice of lemon meringue pie for after, he tried to think what he was missing in this investigation. Information on the victim was the main thing. Carly Walsingham had been surprisingly short of real friends.

He'd spoken to Kirsten Madeley, her best and oldest friend, but other than that, all Carly had were acquaintances. Dylan had spoken to neighbours, people Carly met at her children's school, people she worked out with at a nearby gym and anyone else who might have come into contact with her. Not one of those conversations had lasted more than five minutes and not one of those people had told him anything more interesting than she was likeable, friendly and always willing to help. No one truly knew her.

She'd had her husband and her children, and she'd had Kaminski and a best friend in Birmingham. It didn't seem a lot for the livewire he imagined Carly to be. Perhaps husband, children and lover were enough.

His phone trilled. It was a number he didn't recognise. "Hello?"

"Mr. Scott? Dylan?"

He recognised the voice. "It is, yes."

"Ah, my name's Tinsley. James Tinsley. We met at the Pennine View Rescue Centre. I'm the vet employed at the centre."

Dylan didn't need the longwinded introduction, but it gave him time to gather his thoughts. "Jamie, hi. What can I do for you?"

"Actually, it's more what I can do for you. I'm busy now, about to go into the surgery, but I wondered if you'd be free to meet later. There's something I'd like to tell you about Aleksander Kaminski."

"Suits me. What time?"

"Let me see. Sorry, I'm really busy today. I'll be finished at the surgery around six this evening. Make that six-thirty. Then I'll need to take Monty out for a good run."

He paused, almost as if he expected Dylan to sympathise with his busy schedule.

"I don't suppose," Jamie said, "that you could meet me when I take the dog out? I usually drive out to Crown Point and walk him across the hill there. It's not too far from you, is it? You do know it, don't you?"

"Yes." The bleak hillside was high above the town of Burnley and offered one of the best views in Lancashire. Dylan had been there to inspect a local attraction, the *Singing Ringing Tree,* a steel work of art that was supposed to sing when the wind rattled its carefully designed pipes. "Yes, I know it. What time suits you?"

"Shall we say seven-thirty? Or is that too late for you?"

"Seven-thirty it is."

"Thank you. I appreciate it. If we meet in the car park, we can talk while we walk."

"Okay, Jamie, I'll see you later."

Dylan ordered his lemon meringue and wondered what had possessed him to agree to a meeting on a barren hillside when Lancashire was being battered by strong winds and heavy rain. He was desperate for leads in this case, but there had to be limits.

He wasn't confident that Tinsley would provide those leads. It was more likely that Sue had spoken to him and asked him to stop following her. Dylan would bet he'd be told to stop interfering.

Perhaps he was being more pessimistic than usual. Tinsley had said he had something to tell him about Aleksander Kaminski. Dylan was all ears.

He was drinking a strong coffee when his phone trilled into life again. He was popular this morning.

"Pikey? Thanks for getting back to me, mate. Did you get anything on those vehicles?"

"Good morning, Dylan, and how are you? Me? Oh, I'm good. Thank you so much for asking."

Dylan chuckled. "I'm glad to hear it. So? Did you get those vehicles checked?"

"I did, but people are soon going to start asking me questions about—"

"I know, I know. And I appreciate it. This is the last, you have my word on that."

"It had better be," Pikey said. "Right, have you got a pen?"

"Yes. Fire away."

Dylan jotted down the details of the vehicles' owners with a growing sense of disappointment. The owners' names and addresses meant nothing to him.

"I don't think you'll find a killer in that lot, mate," Pikey said.

Sod it. As a private investigator, Dylan was a joke. He was no further forward than he'd been before he'd heard Carly Walsingham's name mentioned.

"You're probably right, Pikey. But thanks anyway. I appreciate it."

When the call ended, he paid for his food, left the café and ambled through the town. He needed to think of a constructive way to pass the time until he met Tinsley this evening.

His phone trilled again, a reminder that he needed to change his ringtone. The display told him his mother was calling. That was one he could ignore.

After a few seconds, his phone beeped to tell him he had a message. She never left messages. He guessed she was calling for a chat while she enjoyed a marijuana hit, but he played the message. It was difficult to claim he was too busy to listen.

"Dylan, there's nothing to worry about, but I think you should be here. They've taken Freya into hospital. Her breathing's a bit—difficult. As I said, there's nothing at all to worry about, but Bev's a bit, um, uptight."

"Holy shit."

He broke into a run. If there was one thing he hated, it was phone calls that started with *There's nothing to worry about but*... What was there to do but sodding worry?

There was no one on the reception desk when he raced into the hotel. That suited him because he didn't have time to explain. He shoved everything in his bag—it was too bad if he'd missed something—and ran down the stairs. There was still no one on the desk. He'd call them later. If they thought he'd done a runner without paying his bill, well, that was their problem. He had more important things to worry about.

He fired the Morgan and glanced at the fuel gauge. "Sod it."

Why was there never a filling station around when you needed one? He'd have to find one before he reached the motorway. And why did every moron take to the road when you were in a hurry?

After ten minutes, he saw the welcome sign of a Shell garage. There wasn't a free pump and he had to wait while the man in front filled his car, ambled inside the building, looked through the day's newspapers and finally paid for his fuel. The chap strolled back to his car and fastened his seat belt with the speed of a three-year-old still learning to master buckles before pulling away.

Dylan filled the Morgan and ran inside to pay.

He got back in his car and drove toward the exit. In front of him, a driver was waiting for a gap in the traffic. One appeared, one big enough to get four double-decker buses out safely, but the car didn't budge. A female driver, he noticed. Well, no surprise there. How the hell they could claim multitasking among their many talents, he had no idea. This one couldn't even drive and think where she was going at the same time.

Another gap appeared. She edged forward six inches and changed her mind. Dylan gave his horn a fierce blast. She turned in her seat to look at him and promptly missed another gap.

"If you don't get your bloody car out of my way, I won't be responsible for my actions!"

The pedestrian crossing lights fifty yards away changed to red. Thank God. The woman seemed satisfied that the road was clear of cars, boats, planes, stray dogs and sweet wrappers, and finally decided it was safe to pull out.

The motorway was only three miles away so, even if she was heading that way, he wouldn't have to follow her for too long. They crawled along at a mind-numbing twenty-nine miles per hour until she pulled into a side street and Dylan was rid of her.

It was after three o'clock now. If the roads were incident

free and he drove like a maniac, he'd be lucky to be in London by six.

As soon as he was on the motorway, he tried Bev's phone. It went straight to voicemail so either she was talking to someone else or she'd switched it off. There were signs in hospitals asking people to switch off their phones but no one took a blind bit of notice.

Dylan left a message saying he'd be there was soon as he could and tried his mother's phone. Hers rang out unanswered. All the polite notices in the world wouldn't persuade her to switch off her phone. Perhaps she'd raided the hospital store, discovered a new drug of choice and was too high to answer. He left another message.

By six o'clock, he was still an hour away. All he'd had was a text message from his mother saying they were at Hammersmith Hospital, Freya was fine, Bev was a mess, and telling him not to rush as she didn't have time to take him a bunch of grapes if he ended up in a hospital bed.

It was a little after seven o'clock when he finally pulled into the hospital's car park.

The first person he saw was his mother. Outside the main entrance was a group of around twenty people, including one chap in a wheelchair, desperately puffing on cigarettes. His mother was in the midst of the addicts.

Either everything was okay and she was enjoying a relaxing smoke or the news was so bad she needed to be stoned to cope.

She spotted him and came to meet him.

"You made good time, love." She gave him a quick hug. "I thought I'd wait out here for you. I can show you the way up to the ward."

"How is she? Are they?"

"Freya's okay. I told you, there's nothing to worry about."

Dylan couldn't stop worrying. And he couldn't be bothered to waste his breath by explaining that, given the current state of the NHS, you had to be at death's door before they found a spare bed. Even a small bed.

"What about Bev?"

His mother pulled a face and shrugged. "She's okay." She looked a little wistfully at her cigarette before stubbing it out. "Come on, I'll show you where they are. It's a bit complicated."

There couldn't be a more depressing smell than that of disinfectant and rotting food that seemed to pervade every hospital in the land. It clung to everything and everyone, and it made Dylan shudder.

Given the choice between Strangeways and a hospital, he'd have to take his luck with those sixteen-feet-thick prison walls. He wasn't squeamish, or no more than most people, but he loathed hospitals with every fibre of his being. He couldn't bear the thought of Freya being in this place.

Worried visitors walked the long corridors. Doctors who looked no older than Luke dashed about with stethoscopes hanging round their necks. A cleaner was pushing a floor polisher from side to side.

The air was stuffy. And too warm. Sweat trickled down between Dylan's shoulder-blades. He had to get out of here. More important, he had to get his daughter out of here.

THIRTY-ONE

JAMIE ARRIVED IN the small car park that gave access to Crown Point at a quarter to seven. He was early, but Monty had sensed that something different was happening and had been pacing around the house in excitement with his leash in his mouth.

"Okay, let's give you a good run." Jamie let the dog out of the car.

He reached into the glove compartment and pulled out Pete's Glock. He removed the protective black cloth and slipped the gun into his coat pocket.

"Come on then."

The wind tried to blow him off his feet as he walked in the direction of the sculpture, the *Singing Ringing Tree*. At three metres tall, the sculpture took the form of a tree bending in the breeze. Galvanised steel pipes were supposed to harness the wind's energy and produce a choral sound across several octaves, but all Jamie could hear was a low hum.

Monty ran on ahead, only pausing to investigate an interesting scent. The dog was oblivious to the thoughts racing through his master's head.

Jamie often walked up here and, at this time of year, it was deserted in the evenings. On summer days it could be busy with dog walkers and hikers. This evening there wasn't a soul in sight, just as he'd hoped.

The gun weighed heavy in his pocket, but he found it reassuring. He'd planned everything to the last detail. Nothing could go wrong.

He would stay outside with Monty and, as soon as Scott's car drove into the car park, Jamie would approach him. His first thought had been to walk with Scott and find out how far his so-called investigation had progressed. He'd soon dismissed that idea though. Scott was a well-built man. It would take Jamie too long to drag his body back to the car park. The risk of being seen was much too great.

No, he'd approach Scott in the car park and tell him he'd already given Monty his walk. As soon as Scott was out of his car, Jamie would lift the gun and fire. In the unlikely event there was anyone around, he'd make conversation. He'd talk about Kaminski, tell Scott what a piece of shit he was and how rotting in prison was a lot less than he deserved.

The second they were alone, Jamie would put a bullet between Scott's eyes. He would then bundle the body into the boot of his car and drive.

He'd spent sleepless nights wondering how best to dispose of Scott's body. For a while, he'd thought it could go where the euthanised pets ended up. A cremation was by far the best solution. Jamie wasn't sure he could manage it though. Others would be involved. It was too risky.

He'd thought about dumping the body in a local quarry. Lee Quarry at Bacup had appealed to him, but he'd had to forget that idea as it meant dragging Scott's body too far. Impossible.

In the end, he'd come up with the best solution. He would drive north to the Lake District. Thanks to annual summer holidays as a child, he knew the area well.

For two blissful weeks each August, he and Pete had known a kind of freedom only dreamed about the rest of the year. He supposed it was because no one knew them, so his father didn't have to rule with his usual rod of iron and show friends and neighbours that he had the best-behaved kids in the area. Whatever the reason, he and Pete had roamed the lakes and let the sun brown their skin or the rain soak them through.

The downside was that his dog hadn't been allowed to accompany them. Despite Jamie's pleas, Ben had been left in boarding kennels for the fortnight.

Jamie had refreshed his memories of the area by reading up on the murder case that the media had quickly dubbed the Lady in the Lake trial.

Whether Gordon Park actually did murder his wife, Jamie had no idea. The man had claimed he was innocent right up until he hanged himself in his prison cell. Jamie didn't care about that. All he knew was that Carol Ann vanished in 1976 and it wasn't until 1997 that her body was found at the bottom of Coniston Water, the third biggest lake in England. The interesting part, as far as Jamie was concerned, was that her body was dumped from a boat and found on a ledge. Experts claimed that, if her body had landed a few more metres from the shore, it would never have been discovered.

Jamie knew every inch of the area. He knew where to park his car so that it was close enough to the water yet unlikely to be spotted. Small boats were often moored there and it might be possible to borrow one, but that was another risk too far. Instead, he'd bought the small cheap inflatable dinghy that was in the boot of his car.

It was barely big enough for him and Scott, but he'd have to manage. He knew how far he had to row before pushing the body overboard and he should manage it easily enough.

He'd worried about Scott's car. He could dispose of the Morgan easily enough. It wouldn't take too much effort to drive it to a nearby quarry, push it over the cliff and walk back for his own car. Or he could call the police and claim to have seen car and driver being hijacked. In the end, he'd decided to forget about the car. Someone would report Scott missing and it wouldn't be too long before the car was spotted. It didn't matter. By the time that happened, Scott would be at the bottom of the lake. Police would assume Scott had parked up and gone for a stroll. They'd spend days searching the moors for his body.

Jamie's heart raced with excitement. He picked up a stick and threw it for Monty to retrieve. It was impossible to hear any cars over the noise of the wind, but he could see the car park and would know when Scott arrived. He snorted with laughter. It was impossible to miss that yellow Morgan.

Half a dozen plump raindrops landed on him, so he whistled Monty to heel and walked back to the car park. It was seven-fifteen and there was still no sign of the Morgan or its owner.

Jamie was always early for appointments. As a child, punctuality had been drummed into him on a daily basis so that now, as an adult, he couldn't be late for anything. It simply wasn't in his nature. If he had a dental appointment at eleven, he was sitting in the waiting room at ten forty-five. If he needed to be at the airport by eight, he was waiting for the desk to open at seven. Most people didn't bother if they were late, and then complained if people couldn't see them or if they missed their planes. Idiots. Jamie was never late.

Scott didn't have far to come and as they'd arranged to meet at seven-thirty, the private investigator still had fifteen minutes grace.

Jamie passed those minutes by sitting in his car and flicking through radio stations. The presenters irritated him with senseless chat and loud laughter.

The news bulletin came on at seven-thirty. Jamie's watch and the car's clock both agreed it was seven-thirty. There was no sign of Scott.

Jamie drummed angry fingers on the steering wheel as he waited. Scott's behaviour was bloody rude and inconsiderate.

Minutes ticked by slowly. Jamie silenced the radio and the childish presenter.

He wondered if Scott had had the manners to phone him to say he'd been delayed. He'd removed the SIM card from his phone. He knew how easily police could track mobile phones and he hadn't wanted to take any chances.

Cursing, he reached into the glove compartment for his phone and inserted the SIM card. He switched the phone on and waited for the ping that would announce messages. His phone remained stubbornly silent.

He switched it off again.

Rain was bouncing off the car's roof now and Jamie was finding it increasingly difficult to hear himself think.

He waited another five minutes then switched his phone back on. Reception was good out on the hill, but still he received no message alerts. Furious, he switched off the phone and removed the SIM card again.

He took the gun from his pocket and handled it.

Monty was asleep on the passenger seat and Jamie put the gun between the dog's eyes. Monty looked at him questioningly.

"Stupid dog." Jamie was torn between amusement and exasperation. "I could kill you and you're too stupid to realise. Don't worry, though. I won't waste a bullet on you. I need them for Scott."

Monty closed his eyes again and Jamie returned the gun to his pocket. He still wasn't sure about the dog. Monty looked like Ben, but he wasn't Ben. He didn't have that same sense of loyalty. Jamie felt that if anything happened to him, Monty would happily trot off and find someone else daft enough to feed him, shelter him and take him for walks. Ben had been grateful for everything, but Monty seemed to believe he was entitled to food and exercise.

Jamie rubbed at the band of pain tightening around his

forehead. He should be on his way to Coniston Water now. Scott had ruined his meticulous schedule. Damn the man to hell.

Jamie had thought it unlikely that Scott would tell anyone he was meeting him but if, after Scott's disappearance, the police had come to talk to him, Jamie had planned to say that Scott never turned up. Now it was true. The bastard *hadn't* turned up.

Damn him to hell!

THIRTY-TWO

ON THURSDAY MORNING, it arrived. Sue was in the back garden, grooming Lennon, a scruffy spaniel, when she spotted the postman drive up and jump out of his van.

"You might want this one, love!"

Hardly daring to believe it, Sue forgot about Lennon and ran to snatch the envelopes from Mike's hand. He had three for her. Two bills and a much-longed-for letter from Alek.

"Thank you. Thank you so much." She knew she sounded too grateful and a little pathetic. It wasn't as if Mike had written it himself.

"You're welcome. Be seeing you."

Clutching the envelopes to her chest, Sue grabbed Lennon by his collar. "You can come inside while I read this."

She was fit to burst with excitement but she went inside, took off her coat and sat at the kitchen table to carefully slit open the envelope with a knife. Only when she'd read this letter enough times to memorise every word would she put it with his others. She kept them all. One day, when he was home with her, they'd read them together and maybe even smile about these long, lonely days.

She removed the two sheets of paper with fingers that shook.

Dear Sue, he began. She didn't mind that. Although she had no real idea of the prison regime, she could imagine the taunts he'd suffer if someone saw him writing *my darling* or *my dearest*.

Thanks for your letter. Sorry I haven't written before now, but I'm sure you understand how things are. I was glad to hear that your aunt's doing well...

Sue felt a familiar bubble of despair inflate inside her as she read on. There was no *I love you* or *I miss you* or *I'm counting the seconds until your visit.* There was no part of him, the real him, to cling to.

Perhaps he wrote about the mundane to stop her worrying about him. Or worse, perhaps he was struggling to cope and daren't even think about how much he missed her and his home.

Every time she received a letter, she hoped that, this time, Alek's deepest feelings would be spread across the page. And every time, she was disappointed.

He'd told her it was impossible to buy privacy though, so she supposed she could understand why he kept his letters a little impersonal. Added to that, staff at the prison checked all mail. He'd be embarrassed to make his words too flowery.

The only mention made of their hopeless predicament was a reference to Dylan Scott. *I don't suppose there's much point to any of it,* he wrote, *but at least he's interested and at least he's willing to talk to people. We'll just have to put our faith in him.*

He wrote that it was time for breakfast so he needed to get a move on. And that was that. The letter was signed *Love from Alek.* Sue sent birthday and Christmas cards to people she'd only met half a dozen times and signed them *Love from Sue and Alek.*

She dragged herself upstairs to their bedroom. It was becoming less theirs and more hers. A pile of loose change that Alek had taken from his pockets before climbing into bed that last time still sat on the dresser. His jacket hung from the back of the chair and his indoor shoes waited for him by the side of the bed. She couldn't put any of it away.

She lay on their bed, pulled Alek's shirt from beneath his pillow, put it to her face and inhaled deeply. Sometimes she wore the shirt in bed, and sometimes she simply fell asleep with it clutched tight in her fists, but it was always there as a reminder. It was difficult to detect Alek's smell now, though, probably because she'd worn the shirt too often or cried too many tears into it.

She lay on the bed for long minutes, wallowing in her despair and knowing she should pull herself together and get outside. Keeping busy was the only way to survive.

She'd learned that when her dad died. It hadn't stopped her missing him, far from it, but it helped push the pain a little further to the back of her mind. She wondered if she'd ever stop missing him. Probably not, because he'd been everything to her. Even when she'd left home, it was rare that a day passed when she didn't see him or speak to him on the phone. She longed for his gentle warmth and his sense of humour.

She knew he still watched over her though. Two days after his funeral, when the enormity of his death was beginning to hit home, she'd felt a light touch on the back of her head. She'd spun round but there had been no one there. No cat had brushed past her and no door was open to provide a draught. People could say what they liked, but she knew what she knew. Her father had put a gentle hand to her head to comfort her, to remind her that, although his body might be in the ground, his spirit would always be with her.

A car jolted along the track outside and she knelt on the bed to peer out. She'd hoped it was someone wanting a look at the animals, someone willing to offer a good home to a needy and deserving dog or cat, but it was Jamie.

She watched him get out of his car and open the boot for

his bag and a pair of boots. When he'd laced up more appropriate footwear, he strode off to the kennels.

Sue knew she must rouse herself, forget her depression and be her usual bubbly self. It wasn't easy. Sometimes she was so damn perky, she drove herself mad.

She collected Lennon from the kitchen and set off to find Jamie.

He looked so pleased to see her that she decided, there and then, that she must say something. After her chat with Dylan, she'd convinced herself that the PI was imagining things and that any feelings for her Jamie may or may not have were best ignored. Life wasn't that simple though. She'd worried about it, had even started to obsess about it. As difficult as it was, she had to say something for Jamie's sake.

"Hi," he said. "Everything okay?"

She wondered if her bright vivacious self had deserted her, and forced an even wider smile to her face. "Everything's great. I had a letter from Alek this morning."

"Right."

A spark of anger flared briefly, but why should she expect him to talk about Alek? He wasn't the one counting the seconds until he could be with someone again. He was the centre's vet, that was all. He came to the centre to check out the animals, not listen to the owner's problems.

"Any new arrivals?" he asked, dismissing Alek.

"No, thank goodness."

"Okay. I need to give booster inoculations to—" he flicked through his notes "—Sam, the lab cross, and Caesar, the staffie."

"Really? Have the poor things been here a year?"

"'Fraid so."

Sam had been abandoned at the side of the motorway and hit by a passing car. He'd healed physically but, mentally, he was still a handful. It was going to be difficult to rehome him. Caesar was fine, once you got to know him. The problem was that most people didn't have enough time for that. He growled at prospective new owners and they passed quickly to the next kennel.

Sue took a deep breath. "When you've done that, Jamie, could I have a word, please? If you're not too busy, of course."

"I'm never too busy for you." He looked delighted at the prospect. "You know that."

"Thanks. Let's get these dogs sorted then."

By the time the two dogs had been given their boosters and Jamie had checked on a few of the other residents, an hour had passed. They were in the examination room, but it was too small for a difficult chat.

"Would you like to come into the house for a coffee?" Sue asked.

"That would be good. Thanks."

Lord, she was dreading this. On the other hand, she didn't want Jamie getting ideas. He was a lovely young man and he should be dating someone who appreciated him and, more important, someone who didn't have a husband.

She was at the kitchen sink, filling the kettle and trying to find the right words, when Jamie spoke.

"I've been thinking," he said. "We should go out, you and me. To the cinema or something. Perhaps we could take in a show or go for a meal. Or both."

The words startled her. She'd never known Jamie to have a girlfriend and it shocked her to realise that Dylan was right and that he was having thoughts of giving her that title.

"That's what I wanted to talk to you about." She was surprised to hear herself sounding so calm. "I'm married, Jamie—"

"I know that." A nerve twitched at his temple. "I'm not stupid, Sue, and I wasn't asking you to marry me. I was thinking of you, really. I'm just saying that as your husband is in prison for murder, locked up for God knows how many years, you should get out more. I was offering to take you out. I thought it might cheer you up."

He was smiling, but she had the feeling he was angry with her.

"Thank you," she said. "It's good of you to think of me, but I couldn't. I'm married to Alek and the fact that he isn't here at the moment doesn't change that. I wouldn't feel comfortable. I'm sorry, Jamie."

Jamie shrugged. "It's your choice, of course. I just thought it would help take your mind off things. It can't be good for you being stuck here with nothing to do but worry about Alek. And let's face it, that's all you will do until Dylan Scott gets him out of there."

He sounded so confident that Sue leapt on his words. "Do you think he will get him out? Has he said anything to you?"

"He hasn't said anything, no, but I'm sure he's working on it. He always looks—confident."

The kettle switched itself off and Sue gave herself a few moments to think while she made their coffee. This was the first time anyone had shown any belief in Alek's plight or Dylan's ability.

She handed him his coffee and wondered if perhaps some time spent with him would do her good. Perhaps some of his confidence would rub off on her.

"I appreciate the offer, really I do, Jamie."

"It's up to you, of course. I thought it might cheer you up to get out." He blew across the surface of his coffee. "So what did you want to talk to me about?"

"Someone said—" She didn't want to drag Dylan into this. "Someone said they thought you might have feelings for me. They also thought you followed me when I went to put flowers on my dad's grave."

"Who? Who said that? Who's been telling tales behind my back?"

He hadn't denied following her, and an uneasy shiver ran down her spine. "Is it true?"

She'd thought he was angry, but it all melted away and he smiled suddenly. "Who's been saying that?"

"The who doesn't matter. I just wanted to tell you that you're wasting your time, Jamie. You're a really lovely man, and I appreciate everything you do here, for the animals and for me, but there's only one man in my life."

He laughed softly. "I know that, Sue. Good grief, I don't know who's been saying such stupid things. Yes, I did follow you, as you put it, when you went to the cemetery."

"You did? But why?"

"I was setting off on my rounds, on my way to Crags Farm, when I saw you. I was far too early and needed to kill some time, so I thought I'd have a chat with you. I waited in the car park until you'd attended to your father's grave. Then, when you came out, I had a phone call and needed to get out to see a calf urgently."

And now she felt foolish.

"Sue, I don't know what sort of person you think I am, but I don't chase after married women. Good grief." He shook his head and chuckled.

"Of course you don't. I'm sorry." She felt such an idiot and could feel herself blushing to the roots of her hair.

"Don't apologise." He drank some coffee, smiling as he watched her try to recover from her embarrassment. "I thought you needed a friend, that's all. Someone to talk to. I see you here, being all strong and brave, and I simply thought you might like to get away and relax a bit. I thought it might help if you could talk about things, about Alek, about how hard life is for you right now. I always think it helps to talk things over with someone who understands."

"I got it all wrong, didn't I?"

"You did." He still wore that indulgent smile.

It was Dylan who'd got it wrong, though. Not her. If he hadn't said anything, such foolish ideas wouldn't have crossed her mind.

"No harm done," he said. "Forget I ever said anything."

Sue wished it were that simple. It wasn't. All she wanted now was to get away from here where her problems seemed to crowd her, and spend some time relaxing with someone who had faith in Dylan's ability to get Alek freed. That sounded like heaven.

Jamie drank his coffee and put the empty mug on the table. "It's time I was going."

"Jamie." She didn't know what to say. "If the offer is still open—"

"What offer?"

Her skin was burning with embarrassment. "If you wanted to go out for an hour one evening…" Her voice trailed away. She expected him to leap in and say yes, but all he did was gaze at her.

"Perhaps it's not such a good idea," he said. "I wouldn't want you getting silly ideas. Or anyone else getting them, come to that."

"I certainly won't. But if you'd rather not—"

"It's up to you. It doesn't matter to me one way or the other."

Of course it didn't, and she'd have words with Dylan when she next saw him. It was his fault that she was stuttering and stammering like an idiot. Jamie was too polite to say so, of course, but he probably thought she had a very high opinion of herself if she thought he was attracted to her.

She didn't know what to do, but she did know she didn't want to leave things like this. If she did, they would be forever awkward in each other's company and that would be awful.

"Tell you what," she said, sounding a lot braver than she felt, "why don't we drive out to that new pub on Top Road. We both have to eat and it would save us cooking."

"If you like."

"Tomorrow night? Seven o'clock?"

He shook his head. "Sorry, I can't make it tomorrow."

"Oh, right. How about, um, Saturday or Sunday? Monday?"

"I can do Sunday."

She'd thought he was trying to put her off and was relieved to hear him suggest a day. "Good. I'll look forward to it."

"But only as friends," he said. "I don't want anyone getting any stupid ideas."

"I'm sure they won't."

"Okay." He glanced at his watch. "I'll be late if I don't get a move on. Thanks for the coffee, Sue. Be seeing you."

The wind must have caught the front door when he went out, because it slammed so hard she expected the glass to shatter.

THIRTY-THREE

DYLAN WAS TEMPTED to believe that spring had chosen this Sunday morning to arrive in Shepherd's Bush. It was just possible to feel some warmth from the sun. He guessed it would be a few weeks before the improvement was noticed as far north as Dawson's Clough. But he was forgetting northern towns, for today at least.

The unexpected sunshine had brought people out to enjoy the common. Dogs pulled owners along, couples kissed, and children pretended they were planes or trains.

He'd had to phone Pikey and cancel yesterday's planned get-together, but perhaps they could arrange something for next weekend. If the weather stayed like this, they could have a few pints at the local pub and then throw something on the barbecue.

"I hope she's warm enough," Bev said, adjusting Freya's covers.

"Of course she is." Freya was wrapped in enough clothes to undertake a trek across Antarctica.

"The doctor said she'd benefit from fresh air."

"We'll all benefit."

"Yes. It makes you feel glad to be alive, doesn't it? So what are you going to do next? Are you driving north tomorrow?"

"That's up to you."

His son was "chilling at Tom's," his daughter was fit and well and content to be pushed across the common with nothing to do but watch a couple of clouds drift across a blue sky, and his wife was relaxed, or fairly relaxed, and smiling. There was no need for him to be in Shepherd's Bush tomorrow. If Bev wanted him to stay, though, he would.

"You go," she said. "We're fine now. Besides, I have plenty to do."

"Like what?"

"People to see," she said. "There are dozens of people I promised to see after Freya was born and they'll start thinking I've turned into a hermit. I have a lot of catching up to do. Besides, I want to show off our daughter."

Dylan wasn't sure what had happened, but he was pleased with the end result. As soon as the doctors had managed to reassure Bev that they were keeping Freya in hospital overnight as nothing more than a precaution, she'd calmed down. The near hysterical outpourings of self-blame for Freya's sudden illness had ceased. Happy that her daughter was well, Bev had undergone a transformation. She was back to her old self.

He'd thought, as had his mother, that Bev was suffering from post-natal depression. She couldn't have been, though. Or, if she had, it had vanished along with Freya's temperature.

Freya's mild chest infection had probably been responsible for her cranky behaviour. Since her two nights in hospital she'd been angelic. She hadn't screamed through the night. In fact, she'd slept so long that Bev had panicked and prodded her awake.

Bev, instead of not wanting to move, of being constantly tired and irritable, was full of energy. At seven o'clock this morning, she'd been cleaning out kitchen cupboards. Given that she was usually allergic to rising early, this was little short of a miracle.

"If you're sure you'll be okay, I'd better get back to work then," he said. "I'll only be a phone call away." A phone call and the best part of three hundred miles.

"You'd better make your peace with that vet too. What's his name?"

"Jamie Tinsley. Yes, I had."

Amid the panic of getting to the hospital on Wednesday, Dylan had forgotten all about the meeting he'd arranged with Tinsley. He hadn't remembered until Thursday morning and, when he'd phoned to apologise, Tinsley had been less than happy. He'd cut the call short in an icy, abrupt manner.

Dylan wasn't going to lose sleep over that. With or without Tinsley's help, he'd solve this mystery.

"I doubt if he has anything of interest to tell me," he said. "If he had, he'd tell me over the phone. I expect he wants to convince me that Kaminski should rot in jail. That way, he might stand a chance of getting the lovely Sue to himself."

"Is she lovely?"

"Tinsley thinks so."

"That wasn't what I asked."

If Dylan didn't know better, he'd think Bev was jealous. "She's okay. All she seems to care about is Kaminski and her stray animals. I don't know about lovely, but she's quite a tragic figure."

"Tragic?"

"Yes. She strikes me as one of those people who'd do anything for anyone. She takes in strays and would go without food herself rather than turn away a hungry dog. Rain or shine, she visits her great-aunt every week and takes treats for the nursing home staff at Christmas and on her great-aunt's birthday. She's the Good Samaritan and yet life seems to have a habit of kicking her in the teeth. Her first husband was killed in a pileup on the motorway, then her dad died, and I gather they were close, and now her second husband has been locked up for God knows how long."

They moved off the path to let three youngsters on skateboards speed past them.

Dylan set Freya's buggy straight again and they carried on walking.

"Some people are like that, aren't they?" Bev said. "A lo
of people glide through life without a problem yet others seem
to have to deal with all sorts of horrors."

Dylan nodded at the truth of that.

"Is this vet a suspect?" Bev asked. "Do you really thinl
he could have killed Carly Walsingham?"

For the first time since Freya was born, Bev was show
ing an interest in his work. He'd always enjoyed bouncing
ideas off her. Her thought processes were totally different to
his, probably because she was female, and she occasionally
threw out suggestions that wouldn't have occurred to him.

"No, not really." There was something about Tinsley tha
Dylan didn't like. The geek impression he gave off was a
odds with the dozens of emotions that flickered in his eye
every few seconds. He was kind to animals, but didn't seem
to like them much. "He's an odd bugger, and I bet he is ca
pable of murder, but I don't think he killed Carly."

"Why not?"

"Why would he?"

"To get Kaminski out of the way."

That had been a recurring thought, but it was ridiculous.

"It doesn't add up, Bev. Assuming Tinsley is capable o
murder, which he may or may not be, he would kill the per
son he wanted out of the way. That's Kaminski. How coulc
he know Kaminski was seeing Carly? Supposing he did, how
could he possibly know that Kaminski would visit Carly tha
afternoon? Even Kaminski didn't know until the night before
Assuming, by some miracle, that he did know, how coulc
he possibly guess that Kaminski would take the rap for it?"

"He couldn't, could he?" she said. "Even if he had, he
couldn't know how long a sentence Kaminski would serve
These days, prisoners get out years early if they behave them
selves. Your vet wouldn't want that, would he? He'd get him
self nicely settled with Sue and then have to hand her back

to her husband." She shrugged. "Okay, it looks like Tinsley isn't your man. Who else have you got?"

"Just my chief suspect, the Invisible Man." Dylan took off his jacket and draped it over the buggy's handle. The sun was bringing a lot of warmth now and, with no clouds to watch, Freya had fallen asleep.

Bev nudged his arm. "Let's get an ice cream."

It never failed to amaze him how Bev couldn't walk past an ice-cream seller. A gale could be howling, snow could be falling, yet if an ice-cream seller was desperate enough for trade to be out, he was guaranteed a customer in Bev.

Dylan didn't want one, couldn't see the point to ice cream really, but he found himself asking for two when he got to be served.

They carried them to a nearby bench and sat to enjoy the peace and the warm sunshine.

Given an ice cream, Bev turned into a three-year-old. She savoured every mouthful and usually ended up with the stuff plastered across her face.

"It would be awful, wouldn't it," she said, "if after all this, Aleksander Kaminski was guilty?"

"It would certainly be a waste of his parents' money."

"You don't think he could be, do you?"

"No. I'm about ninety percent sure in my own mind that he's innocent."

"Only ninety?"

"Kaminski's in that cell because he was having an affair with the victim, his fingerprints were all over the house, the victim's husband claims his wife was being threatened by Kaminski, and a neighbour saw a man who looked like him leaving the scene."

Then again, Kaminski didn't deny being at the property so of course his prints were there. As for those threats, either Kaminski was refusing to admit they'd had a row or Walsing-

ham was lying. The neighbour may or may not have seen the
killer leave, she may or may not have seen Kaminski leave...

"I suppose Walsingham is chief suspect," he said. "Perhaps
he wanted his wife out of the picture for good. His mistress,
Megan Cole, is another suspect. She probably has the best
motive of all. Get rid of the wife and the grieving widower
would presumably make her the second Mrs. Walsingham."

"What a mess." Bev reached for a baby wipe to clean herself so Dylan wasn't sure if her comment referred to the de-
mise of Carly Walsingham or her own ice-cream-splattered
face. Either way, she was right.

They carried on walking. All around them, people laughed
in the unexpected but welcome sunshine. Children raced
around on bikes or rollerblades, adults attached to iPhones
jogged along the path, pigeons scavenged for crumbs.

"You'll get there in the end," Bev said. "You always do."

Dylan basked in her confidence. He just wished he could
share it.

THIRTY-FOUR

NEIL HAD BEEN dreading this for weeks. Given the choice, he'd let today, Carly's forty-fifth birthday, pass without comment. His sons, as young as they were, had other ideas so he'd been forced to fall in with their wishes. As such, he would shortly be embarking on a trip to Birmingham. That was, if Harry ever finished his breakfast.

"Are you planning to eat that, Harry?" Neil asked, smiling to take the impatience from his words.

"Yes. I was just saying we should take a present to Gran and Granddad as well."

"We'll stop and get something on the way," Neil promised. "Perhaps some flowers for your grandmother and a bottle of whisky for your grandfather. How does that sound?"

"Cool," William said. "We can buy Gran's flowers when we get Mum's."

"Yes, but only if you hurry up, Harry. The longer you delay, the less time you'll have with your grandparents."

As far as Neil was concerned, five minutes with them would be five minutes too long, but Harry was spurred on enough to gobble down his slice of toast and race upstairs to wash his hands and clean his teeth.

Neil drove them to the florist's where it took far longer than necessary to choose flowers, a selection of white blooms for Carly and a suitably tasteless psychedelic concoction for her mother.

William and Harry raced along the paths at the cemetery as if they were involved in a game. They were too young to understand the concept of death, or murder, and perhaps that was a good thing. Both boys missed Carly, but Harry was the more tearful of the two. William was more like Neil, more able to accept and move on. Harry needed answers to all his questions. He had to know where his mother was, what she was doing, if she had lots of friends, if she could see him. Endless questions.

Neil squatted down at the graveside to arrange the flowers to the boys' satisfaction. Both wished her a happy birthday and told her they were being good boys.

Thankfully, to prove there was a god, a couple of fat raindrops landed on them and Neil was able to shoo them back to the car.

They stopped to buy a bottle of malt whisky for Eric Smith. Pearls before swine…

Finally, they were heading for the motorway. The boys had DVDs to watch while Neil concentrated on the traffic and prayed for the day to end. They were no more than ten miles from Dawson's Clough when the sun burst out from behind a cloud. As they drove south, the sky cleared and the temperature rose.

A couple of hours later, they were in Birmingham. Neil drove along leafy suburbs, then streets lined with rundown shops before reaching the area he wanted. Not wanted, needed. Under normal circumstances, he wouldn't be caught dead in a place like this. Houses became smaller and scruffier, and gardens became dumps for litter and unwanted furniture.

"We're nearly there," William piped up, his DVD forgotten.

"Yes." Another mile or so of this despairing, rotting landscape and they would reach the Smiths' house.

Neil often wondered if he would have married Carly if he'd known where she came from. All he'd seen was an exceptionally pretty, extremely bright radiographer who knew how to flirt and who was, he soon found out, great in bed. He'd asked about her past, of course, but she'd been one of those who lived for the moment. It had taken her two minutes to explain how she'd grown up in Birmingham and married her childhood sweetheart.

It wasn't until their wedding day that he met her parents and he'd been appalled by everything about them, from their cheap clothes and broad accents to their loud, uncouth behaviour. Carly was pregnant when he first visited their home and he could still remember the sense of shock he'd experienced. There were council houses and then there was the Smiths' home. Slum didn't even begin to describe it.

All credit to Carly, he supposed. Somehow, she'd managed to drag herself out of this mire.

"Here we are, boys."

Suppressing a shudder, Neil glanced at the grimy windows of the house. God knows what diseases lay in wait behind those walls. The white PVC front door was new and, surprisingly, someone had spent an hour or so tidying the small patch of garden at the front.

That new front door opened and Laura Smith, who was at least sixty pounds overweight, did a fast waddle up the path. Her arms were wide as she waited. Harry and William obliged by racing into those arms and covering her face with kisses.

If Neil lived for another century, he would never understand how the boys could love this woman so much. When Carly had been alive, they'd probably visited this house three times a year and they hadn't seen Laura once since the funeral. Yet they adored her.

She had her good points, Neil couldn't deny that. She'd pushed her daughter to make something of her life. "Qualifications are what you need, Carly. Qualifications. You can do anything then."

If only she didn't live in a slum.

Still holding her grandsons' hands, she reached up and dropped a wet kiss on Neil's cheek. "How's my lovely boy, eh?"

Neil resisted the urge to reach for his handkerchief and rub dry the place her lips had touched. "I'm doing okay, thank you, Laura. How are you?"

"Oh, you know. Good days and bad days. Today—" She glanced down at the boys and gave a wan smile. "These two young scamps will make today better."

As always, she had presents for them. Cheap toys that, if they didn't maim the boys first, would fall to pieces before the day was over.

Neil had hoped that Eric was out, but no such luck. His father-in-law's great bulk was wedged in his usual dirty armchair surrounded by well-read newspapers and an overflowing ashtray. The TV was off for once but the remote control sat on his lap poised for action.

"Well, Neil." He didn't get out of his chair. "Long time no see."

"Yes." It would have been much longer if Neil had had his way. "How are you, Eric?"

"Can't complain. No point, is there? I keep taking the tablets, but they don't do no good. They can't find out what's wrong with me."

Neil's diagnosis was a chronic case of laziness. Eric had hurt his back, or so he claimed, over twenty years ago and he hadn't done a day's work since. He preferred to claim benefits. Let those people daft enough to work pay to keep him, that was his motto. Eric could afford to drink and smoke, to subscribe to Sky Sports channels and bet on the horses. He lacked for nothing.

Laura worked at a couple of local pubs, both as cleaner and occasional barmaid.

"I come bearing gifts," Neil said, seeing Eric spot the whisky. "I hope it's to your taste."

Highland Park whisky would be to anyone's taste, and far superior to the cheap blended stuff Eric served up.

"Thank you. Very kind."

Damn it, there was no way Neil would have asked Carly to marry him if he'd known that she came from this hellhole. By the time he found out, it had been too late. It would always irk him to know that these people's genes had been passed on to his sons.

The living room was awash with photos of Carly from the age of two onwards. It was like a bloody shrine. Neil would have been more impressed if someone had bothered to flick a duster over them now and again.

Eric ran a finger over the bottle's label. "I wish I could afford to drink stuff like this. You're a lucky bugger, Neil."

Neil was tempted to tell him that, if he got off his fat arse and did a day's work, he'd be able to afford lots of life's luxuries. Instead, he muttered something like, "It's good stuff," and left Eric alone.

He joined Laura and the boys in the kitchen. He could tolerate Laura.

She'd been seventeen when Carly was born and Neil didn't suppose she'd changed much over the years. She was vastly overweight, yes, but her complexion would be envied by women twenty years younger. It certainly didn't hint at the life she'd had with Eric. He drank and gambled, and she worked. It was the way it had always been. It had been Laura who'd earned the money to put decent clothes on Carly's back.

She was showing the boys how to make cookies, and the messier the process became, the more they enjoyed themselves.

When the cookies went in the oven, the boys raced into

the garden to explore the wilderness. God knows what they'd find among the tall docks and thistles.

"So how are you really doing, Neil? Are you coping?"

"What else can we do, Laura? As much as we hate it, life has to go on, doesn't it?"

"I suppose it does. It's a bloody horrible life though."

"Yes."

"Has that private investigator spoken to you?" she asked.

"He has, yes."

"Eric won't speak to him. He said we shouldn't."

"It's up to you, of course."

Her fat arms wobbled as she nodded. "I gather he's going to try and get Alek off the hook?"

"He seems to think he could be innocent, yes."

"He can't be, though. Can he?"

He saw the light of hope in her eyes. She'd liked Kaminski and, although she'd turned against him now, nothing would make her happier than hearing he was innocent of her daughter's murder.

"Of course he's not. How can he be? The judge and jury heard everything. Everything. God, I heard him threatening her, and a neighbour saw him leaving the house. For him to protest his innocence is just laughable."

He always lost patience with his in-laws. It wasn't only the mess they lived in, it was the way they were incapable of using the few brain cells they'd been born with. They couldn't think for themselves, it took far more effort than they were willing to expend. Eric and Laura both read the tabloids from cover to cover and believed every sensational word printed, but couldn't or wouldn't make up their own minds about anything.

Thankfully, Harry and William raced back inside to check on their cookies, and the murder of their mother wasn't considered a suitable topic of conversation.

Lunch was soon ready and Neil sat down to a colourful mess of sandwiches, crisps, jelly, ice-cream and an iced sponge cake to celebrate Carly's birthday. He was starving, but he only ate a sliced ham sandwich and a small piece of cake for the sake of politeness. No one noticed. The boys wolfed down the sugar-laden concoctions with glee, and Eric and Laura ate sandwich after sandwich before moving on to the cake. It was like feeding time at the zoo.

When the table was bare, Eric lit a cigarette and the boys returned to the garden. Neil wished he could join them.

"Carly would have loved this, wouldn't she?" Laura said. "She loved birthdays and parties."

"Yes." Neil nodded and smiled, as was expected.

"I'll tell you summat," Eric said. "If that bastard Kaminski ever gets out of jail, he'll wish he bloody hadn't."

"Too right he will," Laura chipped in. "I saw his mother a couple of weeks back. Do you know what? She only tried to speak to me. I soon showed her what I thought of her. If she was on fire, I wouldn't bloody piss on her."

Eric cackled with laughter.

Neil could stand no more. "It's time we were off. It's a long drive and I don't want the boys to be late home. Thank you for lunch and for everything. It's been lovely. We must see each other more often."

"We must," Laura said eagerly. "Me and Eric could get the train up. Stay with you for a few days."

"That would be great." He hoped his horror didn't show. "We'll fix something up. As soon as I can get some free days, we'll arrange something."

"Before you race off, I've got something for you. Can't have you being the only one not to have a present to open, can we?" Laura waddled off and returned clutching a parcel wrapped in pink paper. "Here."

"Thank you."

Guessing what was inside, he pulled off the paper. He was

right. Carly, at least he assumed it was Carly, looked back at him from a cheap plastic frame.

"Thank you," he said again. "I'll treasure it."

"That was her on her first birthday." Laura spoke with pride. "I hunted through the box of snaps and as soon as I saw it, I knew you'd like it. There's a bloke on the market who enlarges them. You take him a photo and, a couple of days later, you collect something like this. It's good, isn't it?"

"It's excellent. Very clever. Thank you, both."

Twenty minutes later, he was driving off and welcoming the relief as the tension gradually ebbed away.

The boys sat in the back, laughing and giggling. From the passenger seat, Carly's face stared up at him. He turned the frame over, putting her facedown, and headed for the motorway.

THIRTY-FIVE

DYLAN PULLED INTO Tesco's car park, switched off the engine and made a mental note to book a service for the Morgan. It was sprinting up and down motorways too much for his liking and, although it hadn't missed so much as a beat, there was no point in feeling smug or pushing his luck.

He grabbed his phone and punched in his home number. Bev answered on the second ring.

"Everything okay?" he asked.

"It's fine. Where are you?"

"Dawson's Clough. I've just arrived."

They spoke for a couple of minutes, just long enough to put Dylan's mind at rest. Luke was at school, Freya was chortling in the background and Bev sounded cheerful enough. All was well with his world.

When he ended the call, he went into the store, grabbed a coffee and wondered what to do for the best. He couldn't decide whether to phone Tinsley or call at the veterinary surgery and hope he was available for a quick chat.

Other than that, he wasn't sure which direction to take. Leads, or even hunches, were distinctly lacking right now. He uncovered a lie at every turn, but as yet he hadn't found a single thing that might prove Kaminski's innocence. He had to hope that, as unlikely as it sounded, Tinsley had something worthwhile to tell him.

There was no point in alienating Tinsley. Dylan would call at the surgery, apologise profusely yet again, and ask if they could meet during Tinsley's lunch break or later in the evening.

Moor Lane Veterinary Practice was an impressive double-fronted, three-storey building in the middle of Cooper Road. A sign pointed to a small car park at the rear, but Dylan parked on the road in front of the building. After a quick look to make sure there weren't any No Parking signs or traffic wardens about, he went inside.

The reception room was large, light and airy, and the walls were dotted with pictures of giant-sized fleas and instructions on how often pets should be wormed. Three young women sat behind a curving counter using state-of-the-art computers that told how well the practice was doing. Behind them were shelves stacked with pills and potions, pet carriers, expensive collars, dog coats and anything else the pampered pet might require.

"Can I help you?"

Dylan turned his best smile on the receptionist. "Sorry to bother you. I'm actually hoping for a word with Jamie. Jamie Tinsley. Is he here?"

"He is, but he's with a client at the moment. If you'd like to take a seat, I'll tell him you're here when he's free. What name is it?"

"Dylan Scott."

"As in Thomas?"

"Sorry?"

"Dylan Thomas?"

"Oh, yes. Yes, that's right."

As he sat to wait, he considered giving the girl a medal. Everyone else asked if he was Dylan as in Bob Dylan. He couldn't remember anyone mentioning Dylan Thomas.

Whenever he asked his mother why she couldn't have called him John or Peter instead of naming him after her favourite singer-songwriter, she just laughed. "I had a soft spot for Engelbert Humperdinck too. Count your blessings, love."

She had a point. Not an excuse, a point.

The large clock ticked on until a woman carrying a caged cat emerged from one of the side doors.

The receptionist picked up the phone, tapped in a number and said, "There's a Dylan Scott to see you, Jamie."

She ended the call and didn't even glance in Dylan's direction. He was about to enquire when that door opened again and Jamie, clad in a green overall, appeared.

"Dylan. Come on through."

Dylan followed him along a corridor, past a couple more doors, and into a small examination room.

Jamie stood behind a rubber covered table. "What can I do for you?"

"I came to apologise again for missing our appointment. I'm so sorry, but my daughter was rushed into hospital and I had to dash down to London. In the panic, it went right out of my head."

Jamie nodded, a sign perhaps that he accepted Dylan's apology. Anyone else would have asked after Freya's health. Not Tinsley.

"I wondered if you had a couple of minutes spare," Dylan said.

"Sorry, this is a busy time and I need to leave soon to go on my rounds."

"I understand that. You said you have something to tell me about Aleksander Kaminski?"

Tinsley gave a short humourless laugh. "I can tell you he's guilty. If you knew him, really knew him, you'd realise that. You're wasting your time. You're also giving Sue false hope and that's unforgivable."

"So you don't know anything about the murder of Carly Walsingham?"

Behind the glasses, Tinsley blinked several times. "I know for a fact that Aleksander Kaminski is guilty. Justice has been done. Leave it alone."

"You know for a fact?"

"Yes. I'm sorry, but I can't tell you more than that. I thought perhaps I could, but I can't. And now, if you'll excuse me—"

"Yes, of course." Dylan walked out of the surgery and back to his car deep in thought. As crazy as it sounded, he'd got the impression back there that Tinsley *did* know something. What the hell could that be?

He'd assumed that Tinsley was determined to convince him of Kaminski's guilt simply because he wanted Sue for himself and liked the idea of Kaminski being behind bars for a good number of years. He should have remembered his own mantra, *Never Assume*. Perhaps Tinsley knew exactly who the killer was.

He put the Morgan in gear and drove to his hotel. It was time to make peace with the staff. He pulled into the hotel's car park and grabbed his bags.

If anyone asked, he'd tell them he loathed hotel life. It had its plus points, though, the main one being the breakfasts. What could be better than waking to sizzling bacon, hot sausages, and eggs fried to perfection?

As a teenager, he'd vowed that when he was old enough to leave home and his mother's hopeless attempts to throw a few seeds in a bowl, he wouldn't get involved with any woman unless she could cook. In the event, of course, he'd ended up with Bev, and her talents ended at stacking an Asda trolley.

"Hi," he greeted the girl on the reception desk. He didn't recognise her and he thought he knew all the staff. "I'm Dylan Scott. I've been staying here but had to rush off on Wednesday."

"Ah, yes." She reached for a key card. "We received your message. Here. Your room's all ready for you."

"The same room?"

"Yes."

"Excellent. Thanks."

"You're welcome. Have a nice day."

Dylan would settle for a fruitful day. A useful day. "Thanks. You too."

He took the lift to his room, threw his bags on the bed to unpack later and decided to spend an hour looking through those CCTV images again. But first he tried Neil Walsingham's mobile.

Much to his surprise, it was answered almost immediately. "Dylan? Hello, how are you? What can I do for you?"

The doctor was a good actor. Dylan must be the last person he wanted to hear from, yet his effusive greeting was almost convincing. Almost.

"Hello, Neil. I'm good, thanks. I was wondering if I could have a chat with you. There are just a couple of points I need clearing up and it would be easier face to face than over the phone."

"Of course. When suits you? Tell you what, I'll be home early this evening. By five or five-thirty at the latest. Well, barring any emergencies. Why don't you call at the house at, say, sixish?"

Trying to fathom Neil Walsingham was more difficult than understanding the meaning of life. "That would be good. Thank you. I appreciate it."

"Any time. See you later then. I'll give you a ring if I'm delayed at the hospital for any reason."

Dylan was so unsettled by the ease with which he'd set up a meeting with Walsingham that he was no longer interested in CCTV images. Besides, he could describe every person, recall every vehicle and name every bird that knew Darwen Road. It was a pointless exercise.

Instead, he grabbed his jacket and walked into the centre

of town. His thought processes worked much better when he walked, and he wanted his intended conversation with Neil Walsingham clear in his mind.

He was in the pedestrianised shopping centre before he knew it.

"Dylan?"

He turned at the sound of Frank's voice and saw his ex-boss striding out to catch him up. He waited, smiling at Frank's erect carriage and military stride.

"Hello, Frank. How's things?"

"About the same. What about you?"

He told Frank about his dash to London, how Freya was fully recovered, and how he'd managed to get an appointment at the doctor's home. "Do you fancy a coffee, Frank?"

"I'd rather have a beer, but I suppose it's a bit early."

"Is it ever too early? I need a clear head though. Walsingham's a slippery individual."

They went inside the crowded coffee bar and ordered cappuccinos. Most of the customers were women who'd decided to take a break from shopping. Some had babies or toddlers with them so peace and quiet was out of the question. Fortunately, the woman with two noisy toddlers at the table next to theirs didn't stay long.

"Help me out, Frank." Dylan spooned the froth from the top of his coffee. "Think of the vet, Tinsley, and how much he wants Sue Kaminski to himself. Why would he kill Carly Walsingham?"

Frank was reaching for his cup but he stopped. "You think he did?"

"It's a possibility. He wants me off the case, that I do know."

"Well, he would, wouldn't he? If, as you say, he has plans for Kaminski's wife, he'll be more than happy for the bloke to stay in Strangeways."

"True." Perhaps that's all there was to it. "And he tells me he doesn't want me raising Sue's hopes. Maybe that's true too."

"You think there's more to it?"

"I didn't until this morning."

His train of thought was interrupted by his phone. He glanced at the display and his brain cells worked at a painfully slow rate. Someone was calling him from that bloody phone box again. The one he was currently sitting less than five hundred yards from.

"Don't go away, Frank."

Phone in hand, Dylan raced out of the coffee bar and dodged dawdling shoppers and mothers pushing buggies, but he was too late. The phone box was empty.

While he stood to catch his breath, he watched the pedestrians. No one looked out of place. He was a jerk. He should have answered the damn phone and kept his anonymous caller talking.

Just as he was about to return to the coffee bar, he spotted a familiar figure hurrying in the opposite direction.

He ran to catch her up. "Hello, Sonia."

"Oh, er, hi. Hi, Dylan." Her face was the colour of the red leather handbag slung over her shoulder.

"Did you just try to call me?"

She had, he was sure of it.

"What?" Eyes wide, she took a step back, as if she expected him to cast a spell and turn her into a frog.

"My phone rang," he said. "I saw you in the phone box at the same moment. Before I could answer it, you rang off."

"Well, yes, as a matter of fact I did." She looked at the ground before concentrating on a group of teenagers outside the bookshop. "I, er, just wanted to apologise for Terry's behaviour. He gets a bit—"

"Jealous?" Dylan asked.

She nodded. "Yes. Usually, he's fine. A good husband. But mention of Neil—" She shrugged.

"I see."

"He thinks Neil stole me from him and nothing I say will make him see sense. I've told him fifty times that it meant nothing, but—" She shrugged again.

"I see," Dylan said again. "And that was all you wanted to talk to me about?"

"Yes. Well, I wondered how you were getting on, of course. Are you having any luck?"

"Not really, no."

"Oh. I'm sorry to hear that." She gave him a bright smile. "Anyway, that was all. I would have left a message for you, but I've just remembered an appointment. I have to dash. Sorry."

He caught her arm to halt her flight. "You do know, don't you, that failing to offer information during a police investigation—"

"I don't have any information. There was nothing I could have told them."

"I don't believe you."

"It's the truth. Look, I have to go."

Again she tried to leave and again Dylan stopped her. "What do you know, Sonia?"

She tossed back her head, her stance suddenly defiant. "I know that lying bastard Neil Walsingham wasn't at the hospital when his wife was murdered. And that's all I do know."

She wrenched her arm from Dylan's grip and strode off.

Dylan walked slowly back to the coffee bar deep in thought. How did she know? And why, bearing in mind she hated Walsingham with every breath in her body, hadn't she mentioned it to the police? She could have landed Walsingham right in the sticky brown stuff. So why hadn't she?

As ever, he had more questions than answers. Still, at least he had something to offer Walsingham when he visited him this evening.

THIRTY-SIX

JAMIE STRODE ALONG the familiar streets with a spring in his step. A playful wind pinched at his face and flicked his hair. A swirl of fallen leaves danced around his feet.

He'd known his chance would come, and his patience was rewarded when his mother phoned him shortly before Dylan Scott visited the surgery that morning.

Jamie had been too excited to care about Scott. Thinking about it afterwards, though, he wished he'd set up a meeting with him tonight. No matter. He'd deal with Scott later.

"Your father's much better, Jamie," his mother had said. "The doctor's just been and said he should be fine now. They don't want to see him again unless he has problems."

"I'm glad, Mum."

"It's a relief, isn't it? He's feeling so good, he's said I must go to the guild meeting this evening. It's the AGM. I thought I'd have to miss it, but no."

"That's excellent news." Better than she could know.

Jack Reynolds would escort his mother to and from the meeting. He was an old fusspot and wouldn't allow her to walk home alone in the dark. He'd even call in for a polite word with the invalid. It couldn't have been better.

Jamie crept round the back of the house, took his key from his pocket and let himself in. All was quiet.

He tiptoed into the sitting room where his father sat with the table light angled to shed light on his book. He was reading the Bible.

"James? What are you doing here? Your mother's out for the evening."

"So I gather. She's at her church guild meeting, isn't she?"

"Yes." He closed the Bible and placed it on the table by his side. "What are you doing here?"

"Euthanasia," Jamie said. "There's a thing, isn't it?"

"What?"

"I deal with that day in, day out, you know. Old dogs with cancer, cats with kidney failure. I put them out of their misery, console their grieving owners and pass on to the next."

"So you do, James, but you haven't answered my question. What are you doing here?"

"It's not just sick animals I deal with," Jamie said. "If an animal is bad-tempered, mean-spirited or just plain vicious, I send it on its way to the next life. It's so easy."

Shaking his head in confusion, Victor Tinsley laughed. "You're full of words, aren't you? Stupid words. You're all talk. Always have been and always will be. You take after—" He broke off and Jamie thought he saw something akin to fear in his expression.

"Who do I take after?"

"Nothing. No one. I didn't say anything."

"Who?" Jamie lunged at him and grabbed a handful of shirt collar and throat. "Who do I take after?"

"Hey, stop this now. I can't breathe."

Jamie gave him a good shake. "Then you'd better answer my question, damn you."

"All right. Daniel Wright. You take after Daniel Wright. Satisfied?"

Jamie released his grip and his father sank back into his chair, pulling air into his lungs.

Daniel Wright. He knew the name. Daniel Wright. He paced the room, dragging up long forgotten memories.

"*Father* Daniel Wright?"

The Roman Catholic Church had its large plot at the en
of this road. The priest's house, a dark, forbidding building
was opposite. Long ago, the resident priest had been on
Daniel Wright.

But the Tinsleys were Church of England. They had noth
ing to do with the priest.

Jamie dragged the man's image to mind. He'd been tal
His hair had been thin and sandy-coloured. His hair had bee
a lot like his own, now he came to think of it.

"Some call him Father." Victor Tinsley was scowling. "
call him the devil's offspring."

Wright had left the area around the time Ben died. It wa
a long time ago, so the image Jamie pulled to mind was prob
ably blurred by the years.

He sank onto the worn sofa and Victor Tinsley laughed.

"Yes, you're a bastard, James. A priest's bastard."

Bile rose in Jamie's throat. He ran to the kitchen, want
ing to be sick, but all he could do was retch. Sweat soake
his shirt.

His father had to be lying. And yet—

He could remember a smiling man in priest's robes givin
him a few coins, talking to him, taking an interest. And wha
had his mother said? That he was the son born out of love?

"You've always thought yourself a cut above the rest o
us, haven't you?" His father had come into the kitchen. H
was leaning against the door frame. "You thought you wer
cleverer than all of us. Cleverer than Peter, cleverer than me
The truth is, you're nothing more than a priest's bastard."

Jamie should kill him now but he felt too weak.

"Your mother acted like a common whore. We hadn't bee
married above a year when she went with that man."

Jamie covered his ears with his hands, but he could sti
hear the hated voice.

"She wanted to keep you. Said it wasn't your fault. W

didn't want the scandal. Who would? He gave us money to keep you. He even gave us money to feed that mangy dog you brought home."

"Don't you dare—" Jamie swallowed the bile that surged into his throat. "Don't you dare call Ben mangy. That dog was worth ten of you. He lived his life with dignity, right up to the end. He wasn't a bullying piece of shit like you. He didn't rape anyone, did he? You raped her, I know you did. I'll tell you something else, too. I'd rather be a priest's bastard than have any of your DNA in me."

Jamie straightened. He pushed past his father and strode into the sitting room. He switched on the TV and turned up the volume till it was so loud, the laughing game show contestants almost deafened him.

His father followed. "What in God's name are you doing?"

"I'm doing fuck all in God's name. This is in my name." Jamie reached into his pocket and pulled out the gun. His father reeled back from him.

"This," Jamie said, "is for Ben."

His father screamed as the bullet shattered his kneecap.

"And this one's from me."

The second bullet left a gaping hole in his father's head.

Jamie stepped over his father's body, crossed to the TV, switched if off and walked out of the house.

THIRTY-SEVEN

DYLAN WAS TAKEN aback when the front door of Neil Walsingham's home was opened by a homely, dark-haired woman in her mid-fifties. She was too young to be his mother, but too old for the doctor's taste and not even close to glamorous enough.

"You'll be Mr. Scott, yes?"

"Yes. And you are?"

"Mary Bell. I'm Dr. Walsingham's housekeeper. Please come in. He is expecting you."

"Thank you." Dylan had assumed that, given the doctor's work shifts, he had reliable babysitters in place. He should have known that, being on call at times, the doctor would need a live-in housekeeper. "How long have you worked for Neil?"

"Coming up to six months." Smiling, she led him into a vast sitting room. "Have a seat, Mr. Scott, and I'll go and tell Neil you're here. He won't be a moment."

The room was as tastefully furnished as Dylan would have expected. Two leather sofas and three chairs didn't boast so much as a scratch. A large, but not too large, TV shared a wall with various works of art. The oak floor was partially hidden with tasteful rugs. Oak coffee tables were spotless. On a bureau in the corner sat the obligatory framed photo of Walsingham and Carly on their wedding day.

"Dylan, good to see you." Neil strode into the room, a broad smile on his face. He was dressed casually in open neck shirt and chinos. "Can I offer you a drink?"

"No, thanks. This won't take long. I just need a couple of things clearing up."

Neil sat, left ankle balanced on right knee. He gave every indication of being relaxed and at ease. A man with nothing to hide. He gestured for Dylan to sit opposite.

After a moment's hesitation, he did so. He decided he might as well get straight to the point. "It would help enormously if you told me where you were on the afternoon your wife was murdered."

Smiling despairingly, Walsingham shook his head. "I've told you fifty times. I've told everyone fifty times. I was at the hospital. We were busy because—"

"I know all about the children and the accident." And he didn't want to hear it again. "But I know for a fact you weren't there. Where were you, Neil?"

"Who says I wasn't there?" The smile had slipped a little.

"I'm sorry, but I can't reveal the witness's name." For now, Sonia would have to be elevated to witness. "Where were you?"

Neil looked at him for long moments and all the while his raised foot danced a merry jig.

"Okay," he said at last. "I wasn't at the hospital."

Hallelujah!

Dylan didn't let him see how surprised he was by the admission. "Where were you?"

"Hasn't your witness told you?"

"I'd rather hear it from you."

Walsingham leapt to his feet. "Are you sure I can't get you a drink?"

"Quite sure. Thanks."

Dylan regretted that as soon as Walsingham reached for a bottle of Laphroaig, but he needed two things—a clear head and the upper hand.

Walsingham poured an extremely generous measure into a

large crystal glass. He took an appreciative sip and returned to his seat. With his legs crossed at the ankle now, he still looked reasonably relaxed.

"I can tell you where I was," he said, "but you won't believe me, the person I was with will deny everything, and it will only serve to muddy the water. Do you still want to know?"

"I do."

"Right." Walsingham took another swig of whisky. "That afternoon, I was supposed to be meeting Megan Cole. Occasionally, we'd sneak away from the hospital for an hour. The emergency department had been busy, but everything was under control by lunchtime. So Megan went home and I was supposed to follow her. Then I had a phone call."

Right on cue, a phone rang in the sitting room. Walsingham cocked an ear until someone, presumably Mary Bell, answered it.

"It was Sonia Trueman," he continued. "There had been no contact between Sonia and me since I broke things off, but someone had told her husband about us, God knows who. She was hysterical when she called me because he'd knocked her about. You won't know him, but he's a piece of scum who makes the Incredible Hulk look normal. Anyway, he'd hit her. She'd managed to flee the house and was on her way to the hospital. She was shouting and screaming, telling me—or warning me—that she was going to tell everyone who asked exactly why her husband had half killed her."

"Had he? Half killed her?"

"Nothing was broken." Walsingham sighed. "She was a mess, but it was only cuts and bruises. Her lip needed stitches."

Dylan winced on Sonia's behalf. "What did you do?"

"I didn't want her coming to the hospital and spreading more ugly rumours about me so I threw a few things in a bag—bandages, sutures, anything else I might need—and went to meet her."

"So you treated her injuries?"

"As stupid as it sounds, yes. There's a small memorial garden behind the hospital. No one uses it. Few people even know it exists. Of course, calming her down was my first priority." He let out a long sigh. "I managed that, cleaned her up, and then her husband called her. He was crying down the phone, saying how sorry he was, begging her to go home, that sort of thing."

Dylan wasn't sure he believed Walsingham's story or not. At least it was a story, though, and he had nothing better to do with his time.

"Did she go home to her husband?" he asked.

"Eventually, yes. Having made me promise not to tell him she'd called me or seen me." He rolled his eyes. "As if I was likely to do that. No one would volunteer for a visit from Terry Trueman. Besides, I wanted the blasted woman out of my life. But yes, she went. I gave her money for a taxi—I didn't think her bruiser of a husband would be too pleased if he saw me drive her home—and she left."

He drained his glass and stood to refill it.

"So there you have it," he said. "That's what happened. What I didn't know was that while I was dealing with Sonia's injuries, Carly was being murdered."

"Okay," Dylan said. "So when Sonia left you, what did you do?"

"I dashed back to the hospital. I was almost there when my sons' teacher called me to say she hadn't been able to reach Carly and that the boys were still at the school. I collected them and drove them home. And Carly was dead."

Dylan was beginning to believe him.

"But why didn't you tell the police all this?"

"Before the police had time to question me, Megan phoned

to ask where I'd been. She wasn't pleased at being stood up. I told her what had happened to Carly, and that the police would be asking questions. Once the shock had worn off, she panicked about her job. She'd been at her house waiting for me, remember?"

"What? You lied to the police just because Megan Cole was worried about her job?"

"No. I lied to the police because I knew damn well Sonia would deny all knowledge. I knew she wouldn't tell the world, or more important her husband, that she'd been with me. The vindictive cow would have made me look like a complete idiot. It was easier to say I'd been at the hospital. It helped Megan out of an awkward situation too."

"So you and Megan Cole gave each other alibis?"

"We said we'd been at the hospital, yes." He sat back in his chair. "To be honest, I can't see it matters where I was, where Megan was or where the hell Sonia was. None of us killed Carly. The important thing, in my mind, was to catch the killer."

In the same situation, Dylan would have been a lot more concerned with coping with his grief. The shock wouldn't have allowed him to worry about colleagues who'd lied to their bosses or about ex-mistresses worried about their husbands' reactions. Not that Dylan had any mistresses, ex-or otherwise.

"Basically, I panicked," Walsingham said. "It sounds ridiculous, I know, but the police were asking questions and I thought—Christ, I thought they'd got me down as someone capable of murdering my own wife, the mother of my children."

"I see."

Dylan would go into a state of shock if he found *anyone* dead in his sodding bath. As a doctor, Walsingham might be more used to dealing with blood and death, but there was a world of difference between treating injured strangers and finding your own wife dead in her bath.

"Is that why you lied about Kaminski threatening her the night before?" Dylan asked.

"What? No. No, of course not. I didn't lie. Maybe he wasn't threatening her, but I know what I heard. And I know she was upset afterwards."

More likely, he'd known she was on the phone and guessed, from some intimate whispering, that she was talking to her lover, Aleksander Kaminski.

"Would Sonia Trueman really lie about being with you that afternoon? Lie to the police, I mean?"

"Yes." Walsingham had no doubts on that score. "She wouldn't want her husband to know she'd been with me that day but, more than that, she'd love to see me behind bars. If she could put a spoke in my proverbial wheel, believe me, she would."

While these people played their petty games, Kaminski was rotting behind Strangeways' thick walls.

"The night before Carly was murdered," Dylan said, "I gather you went out to a restaurant in the town?"

"Yes. I told you that. That's why I didn't press her about the phone call. I guessed it was Kaminski, but I didn't want to spoil the evening."

"Hmm. But I've heard, and sorry, but I can't reveal the name of my source, that you and she quarrelled."

"What?" Walsingham couldn't have looked more shocked if the ghost of his dead wife had walked into the room and helped herself to his whisky. "Who said that?"

"Is it true?" Dylan asked.

"No. No, of course not. Well, we might have had words about something or other, like all married couples do, but we certainly didn't quarrel."

"You didn't pick a fight with her?"

"Of course not. For God's sake, people delight in spreading ugly rumours, don't they? Sorry, Dylan, but if we did have a tiff about something, I can't remember it."

He took a sip of his whisky. The aroma drifted across to Dylan, making him wonder why he hadn't accepted a drink.

"What about Aleksander Kaminski?" he asked. "How many times had you seen him before your wife was murdered?"

"Only once. Why do you ask?"

"Tell me about it."

"Carly wanted to go to a fundraiser at that tumbledown animal centre his wife runs. I didn't know that's where Kaminski lived. As far as I was concerned, he and Carly were divorced. End of. But we went to this bloody thing and bumped into him. It was then I found out he was married to the owner."

"Did you talk to him?"

"We passed the time of day, that's all. We spoke about the weather and the fundraiser for all of two minutes." A smile curved his lips. "His wife was dressed up as Goldilocks. Can you believe that? She had dogs that were supposed to be the three bears. Anyway, someone reversed into her car. Seeing her race across to inspect the damage dressed like that was one of the funniest things I've ever seen. There wasn't much damage done to her car. It was a rust-coloured heap anyway, and one wing mirror was already being held on with gaffer tape."

"With what?"

"Gaffer tape. You know, the stuff they use to cover cables on stages or—"

"Yes. I know what it is."

"It was a wreck, that's what it was. Impossible to know where the paint ended and the rust started. How she had the nerve to have a go at someone for putting a small dent in it, I don't know." He chuckled at the memory, then perhaps renembered that Dylan was investigating his wife's murder nd that laughter was out of order. "But, um, yes, that's the only time I ever saw or spoke to the man."

"Yet you knew he was in contact with your wife?"

"Yes. Yes, I knew that."

"Okay. Thanks for that, Neil. You've been very helpful ndeed."

"You're welcome. Now, about that drink? Are you sure you won't have one?"

"Positive, thanks. I'll bid you goodnight."

Dylan wanted a drink, or four, but he wanted to enjoy it n his own company.

THIRTY-EIGHT

It was raining when Dylan left Walsingham's house and sprinted to the Morgan. This was serious rain, angry rain that tried to beat you senseless.

It wasn't far to Sonia Trueman's house, though, so he'd have a quick chat with her, and it would be quick because he wasn't in the mood for playing games, and then buy himself that pint. He needed to think, and he'd do that a lot better with a drink in his hand.

He parked outside her house. A single light was burning in a ground floor room, suggesting someone was in. With his jacket collar turned up as poor shelter against the rain, he ran from the Morgan to the front door and rang the bell. A light came on in the hall and then he heard the sound of a lock clicking.

She opened the door six inches and gasped when she saw him. "What are you doing here?"

Dylan put his foot in the door to prevent her slamming it in his face. "I'd like a quick word. If you'd rather talk to the police, that's fine, but it might be easier if you talked to me."

"The police? Why?" It took her five seconds to make up her mind. "Perhaps you'd better come in."

She must be alone because she wouldn't have made the offer if the hulk was at home. Dylan was relieved. He didn't want a run-in with him.

He was being invited no further than the hallway. She stood in front of him, arms folded in belligerent fashion, barring him further entry.

"So?" she said.

"So I need to know why you lied to me. I have a witness who says you were with Neil Walsingham on the day his wife was murdered."

Dylan had no idea what she'd expected him to say but it sure as hell wasn't that. Her eyes widened in shock.

"A witness?"

"Yes." One lie deserved another.

For some reason, he'd believed Walsingham's story. He didn't like the bloke, and he couldn't warm to anyone who was busy sorting out his alibi while his wife's body was waiting to be removed from her watery resting place, but he believed that Walsingham had been with Sonia.

"Perhaps you'd like to tell me about it," he said. "The truth this time."

Her arms remained folded and she looked at him as if he had dog shit on his shoe. "I suppose Neil's told you, has he?"

Dylan shrugged. "Is it true?"

"He's a liar. I've told you, only a fool would believe what he said."

"Look, Sonia, I'm really not in the mood to be pissed about. Just tell me the truth. Otherwise, we can take a short drive to the police station and see what they have to say."

She glared at him. "Okay, so he was with me. So what?"

"So what?" Dylan had never hit a woman in his life but his fists longed to put that right. "So you've been trying to convince me that Neil Walsingham is guilty of his wife's murder when, all along, you've known damn well he isn't. So a man is currently serving a life sentence in one of the most depressing places on earth and maybe he shouldn't be there. So people's lives have been wrecked."

She had the decency to flush with shame.

"Neil Walsingham couldn't have killed his wife, could he?" Dylan said. "You know he's innocent, don't you?"

She nodded, eyes on her foot that was tracing an invisible pattern in the carpet.

"Then why? Why did you want to convince me he was guilty?"

Her head flew up. "Because I hate him."

"Why? Because you thought he was going to whisk you off to the sunset and your own happy ever after? Look at yourself, Sonia. You're so bitter and twisted, you're willing to accuse a man of murdering his own wife. Who the hell would want to get involved with someone so vindictive?"

Tears sprang to her eyes, but Dylan couldn't care less. He shook his head in disgust. "I hope you can live with yourself."

Unable to bear her company any longer, he turned for the door.

"I take it you have nothing more to say? Your husband discovered you'd been seeing Neil and knocked you about a bit. Neil patched you up, calmed you down and gave you money for a taxi home. Is that about the height of it?"

She nodded. "Yes."

"That doesn't sound like someone who deserves to be condemned for a murder he didn't commit, does it?" He yanked open the door. "Don't worry, I'll see myself out."

He ran back to his car and sat for a few moments with the rain beating out a tune on the paintwork.

It always surprised him when people didn't share his views. If people committed a crime, they should be punished. Whoever killed Carly Walsingham should be given a life sentence, long enough behind bars to consider their actions and what it had done to Carly's family. Justice was what mattered. It was the only way people could make sense of life.

With a long sigh, he fired the engine and began the drive back to town. He'd park at the hotel and take a taxi out to the Dog and Fox. He needed to think about his chat with Neil Walsingham, and that pint of beer was shouting his name.

He'd driven less than half a mile when he turned into a side street and pulled up. The wipers weren't coping with the rain so he'd give it a few minutes and hope it eased off.

The driver of the car behind had the same idea. It, too, pulled into the side street. The car slowed a little and crawled past the Morgan. Odd.

It was going slowly but it was impossible to see the colour or even the model through the rain. All he could see was a pair of rear lights.

Five minutes later, Dylan drove off. Rain was still hammering on the Morgan's bodywork but visibility was slightly better.

Within a minute, he had a car following him. He turned left and the car followed. He continued on to the traffic lights and sat at the front of the queue. He didn't indicate. The driver behind him wasn't showing any intention of driving left or right. The lights changed to green and Dylan took a right turn. The car behind followed.

Dylan could see a pair of headlights, but it was dark, the road had no streetlights and the rain continued to lash down, making it impossible to guess at the make or model of the vehicle.

Of course, it could be that he was getting paranoid.

He drove back to the centre of town. Despite the tortuous route he took, the car followed.

He turned into the small car park adjoining the shopping centre. The car drove on very slowly.

The rain has eased off a little but, if he left his car, he'd be soaked through to the skin within seconds. He had no choice. There was nothing to be gained by playing cat and mouse.

He grabbed his overcoat, locked the Morgan and walked slowly in the direction of the unlit side streets.

No one else was about. No one else was crazy enough to be out on a night like this. The rain remained steady, but the wind was increasing. Discarded crisps packets blew by and empty beer cans rattled along in their wake.

Deciding this was madness, and that he really was paranoid, he was about to turn into the street that would bring him out by the cinema when he heard footsteps. Those feet had to be close for him to hear them over the noise of the storm.

He crossed the road and headed down a narrow, unlit alley. Every inch of him was soaked. Rain dripped off his hair and ran down his neck. His jeans were weighing heavy. Even his feet were wet. He needed to confront whoever was following him, sort it out, whatever "it" was, get back to his hotel for clean clothes and order that pint of beer.

The alley was only a couple of feet wide and walls either side offered some sort of shelter from the wind.

Halfway along, he stopped and turned round. He saw a shadow press itself against the wall.

He walked back. The shadow jumped out in front of him.

"Well, well, well." Dylan shouldn't have been surprised. "You get your kicks from following people, don't you, Jamie?"

It was too dark to see the expression on Tinsley's face, yet Dylan could sense the man's tension. The alley seemed alive with the other man's excitement.

"You should have phoned, Jamie. We could have met up for a cosy chat."

There was enough light to see Tinsley reach deep into the pocket of a coat that, like his trousers, was the wrong length. It seemed unsure whether to stop above the knee, on the knee or at some place between knee and ankle.

It took a second for Jamie to pull out a gun. And slightly longer for Dylan's brain to register the fact.

It was impossible to guess if Tinsley intended to use it, but Dylan wasn't a betting man. He hurled himself at Tinsley.

A brilliant white light jolted Dylan's body. It dazzled him. White-hot, searing light.

It took a second to decide if he was standing on his head or lying down. He deliberately took a moment to think about this. He didn't think he'd passed out, yet he was lying in the alley and he was alone.

And the bastard had shot him!

He was lying on something. Pain tore through him as he tried to sit up without moving his shoulder.

He'd been lying on Tinsley's gun, which didn't make a lot of sense. Nothing made a lot of sense right now.

"Oh, Christ!" Yes, it did. Everything made sense.

Rain was still falling steadily. He put a gentle exploratory hand to his left shoulder. His coat was covered in blood, as was his hand now.

"Right." He pocketed the gun, staggered to his feet and leaned his forehead against the wet wall until the dizziness subsided. "It's only a graze," he told himself. "You'll probably live."

It didn't feel like it.

He took a moment to remember what had happened. At the exact moment he'd launched himself, Jamie must have pulled the trigger. Presumably, Dylan knocked the gun from his hand as he fell. Jamie wouldn't have hunted for it in the dark. He would have scarpered before anyone heard the shot and came running.

That was a laugh. There wasn't a soul to be seen. No police sirens were screaming to Dylan's rescue.

Sweat poured down his face and his spine as he walked slowly back to his car. He kept his shoulder as still as possible, his arm clamped tight against his side.

The effort of unlocking his car and dropping onto the seat had waves of dizziness threatening to send him to some unknown abyss.

It was only a flesh wound, he was sure of it, but he couldn't take off his coat to inspect the damage. His Arsenal FC scarf

was lying in the passenger footwell. He reached for it and
spent the next ten minutes trying to use it as a bandage. I
wasn't the most skilled piece of work but it would have to suf-
fice until he could get to the hospital. Or the pub. Before that
though, he needed to pay Pennine View Rescue Centre a visit

DYLAN WAS WET, he was sweating and shivering at the same time, and his shoulder was screaming in agony. Christ, he needed a stiff drink. Make that several stiff drinks.

He thought Tinsley might have come here but when he stopped the Morgan outside the Pennine View Rescue Centre, all was in darkness. It was after ten o'clock so perhaps Sue Kaminski had retired to her bed.

Her car was absent, as was Tinsley's.

An outside light lit the front garden. Perhaps Sue had gone out and left the light on for her return.

Dylan reached into the glove compartment for a torch and a small roll of tools that might come in useful. He was about to hide Tinsley's gun, but he decided to keep it in his pocket. Who knew when a gun would come in handy? With mad fuckers like Tinsley on the loose, anything was possible.

He left the Morgan and walked up the front path. Although the rain had eased off a little, the wind was howling around the corners of the house, trying to claw its way inside.

He hammered on the door but no lights appeared and there were no sounds from within. It seemed unlikely that a huge Rottweiler lay in wait behind the door.

He knocked again, gave up and walked to the back of the house. He went through the same procedure. The house had been abandoned.

The back door was blessed with two locks and a couple of bolts. The front door, as far as he could remember, relied on a simple Yale lock to keep out intruders. As it was so long since he'd tested his breaking and entering skills, Dylan decided to test them out on that one.

He winced as he walked round the corner of the house, and a gust of wind grabbed at his shoulder.

He stood for a moment to listen but could hear no approaching vehicles over the roar of the wind. Not that he cared either way.

He took his makeshift torque wrench and picks from his pocket. He inserted the torque wrench and hoped to God he hadn't lost his touch. Not, it had to be said, that he'd ever had a real touch. Cat burglar hadn't featured highly on his list of career choices.

He inserted the pick and began the arduous task of trying to set the pins. It would have been easier if he'd been able to hear the clicks over the angry wind. And a lot easier if his shoulder wasn't throbbing.

Eventually, the lock gave. It had probably taken him fifteen minutes. Not bad for someone out of practice, but no good for anyone wanting to take up burglary.

He stepped inside the house, breath held as he waited for the dog from hell to rip him to pieces. All was quiet. He switched on the light. A cat ambled into the hall, looked at him, spat and, with its back arched, scampered up the stairs.

Dylan followed. He might as well start on the first floor.

He had no real idea of what he was looking for. He wouldn't until he found it.

He switched on the light and the sight of Sue's bedroom took him by surprise. Kaminski's coat hung from the back of a chair. His boots waited to trip someone up or to be put away. It was as if Kaminski had stepped out of the room and would return at any moment to finish dressing.

The wardrobe was split so that Kaminski's clothes took up the right-hand side and Sue's the left. On the shelf in Sue's half was a large shoebox. Dylan opened it and found several letters from Kaminski. He skimmed a couple, but they gave nothing away.

His legs were shaking and he sat on the bed to pull open drawers in an old dresser. On top of the dresser sat a framed photo of the couple taken on their wedding day. Sue looked fit to burst with happiness while her husband wore his usual unfathomable expression.

He rifled through her underwear drawer, but found nothing of interest. A hairdryer had been shoved in another drawer. Belts in another.

Sweat was pouring off him and he was still shivering. He needed to get to a hospital.

He tried the small guest bedroom. Beneath a single bed were boxes crammed with junk. Out-of-date calendars, photos, an old mobile phone, screwdrivers, car air fresheners, picture hooks.

A third room, this one much smaller, was in darkness. The switch worked but the bulb was missing. It didn't matter because he could see enough courtesy of the light on the landing.

The room could have been used as a nursery but the childless Kaminskis chose to store a lifetime's accumulated mementoes in it. It would take Dylan a week to sort through this lot and life was too short.

But he was nosy by nature. He moved a few boxes from the top of a wooden trunk, lifted the lid and peered inside. The contents would have delighted any child who longed to be Little Red Riding Hood or Goldilocks. There were dresses, shoes, hats with feathers and wigs.

A flash of light lit the room as a pair of headlights bounced along the lane outside.

Knowing he had to cut his search short, he walked down the stairs, leaning against the wall for extra support. He'd managed to reach the kitchen when Sue Kaminski let herself in. Her companion was a friendly spaniel, thank God.

He couldn't have coped with that blasted Rottweiler wanting a taste of his blood.

She let out a scream when she saw him. Her hand went to her mouth as she tried to recover from the shock. "Dylan, what the devil are you doing here? How did you get in?"

"The back door was open. I thought you must be out in the kennels." Sometimes, lies come too easily.

She stared at the back door as if expecting it to deny Dylan's statement. "Oh, my God. What's happened to your shoulder? You're bleeding."

He shrugged, and the pain was so intense he wished he'd put twenty thousand volts through his body instead. "Just a bit of an accident. It's fine."

"Are you sure? You look very pale."

He *felt* very pale.

"God," she breathed. "What a night this is turning out to be. You'll never believe what's happened."

"Try me." Nothing would surprise him.

"The police phoned me because they were trying to find Jamie. I drove over to his place to see if he was there. There's no sign of him, but Monty was there. He was barking. Anyway, there was a reporter outside and he said Jamie's father has been shot. According to him, someone broke in to Jamie's parents' house and shot Mr. Tinsley."

Dylan waited. Nope. He wasn't surprised.

"Really," he said. "And you don't know where Jamie is?"

"I've no idea."

"I'm surprised he's far from you." Dylan had to sink onto a chair before he passed out. He took the gun from his pocket, making her gasp. "I imagine the police will be looking for this then. It looks like a murder weapon, don't you think?"

Sue wrapped her arms around herself. "What's going on, Dylan?"

"At a rough guess, I'd say that Jamie killed his father and

decided he liked the experience so much, he'd come after me. He's always wanted me off this case and I couldn't fathom out why."

"Jamie? You think Jamie killed his own father?"

"I do, yes."

"But that's—"

"Against the law? So it is." Dylan tried to relax his shoulder but it was impossible. "He shot me too. That's why I'm bleeding all over your kitchen and why I have his gun."

She shook her head. "No."

"Yes."

"No. Oh, no, Dylan. Not Jamie. He wouldn't do such a thing."

"Wouldn't shoot me? Ah, but he did."

"Surely not. He's good and kind. He's been so good to me."

"I'm sure he has, and by getting rid of me, he believed he was doing you a favour. You see—" He broke off.

He walked over to the notice board, the one festooned with pictures of her great-aunt's ninetieth birthday celebrations. A totally unrelated photo showed Sue with three big dogs, smiling into the camera. Off to her right were the kennels. Off to her left, poking its bonnet into the edge of the picture, was an orange Volkswagen Beetle. One mirror had been fastened to the vehicle with gaffer tape, just as Walsingham had described it. It was the same Volkswagen Beetle Dylan had seen driving along Darwen Road. The same Volkswagen Beetle that DS Pike had checked out.

"Whose is this car?" he asked.

"What? Well, it's mine. Was mine. The one I have now was going cheap so I sold the Beetle."

"You're lying." He didn't have time for this. "I checked this vehicle with a friend of mine, a detective. This car isn't, and never has been, registered in your name."

"Oh, no. It was registered in Aunt Joyce's name. She'd

had it from new but, when she could no longer drive, she let me have it. We never got around to dealing with the paperwork." She frowned at him. "Why are you asking about it?"

"I see." He removed the photo from the board. "We were talking about Jamie, weren't we? Yes. As I was saying, he follows you everywhere."

She was still frowning at him. She had no idea what he was getting at, and his own brain was slowly turning to mush.

"Everywhere," he said again. "He didn't want me here looking into the murder of Carly Walsingham because he didn't want to risk me learning the truth. He knew who killed Carly because he follows you, Sue."

Her eyes widened and all colour drained from her face.

"He knows the truth, Sue, because he followed you that afternoon." He nodded at the photos of the famous ninetieth birthday party. "You called to see your aunt, dropped off the cake, took a couple of photos and, hey presto, you had the perfect alibi. Your great-aunt wouldn't have known if you were there or not, would she? You told me yourself that she was suffering from Alzheimer's. The nursing home staff would have seen you arrive, you'd make sure of that by giving them cake and gifts, but they wouldn't have noticed you leaving almost immediately."

She wasn't saying a word. Her bottom lip was trembling and she clutched the sleeves of her jumper in tense fists.

"You then drove your orange Volkswagen—" He waved the photo under her nose. "You drove along Darwen Road and—yes, I've seen this car on CCTV—and parked on Peebles Road at the back of the Walsingham's property."

A stray tear rolled down her cheek and she brushed it away with her sleeve. She wasn't looking at Dylan. He couldn't even be sure she was listening to him.

"You pulled on a hooded jacket and slipped inside the Walsinghams' home. You'd done your own bit of sleuthing, hadn't you? You knew Alek was having an affair with his ex-wife. You knew that every Monday and Thursday, Alek was enjoying some afternoon delight at Lakeside Drive. So you chose Wednesday. You always visit your great-aunt on Wednesdays so you had the perfect alibi. What could be better than a muddled, confused relative, an Alzheimer's patient, and a couple of photos of a birthday cake?"

Still she didn't speak.

"When you went into the Walsinghams' house, you had no idea that your husband had left only minutes earlier via the front door. You crept inside and you found Carly enjoying a nice hot soak in her bath. You grabbed a cushion, intending to drown her, but you had to see her face, didn't you? You hated her so much that you wanted to watch her suffer. So you slashed her throat and watched her bleed. Then, happy in the knowledge that the competition for your husband's affection had breathed her last, you pulled on your hood and left through the back garden. You jumped in your car and drove home to tell your husband what a wonderful time you'd had celebrating your aunt's milestone birthday."

She gave a choked cry but didn't speak.

"Where's the murder weapon, Sue? What did you use?"

A brief shake of the head said she wasn't going to answer his questions.

"When you discovered that Alek had been there that afternoon, and that he'd left his fingerprints all over what became a crime scene, no one could have been more surprised than you."

She still didn't speak, but tears and snot were running down her face. She dragged her sleeve across her face but fresh tears soon fell.

"That's what happens, Sue. Plans have a nasty habit of backfiring." Dylan swayed on his feet as another wave of dizziness threatened to swamp him. "I suspected Jamie of murder at one point, but I couldn't understand why he'd do such a thing. Then I realised, somewhat belatedly, that he followed you around. He was trying to protect you."

"Jamie came to check out the animals one day." Her voice was husky with tears and emotion. "His bag was open and I saw several scalpels. All different sizes. I stole one. I already knew that the vein in the neck was the best place to cut. Everyone does, don't they?"

Dylan had been wrong. He was still capable of feeling surprise.

He wondered if Bev knew the best place to cut someone if you wanted them to bleed to death in record time. Doubtful. He wondered if she would discuss the mechanics of murder while showing no remorse. Of course she wouldn't. Sue's tears weren't for Carly Walsingham or the terrible deed, they were for herself.

"I put it back," she said.

"Sorry?"

"Jamie's scalpel. I returned it to his bag a few days later."

"How did you find out?" Dylan asked. "About Alek and Carly, I mean."

She was shaking. Her breath was coming in painful gasps.

"A woman came here. She'd adopted a cat and wanted to see if I'd look after it for a week while they went on holiday. We got talking and I realised Alek was doing a job for her." Her teeth were chattering and she wrapped her arms around herself. "She said something about him not being there that afternoon. I thought nothing of it because he'll often leave a job early if he needs to go and price a job for another customer." She fell silent.

"And?" Dylan prompted.

She looked at him as if she'd just remembered he was there. "He was late home, only about half an hour, but he said he'd been finishing the job and didn't want to leave it. He lied to me, Dylan. I knew he was lying."

"But how did you know where he'd been?"

"I followed him the next week. He was where he said he was except for Monday and Thursday afternoon. I assumed he was seeing someone on Lakeside Drive about a job." She took a deep shuddering breath. "There was something in the local paper about residents at Lakeside Drive complaining about a planning application. The report said that one of the residents was Neil Walsingham. I knew then. I knew Alek had been to see that woman. I soon found out he was going there every Monday and Thursday afternoon."

She dropped to her knees and began to howl. Dylan used the time to call the men in blue. It wasn't easy explaining that he'd been shot by Jamie Tinsley, that he was in possession of a murder weapon and that he was with a woman who'd confessed to the murder of Carly Walsingham.

"You can't have me put away, Dylan." She was on her knees, tugging on his wet jeans. "I'm claustrophobic. I'll go mad. You can't have me put away."

"I'm sorry, but the police are on their way."

"Alek shouldn't have gone there that day." She looked up at him. "He shouldn't."

"No, he shouldn't."

"I couldn't tell the truth, could I? What about the animals? Who'll care for them? What about Aunt Joyce? Who'll visit her? Who will care if she's alive or dead?" Her teeth started to chatter. "I can't spend my days and nights locked in a cell. I can't do it. I'll go mad."

She was screaming hysterically when the police arrived.

FORTY

DYLAN FLEXED HIS shoulder and waited for a twinge of pain. It didn't come. He'd be scarred for life, but as the doctor who'd looked Luke's age had told him so cheerfully, he'd live. They'd given him huge painkilling tablets when he left the hospital. He'd only taken a couple because they didn't so much deaden the pain as render him unconscious. He got the same effect from whisky and it tasted better.

He dodged around Bev, who was tidying the kitchen after a rare cake-baking session, poured himself a glass of Lagavulin and took an appreciative sip.

Freya was asleep in the crook of his arm and, given the way her fingers and toes twitched now and again, she was having pleasant dreams. Luke was in the sitting room with half a dozen friends. All was well.

"Have the Kaminskis paid you?" Bev asked.

All *had been* well.

"They sent a cheque by return. Case closed."

The case hadn't been closed in a very satisfactory manner, but justice had been done. Aleksander had his pardon but his wife was now awaiting trial and sentence.

It wasn't the outcome Dylan had expected or wanted yet there was something satisfyingly right when justice was done. Carly Walsingham hadn't deserved to die, and her sons shouldn't be facing a life without their mother. Sue Kaminski, no matter how hurt she was by her husband's infidelity, had no right to decide who lived and who died. Dylan quite liked her, but she'd made her choice and she must live with the consequences.

Aleksander Kaminski was a seething mass of rage spiced with shock. He longed to take his own revenge on the person who'd ended Carly's life, and he was struggling to accept that the object of his hatred was his own wife. He'd never loved Sue, but he had cared about her. He was torn between longing to strangle her and weeping for the future that stretched ahead of her.

His feelings would change, though, Dylan was sure of it. The rescue centre had closed and Kaminski was living in Birmingham with his parents. He'd get his life back together.

Sue's great-aunt would cope without her regular visits. Her absence might not even register with the old lady.

Frederyk and Agata were in a state of shock, but pleased that their son's name had been cleared and even more pleased that they could be with him.

As for the cheque—

Bev had printed out Dylan's final account and Dylan, horrified by the idea of taking such a large amount from the couple's life savings, had then printed out a fresh account. He didn't intend to be out of pocket, but he didn't want the Kaminskis on starvation rations either.

Frederyk had phoned Dylan to query the account.

"It doesn't look right," he'd said. "We only paid you five hundred pounds at the start. There must be more than this owing to you."

Dylan had assured him it was correct. Frederyk had sent the cheque by return, with yet another gushing note of gratitude, and Dylan had banked the cheque. There was no need for Bev to know anything about it.

It did mean they were still broke though.

Thanks to his new all-singing website that hailed him as the greatest private investigator ever—another of Bev's big ideas, which came with a price tag to match—he'd been offered a couple of jobs that he'd have to take. They didn't grab his interest, but they would at least put food on the table.

The sound of the TV burst out as Luke raced into the kitchen. "We're starving."

He grabbed half a dozen bags of crisps from the cupboard and was heading back to the sitting room and his friends when he stopped and looked at his mother. "Have you told Dad about the holiday yet?"

"What?" She blushed. "Oh, no. Not yet."

Grinning, Luke skipped off to his friends.

Dylan's spirits sank.

"What holiday?" And more important. "My mother's not involved, is she?"

"Of course not," Bev replied in an airy what-a-ridiculous-suggestion sort of way. "She's coming with us, though. That's a good thing, isn't it? It means we'll be able to go out for the evening without worrying about Luke and Freya."

Dylan would never describe his mother's presence as a good thing.

"And I haven't booked it yet," she added. "Obviously, I wanted to talk it over with you first."

Obviously.

"So where are you thinking of dragging me?"

Dylan watched her take a long breath before saying, "On a cruise."

Dylan knew one thing about cruises and one thing only. They were hellish expensive.

When you'd just banked a cheque that only covered a month's expenses, you couldn't go booking expensive cruises.

"Where to?"

"Norway."

Perhaps it wasn't as bad as he'd feared. No one would want

to cruise round Norway so it would be cheap. People cruised the Mediterranean or—

"In November," she added.

Even better. She'd obviously spared their finances a thought and found a bargain holiday.

Cheap or not, it couldn't be classed a holiday. A holiday was something you looked forward to, and shivering in Norway would be more penance than treat.

"Bev, your idea of a holiday is reading as many books as possible while slowly roasting until you're medium rare. Norway is—cold. It'll be cheap, yes, but we'd have no fun at all shivering on a boat round Norway. Let's look for something else. There are sure to be cheap offers for Spain, Italy or Greece."

She busied herself putting baking trays in the cupboard.

"It was when I booked a week in Spain that I saw this cruise," she said, and he still couldn't see her face.

"So we're having a week in Spain then—"

"Ten days."

"Ten days in Spain *then* a cruise round Norway?"

She slammed the cupboard door shut and faced him. "You dare utter one word about money not growing on sodding trees and I won't be responsible for my actions. I've had a baby, a sick baby, and life's been hard. It's all right for you swanning around bloody Lancashire, but it's been hard work here. So yes, we're having ten days in Spain in August and a cruise in November."

Before he could say anything, she stormed into the hall and returned with a thick brochure that she banged down on the table in front of him.

Freya, blissfully unaware of her mother's temper, slept on.

"Holy—" He clamped his mouth shut, but bloody hell. "So when you say Norway, you really mean the Arctic Circle."

"No. I mean Norway. The cruise starts and ends in Nor way. You do travel north, yes."

The brochure enticed people to book for the cruise of a lifetime, to celebrate the Northern Lights Festival. Hell, you could even arrange a wakeup call as soon as the aurora bo realis was spotted.

"My mother put this notion in your head, didn't she?"

"It's not a notion, Dylan." The words were forced through gritted teeth. "I want to see the northern lights. That shouldn' be too difficult to understand, even for you. Vicky, Luke Freya and I are going on the cruise. You can stay here and be a miserable git if you so choose."

"Hang on a minute, I thought we were going to talk i over?"

"And that's exactly what we are doing. But I've paid the deposit."

Dylan turned pages that were dotted with photos of spec tacular scenery beneath green swirling skies. He came to a page showing available dates, choice of cabins and suchlike It was supposed to show prices but—surely not. No one in their right mind would pay over two grand for a week on a blasted boat in the frozen north. Not even Bev would be so stupid. His mother might, but not Bev.

The doorbell rang and there followed a flurry of activity for the next hour or so as parents came to collect their off spring and stopped to admire the still-sleeping Freya.

Having shown off his beautiful daughter, Dylan though he could safely put her in room to sleep undisturbed.

"A daughter is a very precious thing," he whispered as he tucked her in, "but I hope to God you grow up with more sense than the rest of your breed."

He dropped a kiss on her unconcerned forehead and walked downstairs in time to hear Bev on the phone to someone.

"Here he is," she said when Dylan walked into the kitchen

She put her hand over the microphone and whispered, "It's
Lewis Cameron."

He took the phone from her. "Hi, Lewis. How are things
in Lancashire?"

"Pretty much as you might imagine."

Yes, Dylan could see how the local media might enjoy
slagging off the inefficiency of the police. Reporters had kept
Dylan's own phone busy.

"I'm ringing," Lewis said, "because I'm getting a little
tired of seeing your quotes splashed all over the papers. You
chose to come up to Lancashire and interfere, that's fine.
But don't presume that you have any idea of how my team
conducted the initial investigation. And don't you dare say
that I rushed through the case because I was eager to retire."

"I never said anything about the investigation being
rushed."

"It's splashed all over today's papers. How do you explain that?"

Dylan couldn't. "You know as well as I do that journalists
have to twist things."

"Ah, so you didn't say that our investigation, *my* investigation was third-rate?"

"Ah."

"Quite. In future, if you have any views about things of
which you're ignorant, I for one would be grateful if you'd
keep them to yourself."

"Fine."

"You have no idea—"

"I know that an innocent man faced a life sentence in
Strangeways." Dylan didn't add "because of your inefficiency" but it hung in the air between them. "Look, Lewis,
I'm sorry for all the crap that's being printed in the papers,
but I can't apologise for seeing justice done."

"I wouldn't expect you to, but don't ever—*ever*—call my

work third-rate. Just take a long hard look at yourself. You'r
an ex-con. Someone judged not fit to be a member of the po
lice force. Look at yourself before you judge other people."

Dylan rolled his eyes in Bev's direction.

"Fine," he said. "Was there anything else you wanted
Lewis?"

"Nothing." The connection was cut.

"What was that about?" Bev asked.

"Ex-DI Cameron wanted to remind me that I'm an ex
con who's not fit to lick his boots. He'd rather have watche
Kaminski rot in jail than have his investigation called int
question." Dylan couldn't care less. In fact, he felt a certai
degree of satisfaction at the idea and couldn't help smiling
"Never mind. I think I'll have another drink."

Bev, furious on Dylan's behalf, was prevented from giv
ing vent to her thoughts by the arrival of Luke.

"When we do Freya's room—" he said, only to receive
warning glance from Bev.

Dylan shook his head in despair. It was far, far easier t
solve a murder case than it was to live in this house.

The thought brought Jamie Tinsley to mind. The vet's fac
was on every news bulletin but police still hadn't traced hin
He'd achieved the impossible and vanished off the face of th
earth. Dylan almost envied him.

"So we're decorating Freya's room, are we?" he sai
"Well, I don't like to say I told you so, but I knew those yel
low elephants would have to go."

Luke grinned. "Bye, bye, yellow elephants. Hello, big ne
room in the roof."

Bev gave him another warning glance.

Luke sampled Bev's cake, hot out of the oven. He chatte
about football—the boring close season was upon them—an
school—too boring to believe—and then decided he'd go t
his bed and chill with his music before sleep.

Bev switched on the small portable TV in the kitchen, a sure sign she didn't want to talk. That was worrying in itself.

"What plans for Freya's bedroom then?" he asked.

"Hmm? Oh nothing, really. I've had some plans drawn up, that's all."

"Plans? It's a twelve by twelve room with a window. What do you need plans for?"

"Well." She thought for a moment. "Your mum's a regular babysitter and it's not fair to expect her to sleep in Freya's bedroom, is it? So, I thought we'd knock Freya's room and the bathroom into one. That way we'd have a nice big bathroom instead of the pokey thing we have now. We could then have a loft conversion and have two rooms up there, one for Freya and one for your mum."

Dylan, who'd been thinking along the lines of choosing paint or wallpaper, despaired. Bev taught English and Drama and she put too much effort into the drama side of life outside school. He'd be eternally thankful when her maternity leave ended and she got back to her pupils. She'd have less time to think.

"I had plans drawn up and got a few quotes, that's all," she said.

"Are any of those quotes under ten grand?" he asked.

"Dylan, don't be ridiculous."

"Are any under twenty grand?"

"One was." She concentrated all her attention on the TV. Chefs were showing viewers how to dish up some exotic concoction which would be of no interest to Bev whatsoever.

Dylan supposed he'd hate a boring life. He didn't know, he'd never had experience of such a thing, but the idea didn't appeal.

His wife was busy making plans that included him and his children, his son was happily listening to his music and dreaming of the giddy heights Arsenal FC would achieve next season, his daughter was contentedly dreaming of yellow elephants, and his mother was in her own home on the other side of the city. Life wasn't bad at all.

Bev spun around and, seeing him looking at her, glared at him. "What?"

"I was just thinking I'd better put my coat on, head out to the streets and see if I can sell my body."

Bev looked him up and down and a smile tried to work its way to her lips. "It might work. I'd give you a couple of quid."

"You would?"

"Yes." She gave him a long appraising look, then walked over to sit on his knee and put her arm round his neck. "I'd want enough change for a coffee though."

The cookery programme ended and a newsreader began updating viewers on the latest headlines. Dylan wasn't paying attention.

If Bev was coming clean about her expensive plans, maybe he should tell her about the revised account he'd given the Kaminskis. But, no. There was little point. All he wanted was a quiet life.

"Fifty pence and my body's all yours," he said, holding out his hand.

She went to her purse, grabbed a fifty-pence piece and dropped it into his hand. "You always were cheap."

She grabbed his hand and led him up the stairs, leaving the newsreader to talk to the empty kitchen.

"A body, believed to be that of James Tinsley, a man wanted by Lancashire CID in connection with the murder of his father, Victor Tinsley, has been found at Coniston Water. Police are not treating the death as suspicious."

* * * * *

REQUEST YOUR FREE BOOKS!

2 FREE NOVELS
PLUS 2 FREE GIFTS!

MYSTERY WORLDWIDE LIBRARY®

Your Partner in Crime